A Deadly Affair at Bobtail Ridge

ALSO BY TERRY SHAMES

A Killing at Cotton Hill

The Last Death of Jack Harbin

Dead Broke in Jarrett Creek

A Samuel Craddock Mystery

A Deadly Affair
at Bobtail Ridge

Terry Shames

SEVENTH STREET BOOKS®
AN IMPRINT OF PROMETHEUS BOOKS
59 JOHN GLENN DRIVE • AMHERST, NY 14228
www.seventhstreetbooks.com

Published 2015 by Seventh Street Books®, an imprint of Prometheus Books

Cover image (top) © Media Bakery
Cover image (bottom) © Shutterstock
Cover design Grace M. Conti-Zilsberger

Inquiries should be addressed to
Seventh Street Books
59 John Glenn Drive
Amherst, New York 14228
VOICE: 716–691–0133 • FAX: 716–691–0137
WWW.SEVENTHSTREETBOOKS.COM

19 18 17 16 15 • 5 4 3 2 1

Library of Congress Cataloging-in-Publication Data

Shames, Terry.
    A deadly affair at Bobtail Ridge : a Samuel Craddock mystery / by Terry Shames.
        pages ; cm
    ISBN 978-1-63388-046-7 (paperback) — ISBN 978-1-63388-047-4 (e-book)
    I. Title.

PS3619.H35425D44 2015
813'.6—dc23

                                                                    2014043688

Printed in the United States of America

To my parents, Adelle and Lloyd Klar

CHAPTER 1

It's six a.m. and I'm lying in bed awake, ready to get up, when a pounding on my front door startles me.

"Hold on!" I holler as I step into my jeans and grab a T-shirt out of the chest of drawers.

My next-door neighbor, Jenny Sandstone, is standing on my front porch, looking like a wild woman. Her face is swollen and tear-stained, and her bundle of curly red hair is out of control. She's a big-boned woman only a couple of inches shorter than my six feet, but she's hunched over like she's in pain.

"What's the matter? You want to come in?"

"I can't come in, I have to go. It's Mamma. They just called me from the hospital in Bobtail. She had a stroke."

I grab her hand and she clutches mine. "You're not fit to drive. Let me take you over there."

"No, no. I can drive. But I have to ask you a favor. I hate to. I know you don't like my horses, but can you call Truly Bennett for me and ask if he can feed and water them? I'd call Truly, but . . ."

"I'll take care of it. You go on and get to the hospital. And call me if you need anything. You know I'll come."

Her mouth starts to tremble and a whimper escapes, and then she's off down the steps.

I make do with cereal so I can take care of my cows and then deal with her horses before I drive over to the hospital. What I didn't tell Jenny was that Truly Bennett has gone off to handle a cattle auction down in San Antonio, so I have to take care of the horses myself. Jenny's right, I don't like horses, but I owe a debt to her that can never be repaid: she saved my art collection from being destroyed in a fire.

As soon as I'm done feeding and watering my cows, I go up to Jenny's barn and do the same for her horses and then turn them out to pasture. I've never paid a lot of attention to them, but I know the bigger one, brown with a black mane and tail, is named Mahogany, and the black one goes by the unoriginal name of Blackie. Mahogany is the one I'm most wary of. He's a huge, retired racehorse, which Jenny says makes him more skittish than the average steed. She rides both of them, but because of her size, she looks more comfortable on Mahogany.

The whole time I'm with them, both horses look at me like they know I think they're stupid and they're figuring out how to let me know they're smarter than I think. But in the end, they can't seem to come up with a plan, so I escape while they're still mulling it over.

I wonder if I ought to take something to the hospital for Jenny. I wish Loretta Singletary was in town so I could get her to fix me up a care package of cinnamon rolls or coffee cake. But Loretta's son surprised her with a trip to Washington, DC, with his family, and she won't be back for a few more days. I stop by Flower Power and have Justine make me up a suitable bouquet to take to Jenny's mother.

At the hospital the receptionist tells me only family can visit Mrs. Sandstone, but she gives me the room number so I can wait outside for Jenny. As I turn the corner into the east wing hallway, I see Jenny standing in the corridor facing a lanky man a little taller than she is. Dressed in a lawyerly suit with a striped tie, his hair is longish and he wears rimless glasses. He looks like a throwback from the '60s.

I pause because it's clear the two of them are having a disagreement. Jenny has her hands on her hips, and the man is gesturing in appeal. Apparently getting nowhere with his argument, he runs his hands across his hair and spins away from her. She says something, and he turns back and grabs her arm. She pulls away from him, and I figure it's time to make my presence known.

"Hey, there!" I say sharply. "What's going on?"

They both turn to look at me, startled, faces guilty, like they've been caught doing something wrong.

The man steps toward me. "Who are you?"

"Will, he's my next-door neighbor, Samuel Craddock. Samuel, this is one of the county public defenders, Wilson Landreau."

Landreau shakes my hand. "Sorry, I'm a little on edge." He shoots a look at Jenny and she shakes her head.

"You don't need to burden Samuel with office politics."

"It's not . . ."

"Will, I mean it."

Jenny takes Landreau by the arm and says to me, "Samuel, would you mind going in and staying with Mamma for a minute while I see Will out to the parking lot?"

As they walk away they resume their angry whispers.

I met Jenny's mother once a few months ago when she was leaving Jenny's place. Like Jenny, Vera Sandstone is a big-boned woman, but lying in the hospital bed she looks shrunken and weathered. She taught school her whole life, and Jenny said when she retired a few years ago she took up gardening with a vengeance. That's why her face is a nice color of tan. When I met her, she had her gray hair done up in a bun, but now it's straggling down beside her face. I suspect she wouldn't like anybody seeing her like this.

The sight of her hooked up with all the tubes and contraptions makes me a little queasy. It reminds me of the way my wife Jeanne looked in the weeks before cancer claimed her. Mrs. Sandstone's eyes are closed, and the left side of her face is slack. I see no reason to wake her. But she heard me come in because she struggles to open her eyes— at least the right one. The left one barely flutters. "Who's there?" Her voice is slurred.

"Mrs. Sandstone, I'm Samuel Craddock. I live next door to Jenny. I met you a while back."

"Samuel." She frowns and moves one hand restlessly. "Thank God. Jenny trusts you." She turns her face toward me and struggles to bring me into focus with her good eye.

"Listen, you stay still. No need to get stirred up. Jenny will be back in a minute."

A frown flits across her face and she waves her right hand as if shooing a fly. "Jenny's not here?" Her voice is agitated and again she tries to focus on me.

"She'll be right back."

"Come on over here. I need to tell you something. Before she gets back." She beckons, her voice is an urgent whisper.

"Lie down now. Don't try to get up. I'm right here."

I reach out and touch her hand gently, but she grabs on to it stronger than I thought possible. "I need to tell you something." Her lips don't work the way she wants and her good side grimaces. "You need to know in case I don't make it."

"I'm sure you're going to be fine."

"No!" She tightens her grip. "Before Jenny comes back I need to tell you something." She pants with the effort of speaking. "Jenny could be in danger."

"Danger from whom?"

Her grip loosens and she sags. "I think he did something bad." Her eyes blink open again and she strains to bring me into focus.

"You need to take it easy," I say, patting her hand.

"She doesn't know what he did." Her voice rises in a moan.

"What who did?"

Her breathing quickens, and one of the machines starts to beep softly. "Listen to me. Listen to me." She pulls at my hand and I lean down. I can barely make out her words. "Will you try to find Howard? I'd feel better if I knew where he went. And . . . and," she's searching for words, "find his first wife."

The door opens and a short, heavy Hispanic nurse bustles in. "Mrs.

Sandstone? Vera?" She looks at the machine that's beeping, presses a button to switch off the alarm, and turns a stern eye toward me. "Who are you and what are you doing in here? It's supposed to be only family here. Where's Vera's daughter?"

Before I can answer, Jenny comes back. "It's okay, Monica, I asked Mr. Craddock to keep an eye on Mamma while I stepped out."

"He must have said something to upset her. Her pulse rate is up. She needs to stay as quiet as possible." She shoots another accusing look at me and I try to look innocent.

Jenny's face is red and perspiring, and her hair, always a little unruly, is a tangle of damp curls. She bites her lip and says, "I had a friend here and Mamma probably heard us arguing. That might have upset her."

Vera seems to have drifted back to sleep. Jenny smoothes her mother's hair away from her forehead. She hasn't looked at me since she came into the room. I wonder if the man she was arguing with is more than just a colleague and she's embarrassed.

"I'm going to the waiting room," I say. "When you take a break come and find me."

"You go on with him," the nurse orders Jenny. "I need to do a few things for your mamma. She'll be fine until you get back."

I steer Jenny to the elevator. "Let's get you down to the cafeteria," I say. "You need a bite to eat."

"I couldn't eat anything."

"You have to. It won't help your mother if you faint and crack your head and end up in the bed next to her."

She manages a tired smile. "Some coffee would be good."

When I have Jenny sitting in front of coffee, pecking at watery scrambled eggs, I ask how Vera ended up in the hospital. "Who found her?"

"The nurse told me Mamma called EMS at four o'clock this morning. Said she wasn't feeling good and she thought they better come and get her." She shakes her head. "If you knew Mamma, you'd know she had to be in bad shape to make that call. Anyway, by the time they got to her place she was unconscious."

"They think it's a stroke?"

Jenny frowns and pokes the eggs. "Yes. They said it's a good thing she called when she did. The faster they get to a stroke victim, the better the chance of recovery."

"What does the doctor say about her prognosis?"

"You know how they are. He didn't say much—just that they got to her in good time." She swallows. "All I know is I don't know what I'll do if something happens to Mamma." She looks into the distance. "I can't stand to see her lying there looking so helpless."

I reach over and pat her hand. "How old is Vera?"

"She's only seventy-five. And vigorous. I told you she gardens and she walks with a couple of friends every day. Vigorous!" Jenny's talking as if she's trying to persuade me—or maybe she's trying to persuade fate to pass her mamma by.

"Jenny, you've never mentioned any family but your mamma. Do you have anybody else?"

She tucks a few of her escaped curls back behind her ears. "Just an aunt and uncle out in Lubbock. We see them a couple of times a year. I guess I'd better call Aunt Susie. She's a good bit younger than my mamma and they aren't close."

"Your daddy still living?"

She sets her fork down precisely, and her face closes up like a door that's been slammed. "I wouldn't know about that. He left us when I was a teenager. Walked out and never came back."

"What was his name?"

"Howard. That was a long time ago." She shoves her coffee away. "I need to get back up there. I'm nervous as a cat when I'm away from Mamma."

"Wait." I wrap up the biscuit she left on her plate in a napkin. "Take this with you so you have something to nibble on later."

She shoves it into her bag and starts to walk away but turns back. "Thank you for coming. You got Truly to take care of the horses?"

"The horses are taken care of. Let me know when you'll be home and I'll stir up a meal for you."

When I get to my pickup, I open my cell phone and find two messages from people needing me. As acting chief of police for the past few months, I've gotten back in the saddle. I was chief years ago but never thought I'd serve in that capacity again. But when the town of Jarrett Creek went bankrupt, the mayor asked me to come back as a temporary measure, since I had the experience and didn't need the salary. Turns out the job suits me better than I thought it would.

CHAPTER 2

I'm on the phone with my nephew Tom at six in the evening when I hear banging on my door for the second time today.

James Harley Krueger is standing on my doorstep looking hot and bothered. Krueger was acting chief of police before I took over, and although he has found a different calling, he still resents me.

"What can I do for you?" I say.

"You can call that friend of yours, Jenny Sandstone, and tell her to come round up her damn horses. They're out on the street headed for town and there's gonna be hell to pay if they get on the highway."

"You sure it's her horses? How'd they get out?"

"How should I know? All I know is the two of them are trotting down the street in front of Buzz Carter's house. I don't know anybody else who keeps a horse around here. Jenny's not home, though. I tried knocking on her door first."

I tell him where Jenny is, and then I snatch up my hat and head out to my truck. "I'd appreciate it if you'd follow and maybe between the two of us we can get them rounded up."

I don't listen to his reply. I doubt he'll stop to help. He has an aversion to all things physical. The way his belly has continued to grow over his belt, it wouldn't hurt him to chase some horses. Sure enough, he drives right on past me. Although he's leaving me in the lurch, at least I'm grateful that he went to the trouble to let me know the horses are out.

I head over to Fourth Street and find Buzz Carter standing out in his yard looking down the street where the horses have stopped to sample the grass on a vacant lot. I pull up to the curb next to him and roll down my window. "You know anything about horses?"

Buzz has a boat rental place out at the lake. He's fifty, built small and compact, with a peaceful way about him. He grins. "All I know is, you can't get a horse into a motorboat."

I tell him that Jenny is at the hospital in Bobtail with her mamma. "I don't know how those two got out, but I have to round them up and that's going to present a challenge."

"Say no more. My boy Alvin is here. He's got a good feel for horses, though I don't know how he came by it."

Buzz's son, the image of his daddy, says he'll take care of the horses. He goes into their garage and comes out with a couple of lengths of rope that he fashions into makeshift halters as we walk down to the vacant lot. By the time I would have mustered the courage to approach Mahogany and Blackie, Alvin has them haltered and ready to lead them back home. They shied and jumped around a little bit at first, but it didn't seem to bother him a bit. He talked to them in a firm, kind voice that settled them right down. I tell him where Jenny lives and get back in my truck.

On the short drive back to Jenny's I try to think how they could have gotten out. There's only one gate that leads to the street, and the only time I've seen it open is when Jenny goes out for a ride.

Sure enough, the gate is standing open. Some youngster must have opened it as a prank. I'm grateful that the horses didn't come to any harm. I would have been mortified to have to explain that to Jenny.

Alvin takes the horses straight into the barn. I follow and watch him as he looks them over nose to tail, patting them and prodding them and calling them by name. "I want to be sure they're okay." When he's finished he says, "They look fine. Funny that they got out, though. Better make sure that gate is padlocked."

And then I remember that Jenny always keeps the gate padlocked. To open the gate, someone would have had to get the padlock off. I wonder if Jenny took it off for some reason and forgot to put it back on.

By the time we walk out to the street it's dark. I thank Alvin for his help and run him back over to his daddy's house in my truck. When I get back home, my repaired knee is starting to swell a little, as it still does some nights when I've had an active day. "You're going to have to put up with me moving around a little longer," I tell it.

I take my big flashlight over to Jenny's and shine it around on the ground near the gate. Over by the house, I catch a glint of steel, and sure enough it's the lock. It has been sheared open. Must have taken heavy-duty bolt cutters. Seems like a strange bit of mischief. Who would have done something like that? Not kids. Maybe somebody who doesn't like horses, or maybe doesn't like Jenny?

In my garage I locate a couple of spare padlocks and put one at the top and one at the bottom of the gate.

Back at my house I close up for the night, but the question of the lock nags at me. I'm usually a good sleeper, but tonight I jerk awake a few times, restless, thinking I hear sounds from the horse stable. The third time it happens I get up, ease out the back door, and stand in the yard, eyes straining in the direction of the stable. I don't hear or see anything out of the ordinary.

When I go back to bed, I'm wide awake and I lie there remembering the crazy talk today from Jenny's mamma. Drugs talking. Sometimes when my wife Jeanne was under the influence of the drugs that kept her pain at bay, she would mutter wild ideas. Complaining that people were sitting on her bed or standing by the window when there was no one there. But Vera Sandstone seemed very certain of what she was saying.

Jenny's horses are fine this morning. If anything, they look pleased with themselves for their adventure yesterday. The padlocks are still secure. I'll check them again later in the day.

I swing by police headquarters to make sure nothing out of the ordinary needs seeing to. The young part-time deputy, Bill Odum, is on duty today. He's fresh out of the police academy but is a quick learner. He says he'll keep an eye on things and call me if he needs help. I'm glad I finally got a cell phone. It makes a big difference not having to stick by the telephone.

I go over to Jenny's again to check on the gate locks. They're still in place. There's a man I don't recognize sitting in a beat-up old white Chevy outside her house. I'm uneasy about him, but before I can walk over and find out what he's up to, he fires up the engine and takes off.

CHAPTER 3

Sunday Jenny says Vera seems better, so the next morning, with Jenny off at work, I visit Vera in the hospital. As I approach the front entrance a man who looks vaguely familiar is hurrying out the sliding glass doors—he's a big man with wiry reddish hair peppered with gray. He's football-player big, but unlike a lot of aging men with his build, he's kept his muscle tone. From the leathery look of his skin, I'd guess that he works outdoors. I nod to him, but he takes no notice. He pauses at the top of the steps, looks out over the parking lot like he's surveying his territory, and heads down to the lot. He climbs into a black Lincoln town car and whips out onto the road like he's got someplace important to be.

There's no sign on Vera's door telling visitors to check in at the desk, so I knock on the door and step in. Vera is propped up on pillows holding a tissue to her eyes that she takes away hastily when she sees me. Her skin is blotchy and her eyes red. She gives me a determined smile that is still lopsided. Her left eye is still droopy, but her color looks better. She has pulled her hair back in a bun and donned a quilted, blue bed jacket. "Wait, don't tell me. I know who you are. You're Jenny's next-door neighbor, Samuel, isn't that right?"

"Yes. I came by to see how you're feeling. Jenny says you're on the mend. I have to say you're looking a whole lot better than you did the last time I saw you."

She searches my face. "You were here before?"

"That's right. The day after you came to the hospital. You don't remember?"

She hesitates. "I'm afraid I don't. Was I making any sense?"

"You were fine."

We make a little small talk about when she'll get out of the hospital and how much she imagines her garden has suffered. "Jenny's a good girl, but she doesn't know a thing about keeping a garden. Thank goodness I've got a sweet neighbor man who looks out for the garden when I can't do it."

"Speaking of Jenny," I say, "I'd like to ask you about something you said to me when I was here last week."

"I was so out of it, there's no telling what I said." She gives a strained little laugh. Her expression is wary.

"You said you think Jenny is in danger. What did you mean?"

"I said that? I don't know what was going through my mind. I must have been dreaming." She blushes. Her hand flutters to her hair, and she glances at the door.

"You also asked me to look for your husband, Howard."

"Now I know I was out of it," she says. "Howard has been gone a long time. I don't know why I'd ask you to find him."

"And you wanted me to locate his first wife."

She starts and her right arm jerks, sending a novel lying next to her spinning to the floor. I notice that her hand is shaking.

"I'll get that." I walk around the bed, pick up the novel, and set it back near her.

Her eyes dart toward the door again, and as if she has conjured a rescue, the same nurse who chased me out last time flounces in.

"Vera, is this man bothering you again?" She cocks her head at me as if trying to decide whether I actually constitute a danger to her patient.

"I'm totally innocent," I say. "I only stopped by to tell Vera I'm glad she's feeling better."

There's no mistaking the relief in Vera's voice. "I'm so glad you came, Samuel. And regarding that matter we were discussing, please don't mention it to Jenny." Her look is stern. She was a schoolteacher and sounds like she assumes people will obey when she lays down the law.

CHAPTER 4

"Truly, I wish to hell you'd settle down and stop acting like the KKK is coming in to grab you," I say.

"Oh, you know how I am. I like to eat home. Simple food."

"How much simpler can you get than fried chicken, rice, and beans with cornbread?" I gesture toward his plate. "They even have your pepper sauce."

He finally loosens up enough to grin. "You're right. The pepper sauce fixes it right up." Truly Bennett is not an old man. He's several years younger than me, but he has never gotten used to the idea that it's all right for a black man to sit in Town Café and have a meal. Small towns like Jarrett Creek took a good bit longer than the big cities to come to terms with equal treatment for blacks. Even though Truly went to the local school, which was always integrated, his generation didn't think to go to the café and make themselves comfortable. The fact that Dilly Bolton, a black man in his forties, is sitting two tables over from us doesn't ease Truly's discomfort.

"Tell me what you were doing in San Antonio last week," I say. Truly is in demand all over the area because of his sure-handed way with cattle and horses. He's a little old to break a horse, but he knows how to talk to them and handle them to soften them up so a younger man can get into the saddle. Some people call him a horse whisperer, which irritates him because it's a silly idea.

"This man outside San Anton' had a pasture full of horses—good-looking horses. More than a dozen. Kept them up well, but he never rode them."

"What did he keep them for then?"

Truly laughs and scratches his chin. He knows that feeding and housing a dozen horses that you can't ride or put to work must be

21

the most ridiculous thing I ever heard. "I asked him that. He said he rescued those horses a few years ago. Can you imagine that? They was wild. He fed them up and gave them a good place to live."

"Can't have been cheap."

"No, sir. But in the long run, he's going to get something out of it. They'll bring a good price."

"Truly, you might have figured I didn't get you down here to find out what some crazy rancher is doing with his horses." I tell him about the incident with the padlock being cut and Jenny's horses getting out. "I want to make sure that kind of nonsense doesn't happen anymore while Jenny is distracted with her mamma."

Truly takes his time answering. He mops up the last of his beans with the last of the cornbread. He's a slow eater. I've long since finished up my enchiladas. "Chief Craddock, I know you don't think horses are smart, but if something doesn't seem right to them they'll make enough of a fuss to alert you."

"They wandered up the street when somebody left the gate open. I don't know how smart that is."

He nods. "They will wander, but like you say, they didn't go far."

"I suppose."

"And you haven't mentioned this problem to Ms. Sandstone?"

"I don't want to. She has enough to worry about with her mother in the hospital."

"I hear that." He nods several times. "Tell you what I'll do. I'll get me a bedroll and sleep in the barn nights until things settle down."

"Come on, Truly, you don't need to do that. We're too old to sleep on the ground."

"Speak for yourself."

We laugh. That's as close to humor as Truly gets. "The problem is, I don't want Jenny to find you there. Then I'd have to tell her what's going on. I don't want to worry her if I don't have to."

"Put it out of your mind. I'll get down there after dark and be up and out before daylight."

"You know I'm going to insist on paying you for your time."

"No, sir. You're incurring no debt to me. Never have, never will." When I was chief the first time around, I saved Truly from spending the rest of his life in jail, and he's never forgotten it. He stands and picks up his hat. It'd be a contest to decide which of us has a shabbier hat. "Let me know when you think the danger has passed."

I'm following Truly out the door when Gabe LoPresto steps up to us. "Samuel, you got a minute?" Ever since Gabe went off on a tear with a young girl and got his ego whipped, he's been less blustery.

"Sure, what's up?"

"I want to mention something to you. I saw Ellen Forester's husband in town a couple of days ago. He behaving himself?"

Ellen moved into town recently and opened an art gallery and workshop where she teaches art. The business is thriving. Who would have guessed there were so many would-be artists in a small town? The only problem is her ex-husband keeps showing up and hounding her to "stop her foolishness" and move back to Houston where they used to live. He can't seem to accept that she divorced him, and he seems to think if he puts up enough of a fuss, she'll relent. Both LoPresto and I have had a couple of dust-ups with him. LoPresto's construction company renovated the house Ellen bought, and the ex-husband had threatened him and his workers more than once.

"As far as I know," I say, "Ellen hasn't complained, but you know how she is." Stubborn is what I mean. And determined to be brave. You had to admire a woman like that. Makes you want to protect her. "I'll stop by and make sure everything's okay."

"There's one more thing." He looks like a cat that's been at the cream. "If you know anybody looking for a construction job, send them my way."

I can't resist wanting to know more since he looks so pleased with himself. "Any particular reason?"

"I'm going to make a big announcement before too long. Can't spill the beans yet, though."

CHAPTER 5

"**S**he's gone."

At the hollow sound in Jenny's voice on the phone, I sit bolt up in bed. It's 5:30 a.m. "Jenny?"

"Mamma's gone. She died an hour ago." She draws a shaky breath. "Can you come?"

"She was so much better when I saw her."

"Just come."

It's late April and there should be some cool air so early in the morning, but it's already in the 80s. I'm unlocking the gate to Jenny's yard when I see Truly Bennett walking toward me, holding his bedroll. "Chief, what are you doing here? Can't sleep?"

I tell him about the call from Jenny and ask him to take care of my cows.

"I'm so sorry to hear that. Seems like Ms. Sandstone was a good daughter, spending all that time with her mamma."

At the hospital Jenny is in the hallway talking to a doctor, a dusky-skinned man who looks to be East Indian. Jenny looks spent, but she's dry-eyed and seems to have gone to some trouble with her appearance. Her hair is pulled back and she has makeup on. When she sees me, she puts a hand to her mouth and struggles to maintain some dignity.

The doctor turns my way and looks at me with kind eyes. "I'm Dr. Patel. Are you a friend of the family?"

"My neighbor," Jenny says. "And friend."

My impulse is to embrace Jenny to comfort her, but she isn't one for physical connection. Even if she were, sometimes it's hard for a grieving person to let themselves be physically comforted for fear of falling apart and not being able to stop crying. "Jenny, I'm so sorry," I say.

She swallows and nods a couple of times, but she doesn't move toward me, and I know I've made the right decision to hold back.

I introduce myself to Dr. Patel. "What happened? Vera seemed to be doing pretty well."

"She was. She was recovering well, but she took a turn for the worse yesterday afternoon. It happens that way sometimes. An undiagnosed infection can overwhelm the system, or perhaps there was another stroke."

Although I know he's right, and I've heard the same claim before, something about Vera's death doesn't feel right. She was doing well in general, but she seemed upset when I was here yesterday. She'd been crying, and when she said she didn't remember the things she said to me when I was here before, she seemed almost frightened.

"Are you planning to do an autopsy?" I ask.

Patel hesitates. "I had planned to request one." His glance flits toward Jenny. "It's really up to the family."

Jenny shakes her head. "Do we really need to know every single thing? It's not like there's anything to be done now."

Jenny may be the most down-to-earth person I know and this doesn't sound like her. The idea of autopsies makes some people squeamish, as if it violates their loved one. I suspect Jenny wants to protect Vera, even in death.

"You're right," Patel says to Jenny. "We don't have to know everything. But it could be useful. It adds to the body of knowledge to know why someone who is recovering suddenly succumbs."

Jenny turns miserable eyes to me in silent appeal. What I know as a lawman is that Patel could declare the cause of death unknown and therefore invoke an autopsy. But I don't want to push it. I'd rather Jenny make the decision herself.

"How soon do you have to know if Jenny decides to okay it?" I ask.

"The sooner the better, but she has time think it over." The doctor looks at his watch. "Perhaps we can meet in an hour?"

We agree to meet him back here. He tells us where the chapel is, and, even though neither Jenny nor I is religious, we go there to have a quiet place to sit and talk. It's a small room with a cross on the wall at one end. Under the cross is a small table with a Bible on it and a statue of the Virgin Mary, head bowed in prayer. Instead of pews, there are armchairs facing the cross. We sit down, Jenny sinking into her chair as if she will never get up again.

"I'm sorry I made you come to the hospital," Jenny says. "I know you have a lot to do. When it first happened, I thought I was going to fall apart."

"It's no problem for me to be here. Some little old lady may have to wait for me to catch whoever ran through her flowerbed, that's all." Being chief of police in Jarrett Creek doesn't require much in the way of heavy police work. My two deputies can handle most anything that comes around, especially Zeke Dibble, who put in twenty-five years on the force in Houston. He didn't take to retirement and we hired him part-time.

Jenny tries to smile. "I don't know what to do. I can't believe Mamma's gone. I can't wrap my head around it."

"Were you with her when she died?"

"Thank goodness I was. I never would have forgiven myself if I hadn't been there."

"Tell me the details."

Some people assume that a newly bereaved person doesn't want to discuss the death of someone they were close to. I know from experience that it's a gift to be able to talk about it while it's fresh in your mind. It's a way to bring back the person who died, if only for a few moments.

Jenny takes a deep breath. "Dr. Patel called me at work late yesterday and told me Mamma was struggling a bit, so I left work and came on over to the hospital. She was restless and seemed not to even see me when I came into the room. That gave me a bad feeling. I knew things weren't going well."

She's quiet for several seconds, lost in thought.

"Was she in pain?"

"No, I don't think so. But you know what? She seemed sad. Like maybe she knew things weren't going her way. And as the evening wore on she sank further and further. After a while she started mumbling crazy things. Sometimes she'd be clear, and then she'd seem confused. The nurses kept taking her blood pressure and they kept saying it was normal. They did some blood tests and said the white cells were elevated a little, but nothing alarming. But she just kept sinking." She shakes her head and wipes away tears.

"Your mamma was in her mid-seventies. She had a long life."

"It should have been longer." Suddenly Jenny smiles. "She was scared she'd be a burden to me if she got too old. I told her she'd never be a burden."

"You were lucky to have a good mother like that."

Jenny nods. We've had a lot of good talks, and she understands that my situation was the opposite. My mamma was a difficult woman, and when she became ill at the end of her life, she resented all the well people around her and anything they tried to do for her. Jeanne and I took good care of her in circumstances where a lot of people would have left her alone.

"You said she was talking crazy. What kind of things was she saying?"

"She kept telling me to find my daddy. I don't think she ever talked like that—not to me, anyway. And she kept telling me to be careful and take care of myself." She starts to cry again, tears slipping down her cheeks. "That's the way she was, always worrying about me instead of herself."

"She asked me to find your daddy, too."

"I don't know what she was thinking. Poor thing."

I decide to plunge in. "There was something else, too. She wanted me to find your daddy's first wife?"

Jenny sits bolt upright. "What? What first wife? My daddy wasn't married before. Like I said, she was talking crazy."

"What do you think about the autopsy?"

"I don't know."

"What would your mamma have wanted?"

Jenny ponders for a few seconds and begins to nod. She squares her shoulders, and her eyes lose some of their misery. "That's exactly the right question to ask. You're right. She was an educator through and through. She would want her death to be used to teach somebody something, and she would have fussed at me for dragging my feet." She stands up. "Let's go talk to the doctor."

Half a dozen people are huddled near the nurses' station and they all turn toward Jenny when we walk up. Wilson Landreau, the man Jenny was arguing with at the hospital last week, is here. He walks up to us and says, "The nurse said you were in the chapel and we wanted to give you time to be alone." He casts a curious look at me.

"Thank you, Will." Jenny grabs his hand for a brief moment, and he puts his hand on top of hers.

Two elderly women and a couple move to Jenny's side, murmuring their condolences. One of the women, rail thin and with sharp features, says, "Jennifer, I don't know what I'm going to do without your mamma. She was my best friend for forty years. It's going to take its toll on me."

Jenny puts her arm around the woman's shoulders. "Mrs. Matthews, I know how much Mamma loved you. It's going to be hard for all of us to get along without her."

Mrs. Matthews takes a tissue out of her sleeve and dabs her eyes. She looks sharply at Will and then at me. She may be grief-stricken, but not so much that she can't assess who Jenny's men friends are. Seeing that Jenny is well taken care of, I bow out, telling Jenny to call if she needs anything.

I'm at the juncture of two hallways, headed to the elevators when I see Dr. Patel hurrying down to meet Jenny for their appointment. I flag him down.

"Jenny would like to go ahead with the autopsy," I say.

"Good, I'll take care of it right away." He starts to walk away, and I put my hand up to stop him.

"A question. When I came here to visit Vera yesterday, she seemed agitated. If someone said something to upset her, could that have caused another stroke?"

He hesitates. "It isn't unheard of for someone with high blood pressure or with a weak immune system to be affected adversely by anger or from some terrible event. But Mrs. Sandstone was not an elderly woman and she was in generally good health. She should have recovered. I'll be glad of the opportunity to find out more from the autopsy."

"I'm glad Jenny decided to go ahead then."

"There is one thing. You were right, Mrs. Sandstone did have a visitor who upset her. One of my nurses told me there was an incident."

"What kind of incident?"

Patel grimaces. "I can't say more than that. It's a privacy issue, but I wanted you to know that your question was not out of line."

Back home, I call a few people Jenny is friendly with in town and tell them her mother passed away. In the best of times, Jenny is not a cook, and the food that people will bring her will be helpful. I make a fair beef stew myself, and I throw the ingredients into a Crockpot.

As I'm leaving for headquarters, Jenny calls and asks if I'll come to her mother's house later. Some of her mother's friends will be visiting this afternoon. "I need somebody to help me entertain them. You've got a gift of gab."

I spend a couple of hours at work and then go over to Vera's house to help Jenny slog through conversations with the mourners. They all press to know when the funeral will be and what they can do to help. Jenny tells them she'll decide with the preacher tomorrow and let them know.

Mrs. Matthews has been fluttering around Jenny like a humming-bird and suddenly she says, "Jennifer, I hope I'm not out of line. Have you phoned your brother and told him Vera passed?"

Jenny's reaction takes me by surprise. Usually unflappable, she couldn't look any more stunned if the woman had slapped her across the face. When it's clear that she isn't going to reply, one of the other ladies says, "I'm sure Jenny will do what's right. This isn't the time to bother her."

"I just meant . . ." Mrs. Matthews's voice trails away, and then she looks around the room. "Can I get anybody a refill of coffee?"

When the conversation returns to normal, Jenny signals me that she wants me to follow her. She takes me out onto the back porch. We stand looking out over the yard. "I just need a minute to collect myself," she says.

The grass is freshly mowed. "Smells good out here," I say. "You mow this yourself?"

She smiles and says, "You know me better than that. It was Nate Holloway from next door. As soon as I got here and told him Mamma was gone, he came over to clean up the yard and mow. He said he wanted everything to look as nice as Mamma would have wanted it to."

"Sounds like a nice young man," I say.

"You wouldn't think a twenty-five-year-old man would take any notice of an old woman like Mamma. Shows how much everyone loved her." She crosses her arms, hugging herself. "Listen, I called you out here to ask you something. Did Dr. Patel have a particular reason for requesting an autopsy?"

"I think he just wanted to get as much information as he could. Why do you ask?"

"I don't know. He just seemed like he had something particular in mind."

"He did mention one thing." I tell Jenny her mother had a visitor who upset her.

"What do you mean he wouldn't tell you who it was? Why not?"

"He said it was a privacy issue."

"She's dead. How much privacy does she need?"

"Maybe he'll tell you; just not me. Now, you want to tell me what that was all about in there? I didn't know you had a brother."

She gets that same strained look on her face, but at least she doesn't stonewall me the way she did Mrs. Matthews. "For all intents and purposes, I don't," she says.

I've become more accustomed to the horses in the past week and feel comfortable leading them into their stalls for the night. I could get Truly to do it, but I don't want to put him out, and besides, I haven't minded getting to know the horses. So when I get Mahogany to the door of his stall at dusk, I'm surprised when he balks and dances backward. "Come on in here. I'm not doing anything different," I say, hoping the sound of my voice will calm him.

I pull on his lead, and he takes a few steps in, but he stamps his feet and blows through his nostrils, something he's never done before. His eyes are rolling and he looks frightened. I could let him stay in the pasture and have Truly come by later and put him away, but it hurts my pride to think I can't outsmart a cranky horse. I step deeper into the stall, speaking calmly, and Mahogany takes another step or two. He's halfway in now, and I move to the side to get out of his way. Suddenly he screams and rears. I jump back, dropping the lead. And that's when I see a huge rattlesnake on the floor of the stall. He's half-hidden by straw strewn on the floor.

"Son of a bitch!" I yell. Mahogany rears again, panicked. In the stall next door, Blackie takes up the panic and begins blowing and flailing around, kicking and butting up against the sides of the stall.

Mahogany continues to rear and stamp, his eyes wild. I fling myself up against the far wall to avoid his hooves—and to avoid the snake, which has begun to coil itself. "Whoa, boy," I say. "Easy does it. Back on up. Take it easy." I try to keep my voice even, although I'm as alarmed as the horse is. I'm relieved when Mahogany moves backward far enough to turn around and bolt out of the stall.

Now it's me and the snake, which is fully coiled and making that rattling noise that chills the blood. The snake is so long that he might be able to reach me if he strikes. I've got sturdy boots on, but I don't know how high up he can lunge. All he has to do is hit my femoral artery and I'm done for. I look for something to defend myself with and see a pitchfork on the wall just out of reach. Should I lunge for it or stay still? The slightest movement could set the snake off.

Knowing a bit about rattlers, I opt for stillness. It's a waiting game that has my legs shaking and gives me plenty of time to get a good look at the snake. This isn't your central Texas rattlesnake. It's thicker and longer. If I'm not mistaken this is a timber rattler, which you sometimes find in east Texas but not so much around here. When I worked as a land man and did a lot of land surveys, I made it my business to know the habits of the poisonous snakes in Texas—which are many. The timber rattler is less aggressive than some others. Sure enough, after a time of seeing no movement from me, he uncoils himself and slithers back under the straw.

I wait until my breathing is quieter and my legs less rubbery before I ease out of the stall, keeping my back to the wall and my eye on the straw where the snake disappeared. Out of the barn, I hunch over with my hands on my knees, taking deep breaths, waiting for my heart rate to slow down. The sun has set, but there's still a good bit of light in the sky. I'm relieved to see that Mahogany has retreated far down into the pasture, still blowing and dancing skittishly.

I go back into the barn and lead Blackie out to the pasture. I don't know what that rattlesnake has in mind, but I don't want it to corner Blackie. The horse is reluctant to leave and tries to go back into the barn, so I have to swat him on the rump to get him to move away.

I waste no time going back to my place for a shotgun. I come back and find a long-handled hoe, which I use to push straw aside until I uncover the rattlesnake. Then I dispatch it with a couple of shots. Normally I wouldn't bother a snake, but this one was in the wrong place at the wrong time. I feel sick thinking what could have happened if Jenny had come home, distracted, and tried to put the horses away.

After I hang the snake's body on the fence, I try to get the horses back in, but Mahogany is having none of it. I get Blackie in and then go back to my house and call Truly Bennett and tell him what happened. "I'd appreciate it if you'd help me get Mahogany in the stall. He's pretty spooked."

"I don't blame him," Truly says. "I'm glad it was you and not me found that rattler. You know I hate snakes."

"I know you do, and I can't say I was too fond of this one myself."

"What'd you do with the carcass?"

"I hung it on the fence."

"Good. I'll take it to a lady I know who makes things with snakeskin. How about lye soap? Did you put some in the stall?"

"I'll take a bar over there now."

I don't really believe in the old tale that says where there's one snake there's two and that a bar of lye soap will keep the second one away. But it can't hurt to put the soap out. I take the pitchfork and toss the straw in the stall around to make sure there are no more surprises.

When Truly arrives we coax Mahogany into the stall. Between the cut lock and the timber rattler that's out of its territory, I can't help wondering if somebody has it in for these horses—someone who knows how much Jenny cares for them.

CHAPTER 6

I'm glad that Truly is spending the night with the horses so I don't have to worry about them and can get a good night's sleep. Early the next morning I get a call from a jogger who says that Ellen Forester's art gallery has been vandalized. I call her and she says she'll meet me there.

She's there when I arrive, standing in front of the store with the look of someone who has been punched in the stomach. Her face is splotchy from crying, although she's dry-eyed now. She's pretty, even with the traces of tears on her face and no makeup. She's wearing jeans and an oversized shirt that makes her look even more petite than she is.

Hands on our hips, we survey the considerable damage to the front of the building. The big picture window that displays art has been smashed, and a couple of the paintings near the window have big splashes of red paint on them. The door and front of the building are also splashed with paint.

"This makes me so mad," Ellen says. "I can hardly stand to look at it. Why would anybody be so mean?"

"You have insurance, right?"

She looks up at me, her dark eyes angry. "Of course, but it's got a high deductible. That's not the point anyway. The window can be replaced, but people have worked on those paintings, and even though they may not have any monetary value, they're important to somebody." She surveys the damage again. "What's the chance of catching whoever did it?"

"I'm not going to lay any odds, but you'd be surprised how one thing leads to another and before you know it . . ." I shrug and then try to lighten her mood. "And it's always possible that someone will get a guilty conscience and tattle."

She smiles. "You're thinking it might be teenagers?"

"It is that time of year." It's prom, finals, and graduation in rapid succession. Kids get amped up, and there's no telling what they will get up to. But that's not actually who I think is likely to have done this. The damage to the window is so thorough that it has to have been more than somebody randomly throwing a rock from a car. It looks like somebody took a hammer and smashed out as much of the window as he could reach. "You got any other ideas. Had any threats?"

She shakes her head, eyes narrowed. She knows what I'm referring to.

"Could this be the work of your husband?"

"*Ex*-husband! I swear I'm going to convince everybody to call him that. And there's no reason he would do something so low."

A crowd is forming, courtesy of Jarrett Creek's lively grapevine, all angry at the destruction. The gallery hasn't been open that long, but it already has a following of would-be artists who jumped at the chance to take classes from Ellen. Many of them huddle around her, commiserating.

Gabe LoPresto storms up to Ellen, "I bet this is the work of that husband of yours—or somebody he hired to do it."

"We were just discussing that," I say. "Let's not jump to conclusions." Although I have to admit that I agree with him.

LoPresto considers himself witty, and a smirk comes to his face. "I don't suppose this is somebody's critical commentary on people's artwork?"

Ellen grins. "Gabe, if everybody who doesn't like my art expressed it this way, I'd have to fold up business."

"Well, don't you worry," he says. "I'm going to have a crew out here the minute the insurance people say I can get started, and I'll fix you up in no time."

Gabe's words sound like he's the soul of charity, but I know his wife Sandy takes classes here. She brags that she has discovered a previously untapped talent. Gabe has been working hard to get back in Sandy's good graces ever since he strayed. If he wasted ten minutes repairing the damage to the gallery, she'd give him hell.

I poke into the glass a little bit, but there's nothing in the rubble that could have been used as a missile. "Have you been inside?" I ask Ellen.

"No. I guess I should. The door was still locked, so I assumed everything was fine inside." She pulls out a key and heads for the door.

"Hold it," I say. "I need to go in there first."

Not only do I want to be sure the crime scene is secure, but also having had the recent run-in with the snake, I want to check things out. I can imagine somebody throwing a snake through the window and it lying in wait inside. But when I check the gallery and workshop area, Ellen's office, and the restroom, everything looks undisturbed—and there are no vipers in sight. I bring her inside to see if anything is missing.

Ellen's art is prominently displayed in the gallery, along with pieces from other Texas artists, mostly landscapes. None of it is to my taste, but I haven't said so. I used to like representational art—the Texas school of cactus, cows, and bluebonnets. But my wife Jeanne gradually won me over to modern art. I have a pretty fair collection that gives me great pleasure. Ellen doesn't carry that kind of art because most people don't have a taste for it. She's got a business to run, and there's no point in carrying things people won't buy.

"At least everything is okay in here," she says. She looks like she's going to start crying again but turns to me with a fierce look instead. "I'm not going to cry! I won't give anyone the satisfaction."

It's late afternoon when I get a call from Jenny. "I wanted to let you know that Dr. Patel called and he said Mamma died of a stroke, pure and simple. Apparently the autopsy set his mind at rest."

"That's good to know. Where are you? You sound like you're calling from the bottom of a well."

"I'm at Mamma's house in the garage. I'm looking through all the stuff out here wondering what I'm going to do with it." I hear the scrape of a box being shoved.

"Do you have anybody there helping you to organize your mamma's stuff?"

"I don't really feel like being around anybody right now, although . . . I know you're busy, but do you have time to come over here later? You won't poke at me the way most people do."

"I'll be there as soon as I can get away. And I'll bring food."

"Oh, Lord, no! I could open a soup kitchen with all the dishes people have brought over. Between the church ladies and the school-teachers, I don't have enough room in the refrigerator."

"I hate to be picky, but is there anything edible in the mix?" I'm thinking of the endless tuna casseroles that seem to show up anytime someone dies. "I have some beef stew I could bring."

"You save that. We can't let this stuff go to waste. There's bound to be something here you can eat. I know your eating habits aren't as elegant as you pretend they are."

When I hang up I realize I've been worried, wondering how Jenny was going to go forward with her mother gone. Jenny talked to Vera every day and consulted her on every little thing. She sounded good just now, but I can't shake the memory of Vera telling me she thought Jenny was in danger. She was upset the last time I saw her, and even though she claimed to have been unaware of what she was saying, I can't help thinking she was hiding something. Maybe Jenny will be able to tell me more.

CHAPTER 7

I find Jenny out in the backyard at Vera's place. She looks pale and drawn. Her red hair is wrestled back into a band low on her neck. Hands on her hips, she's staring at her mamma's beds of zinnias, lantana, lavender, and black-eyed Susans. There's also a big Pride of Barbados and several rosebushes. "I don't know what to do with all these plants. I'm not a gardener, but Mamma would've had a fit if she knew I'd let all them go."

"It will certainly help sell the place if the plants aren't all dead," I say.

"That's not funny." She shoots me an exasperated look.

"Can you hire somebody to take care of it?"

She squints. "I guess I'll have to. One more thing to add to the list."

"Maybe get Nate Holloway from next door."

She runs her hand across her forehead, smearing a streak of dirt. "That's a perfect idea."

I brandish the bottle of red wine I brought. "Thought maybe you could use this."

"I hope you brought one for yourself, too. I could polish that off in ten minutes." She looks down at her clothes. One shoulder of her T-shirt is matted with cobwebs. "I ought to get cleaned up."

"Why don't you take a shower and I'll organize some food."

Jenny disappears while I attack the refrigerator. I pull out a roast chicken, bean salad, and potato salad, and set everything out on the little glass-top table on the patio outside the kitchen. I don't find wineglasses, so I grab water glasses.

"That looks downright civilized," Jenny says, when she comes back looking and smelling fresher. "I think I scrubbed a pound of dirt off."

She sighs when she sips the wine. "I wish Mamma could be here to enjoy this."

"I didn't find any wineglasses, so I wondered if she was a teetotaler."

Jenny laughs. "She didn't drink wine, but she liked a gin and tonic now and again. That's not something she'd want spread around her church friends, you understand."

"You figure out the funeral arrangements yet?"

"Oh, Lord, I should have called you so you could let people know. My mind is a sieve. The funeral is going to be Thursday. Should have been tomorrow, but they already have two scheduled. It's like an epidemic."

"You said you had an aunt and uncle in Lubbock. Are they coming out for the services?"

There's the barest moment of hesitation before Jenny shakes her head. "Mamma and Aunt Susie and her husband were friendly enough with each other, but I hardly knew them. They have two sons that I haven't seen in years. I'll call and let them know when the funeral is, but I don't expect they'll come all this way. I'll be okay."

"Anybody you want me to call?"

She tells me she's already got a team of her mamma's friends but asks me to call a couple of our neighbors.

I tell Jenny about the vandalism at the art store and my suspicion that Ellen's husband was involved. By the way she keeps staring off into the backyard, I can tell she's struggling to focus on my chatter. When I finish the story, we fall quiet and drink our wine peaceably as the light goes soft and a little breeze cools the air.

"There's something I need to bring up with you," I say. "There've been some things going on that I've kept from you because I know you've had a lot on your mind."

She jerks upright and turns to look at me. "Is everything okay with my horses?"

"Yes, but that's because Truly Bennett and I have been handling things. Something happened that has me worried." I tell her about the horses getting out and the snake getting in. "It was a timber rattler."

She shudders and sinks back into her chair and puts her hands over her face. "Oh, my God. Where did a snake like that come from? I've never seen anything that big around here."

"That's the point. They don't live much farther south than east Texas. I think somebody might have brought it in."

"I don't know why . . ." And then she nods abruptly. "I'll look into it."

"What does that mean? You have some idea who did it?"

"I'm not sure. I have to talk to some people." Jenny can be hard to read and hardheaded.

"Jenny, if you have some idea of who did it, you have to tell me."

She stops me with a look.

I've known Jenny long enough to understand that she is fiercely independent. Her personal life is off-limits. I have no idea who her good friends are, just that she spends a lot of time at work. I don't know if she has anybody special in her life—or ever had, for that matter. She has a personal line that isn't to be crossed. But I'm going to have to put a toe over that line.

"All right, I'll let that go for now. But there's another issue I need to bring up."

The light is dim now, but I can still see the wariness that narrows her eyes when she turns her head in my direction. "What is it?"

"Something your mamma said to me at the hospital. Remember when I found you having words with your friend and you asked me to stay with her?"

She relaxes a little. "Of course I do. When I got back to her room, she was all riled up and the nurse kicked you out." She laughs.

"Do you have any reason to believe you'd be in danger from anyone?"

Jenny draws in a sharp breath. For a few seconds it's like she's turned to stone. Finally she picks up her glass but doesn't bring it to her lips. "What did Mamma say exactly?"

"She said she thought you were in danger and wanted me to look out for you. With all this stuff going on with your horses, I wondered if there was a connection. That's why I want to know who you suspect of messing with your horses."

"I doubt there's a connection. She didn't say who she was worried about?"

"No, and when she was feeling better, I asked her why she was worried about you. She said she must have been out of her head, but I had a feeling she was holding something back."

Jenny lifts the glass and sips, but when she puts it down she runs her hands back and forth across the tops of her thighs. "I don't know what she was talking about. Is that it?"

"You're not making this easy."

"There's no reason for you to be involved."

"It was a pretty specific warning."

"I don't think you need to take it seriously."

"She seemed to." The longer we've been talking, the more I feel tension radiating off Jenny. We've always gotten along well, and I'm at a loss how to deal with this sharper, angrier version. "Why haven't you ever told me you have a brother? Is there bad blood between you?"

She gives a sharp, bitter bark of laughter and when she speaks, her voice is unlike anything I've heard come from her. "Sometimes you dance around a subject a little too delicately for my taste, Samuel." Abruptly she gets up from the table. "Let's go inside. I'm starting to get eaten up by mosquitoes."

I get up, too. "That doesn't answer my question about your brother."

"How's this for an answer—it's none of your business. I won't discuss my brother with anyone, not even you."

On the way home, I mull over Jenny's harsh response and what she isn't telling me. Maybe I'm making too much of the incidents with the horses. The snake could have hitched a ride on someone's pickup, or may have been somebody's escaped snake. But the cut lock was no accident. I don't want to intrude on Jenny's privacy, but somehow I've got to find out who she thinks has a reason for the attacks, before they graduate to attacking her as well.

Back home, Truly Bennett's truck is parked outside of Jenny's place. He usually doesn't come until after dark, but I asked him to put the horses away this evening since I'd be with Jenny, and he must have decided there was no sense in going home afterward. I check in by phone with Zeke Dibble, who was on duty today, but he says it was a slow day. He had to settle a problem between a couple of boys down at the Two Dog bar in the late afternoon, but that was the only ripple in his day.

I'm settling down to watch the news on TV when I hear a cry from Jenny's place. It sounds like somebody yelling, "Help me!" At first I think it's probably Mrs. Summerville's TV next door. She's hard of hearing, and sometimes the TV gets loud. But it's too late for Mrs. Summerville and her daughter to be up. And besides, my cat Zelda, who's been keeping me company, is alert, staring in the direction the sound came from. I hold my breath, straining, and I hear it again.

I jump to my feet and head for the door, but then I stop myself. This is no time to rush in without protection. I get my heavy flashlight and slip my shoulder holster on, checking first to make sure the gun is loaded.

Instead of going out the front, I head into my back pasture. There's a gate between my place and Jenny's, and I can slip into Jenny's property that way. As I approach the stable, I hear the sound again, this time with a moan. I shine the light around the outside of the barn but don't see anything wrong.

"Truly?" I call out.

"Chief Craddock. I'm in here." His voice sounds weak.

I fumble around on the inside wall of the stable and turn on the lights. Truly is sitting, propped up against the wall that holds riding gear—halters and such. Blood is seeping from a head wound down the side of his face, and he's holding his arm tight against his side. A length of pipe lies a few feet away next to his bedroll.

"I'm glad to see you," he says.

"Hold on, Truly, let me check first and make sure nobody is lurking around here."

"I think he's gone," he says.

Both horses are awake and have poked their heads over the stall gates, ears pricked forward like a couple of gossips, but they're quiet, so I suspect Truly is right. Still I check the stalls and the tack room before I come back and crouch down next to him to look closer at the wound. His hair is short, so I see that he's bleeding from two places. "What happened? Who did this?"

He groans. "I didn't see who it was. I got the horses put away and went to my truck to fetch my bedroll, and when I got back somebody jumped me."

"How many were there?"

"I think it was only one. He hit me with something that felt like a lead pipe before I had a chance to fight back."

"The pipe's right here. Not too clever of somebody to leave it lying around. Did you get in any licks?"

"Naw, it happened too fast."

It's possible whoever did this was wearing gloves, but I'll have the pipe examined for fingerprints anyway. "Did your attacker say anything?"

Truly gives a half-groan, half-laugh. "Yes, sir, he said, 'That'll teach you, nigger.' I'm not sure what I was supposed to learn from getting beat up."

"Well, you've still got your sense of humor so I guess you're not hurt too bad."

"Feels like it, though." He shifts his position and groans. "I'm glad they picked on me and not those horses. They look okay, don't they?"

"They're fine. Can you walk?"

"I think he might have broken my shoulder, but at least I've still got my legs."

"Hold on, I've got to find something to carry this pipe in so I can have it examined for prints." In the tack room I find a box of plastic bags in a drawer. I use a couple of them to wrap the pipe.

On the way to the emergency room in Bobtail, I call Zeke Dibble and tell him what happened and ask him to go keep an eye on Jenny's place until I get back there. I think about calling Jenny, but I hate to rile her up any more than she was tonight. She needs some rest.

CHAPTER 8

With Truly Bennett out of commission, I've got a problem. I can't keep an eye on Jenny and her horses alone. And I can't keep this latest incident from her. I'll have to tell her so she'll be careful, and she'll need to decide whether she wants to hire someone to watch her horses or if she wants to board them somewhere else for a while.

On the way out of town I stop by Art Visions to check in on Ellen Forester. She's in the middle of a class but comes outside to talk. She has dark circles under her eyes. "Gabe's crew did all the repairs yesterday," she says. "That was really nice of them to get to it so fast." She sounds overly cheerful. She's worried.

"Have you thought anymore about who might have done the damage?"

She shrugs but doesn't meet my eyes. "I was hoping you might have turned up something."

I talked with Bill Odum yesterday. He's a young deputy and has a good way with our habitual troublemakers. He said he'll poke around and see if he can get anybody to point him in the right direction. But I'm still putting my money on Ellen's ex.

"Ellen, if you think your ex-husband did this, I need to know. He doesn't seem to be getting the message that you're not going back. And he needs to stop harassing you."

She rubs at a spot of paint on one of her hands. "I called Seth and asked if he had anything to do with it. He said he didn't, but . . ." She clasps her arms to herself and shakes her head.

"But you didn't believe him?"

"He said it may be the lesson I need to get me off my high horse."

He has a different idea of her than I do. "You consider getting a restraining order against him?"

She shakes her head. "I don't want to do that. I'm still holding out that it was high school kids."

"Maybe so. I'll keep my ears open and hope this is a one-time thing."

Without thinking, I reach out and touch her arm to reassure her. She jumps like she's been burned.

"Sorry, I didn't mean to startle you."

She flushes deep red. "No, no, it's okay. I'm just . . ."

"You take care," I say.

When I go to Vera Sandstone's house to tell Jenny what happened to Truly last night, I find her in the garage staring at a wall of rusted tools. "These tools belonged to my daddy and I don't think anybody has touched them since he left," she says. "I don't know whether anybody would want them, or if I should pitch them out. I don't think they're old enough to be antiques, but they're probably too old to be useful to anyone." She's not looking at me. I expect she's still mad that I pressed her too hard yesterday asking about her brother.

"Leave this until after the funeral, when you've had time to catch your breath," I say to her. I persuade her to go back into the house, where I make some coffee. We sit down in the living room, surrounded by empty packing boxes.

I give her a short version of the attack on Truly. I don't want her to feel guilty that something happened to him, but she has to know that there's been another incident.

"Why would somebody attack Truly?"

"It seems obvious they were after your horses, and when they found Truly there, they attacked him instead. Now that's the third incident involving your horses. It's time we got to the bottom of it."

She draws a sharp breath. "With Mamma being gone, I don't know what I'd do if something happened to those horses. They're okay? They weren't hurt?"

"They're fine. I checked again this morning."

She gets up from her chair and walks around, agitated. "You're right. Something's got to be done. With my mind on Mamma, I haven't paid enough attention."

"Settle down, now. That's why Truly and I have been keeping watch over them, so nothing would happen. But with Truly being injured, we need to come up with another plan. If you want to hire somebody to look out for them, I can recommend Buzz Carter's son Alvin, who helped me corral the horses when they got out last week."

"He sounds perfect. As soon as I get Mamma's house cleared up, I'll be spending more time at home."

"Jenny, until we figure out who's behind these pranks, I don't think you or the horses are safe. The last time I talked to you, you seemed to have an idea who's behind it, and I don't understand why you won't tell me."

She stops her pacing and glares at me. "I told you I'd take care of it, and I'll get right on it. Meanwhile, if you'll hire Alvin for me, I'd appreciate it. Right now I need to get over to the funeral home to finish up arrangements."

"Okay, I'll be on my way."

Apparently I don't hide my frustration very well, because her expression softens. "I'm sorry. I don't mean to be short with you, but I don't want you to worry about me. I can take care of myself." She hesitates. "Do you mind running a couple of errands for me while I'm gone? When I get back I'll bring us some lunch." She's asking for my help as a way to put aside our spat, and I'm glad to comply.

I go to the grocery store and the hardware store to pick up things on Jenny's list, but I'm still back before she is. She left the back door open, so I go in and put things away and then wander through the house, trying to see if there's anything I can do to help.

In the bedroom there are boxes in various stages of packing. Photo albums and loose photos are piled on the bed, and I look at a few of them. Jenny was a tall, gangly girl. There's a photo of her fifth-grade class, and she and one other girl tower over the others, both wearing that same expression that says they wish they could disappear into the earth rather than having their picture taken with their pint-sized classmates.

Time didn't improve things much. A teenage school photo shows her face as too long, her nose too big, and her eyes hidden behind unflattering glasses. The scowl on her face doesn't help. She always told me that she was a wallflower in high school because she was self-conscious about her height and her looks. It's too bad she couldn't see into the future: that her face would settle into good proportion as she got older, and that contact lenses and a little makeup would turn her into an attractive woman.

One photo that catches my interest shows a family of four—Vera and a man I take to be her husband stand behind two kids, Jenny, who is scowling as usual, and a boy who looks to be a few years older, who has a devilish grin. Jenny's around eight in the picture. The kids look alike, although the boy is better-looking. On the back someone has written four names: Vera, Howard, Edward, and Jenny. Edward must be Jenny's brother. Why won't she talk about her brother? Did he get in some kind of trouble? Did he disgrace the family in some way?

I'm interested in the way Howard looks in the photo. Jenny said he walked out on the family, but you would never have guessed it from the way he beams into the camera. What made him decide to leave? Probably that old story of the kids getting old enough to talk back, and the dad starts to feel trapped, and then he meets someone younger who makes him feel like his old self, and he decides he should start over and get it right this time. Vera asked me to locate him. Although Jenny doesn't seem enthusiastic, I can't help thinking it would be a fine thing for her to at least know where Howard is. And then I remember the other thing Vera asked me—to find Howard's first wife. Jenny said he wasn't married before, but she might not have known. But the question is, why did Vera want me to find her?

I flip through other photos and they're versions of the same picture, as if it was a ritual to have their family picture taken every year to mark the passage of time. The last picture in the stack was taken when the kids were in their teens, both of the children towering over their parents. But what stops me in my tracks is that I recognize Eddie Sandstone. He was the man coming out of the hospital the day I last went to visit Vera.

I hear Jenny drive up and make a hasty exit from the bedroom. I've put myself in an awkward position. Now I know that her brother was at the hospital, but if I tell Jenny I saw the photos, she'll know I was snooping.

Jenny has brought some barbecue brisket for lunch and we eat on the kitchen table. Neither of us has much appetite and we have a hard time keeping up a conversation.

When I get home midafternoon, I turn on the computer. I'm curious to know if there's an obvious reason for Jenny to be ashamed of her brother. In no time I'm staring at a string of entries for people named Eddie Sandstone. It's amazing how many people have the same name—even an unusual name like Sandstone. I narrow it down to Texas and query the state files that I can access through the Texas Public Safety sites. Apparently Jenny's brother has lived in Temple for many years—a couple of hours' drive from here. Although he has a contractor's license, he seems mostly to do sheetrock work. He's been married for two years, with no children, and was married once before. Except for a few traffic tickets over the years, he has had one run-in with the law, an assault charge, which was dropped later. In other words, I find nothing to account for Jenny's animosity toward her brother. But family feuds don't have to have much of a reason.

CHAPTER 9

I wondered if Jenny's brother was going to show up at the funeral, but I don't see him in the considerable crowd. Jenny is down front surrounded by her mother's friends. She contacted her aunt and found out she'd recently had back surgery and wasn't able to travel, so there's no family to mourn Vera except Jenny. I go down and say hello to her before I take a seat farther back.

The service is ready to start when I hear a bit of buzz at the back of the room, and I turn to see the man I recognize as Eddie Sandstone walk in, alone. He makes his way down the aisle, and I wonder if he plans to sit next to Jenny. He slows, though, and tucks in a few rows back. But the stir caused by his arrival has alerted Jenny. She cranes her head to look and then snaps back, fast. You don't have to be a genius at reading body language to notice her shoulders stiffen. Whatever happened between the two siblings, the death of their mother has not patched up anything.

At the reception, there's no sign of Eddie. I was hoping to have a few words with him to find out if he ever heard anything from his daddy. If he and Jenny were on the outs, I wonder how he knew his mamma was in the hospital and that she died.

I go through the receiving line that consists of Jenny and a couple of Vera's closest friends, and I overhear some of Vera's students describing to Jenny what they learned from Vera. One says, "She was my favorite teacher. She was a wonderful lady." Jenny is dignified and gracious, but I can see that having to interact with all these people is a strain.

Although Jarrett Creek and Bobtail are only fifteen miles apart, there isn't much comingling, so I don't know many of the people attending. But suddenly I spy someone I do know, a young woman who works in the flower shop in Jarrett Creek. She's very pregnant, with that glow some women get when they are nearly ready to deliver. She's standing alone, so I walk up to her. "Rowena, you grew up in Jarrett Creek. How did you know Vera?"

She beams at me. "My husband was one of her students. Here he comes with my punch." A tall, lanky man in his forties, several years older than Rowena, comes over with two cups of punch. He barely registers my presence and says to his wife, "I wish you'd go sit down. It's not good for you to be standing so much."

"Oh, now stop it, Doyle," she giggles. "If standing around means I get this baby out earlier, then I'll stand up while I sleep tonight. But here, let me introduce you to Chief Craddock."

Doyle Hancock tells me he grew up in Bobtail and never wanted to live anywhere else. "Rowena works part-time at the flower shop in Jarrett Creek so she can learn the trade. She's bound and determined to learn how to arrange flowers."

"I want to learn everything I can from Justine so I can open my own florist shop one day here in Bobtail."

"That's not going to be for a while," her husband says, "not until our kids are in school."

They prattle on, sparring in that easy way some couples have. I wait until I have an opening. "Doyle, Rowena says you were one of Vera Sandstone's students."

"That's right, and lucky to be. She was fair, but she didn't let anybody off easy—I teach English over at Bobtail JC, and she's the person who got me there."

"Let me ask you something. Did you know her kids? You'd be about Jenny and Edward's age."

He grins. "Yeah, I was in the same grade with Jenny."

"And how about Eddie? Did you know him?"

"He was two grades above me. Can't say we ran in the same circles though. He was a jock and I was more the studious type."

"He was popular?"

"One hundred percent. He was one of those guys that seemed to be good at everything. He didn't have time for a kid like me." He smirks. "If you want to know something about him, ask Careen Hudson."

"Doyle!" Rowena puts her hands on her hips. "That's just pure old gossip."

"Who's Careen Hudson?" I ask.

"Go ahead and tell it," Rowena says, laughing.

He shrugs. "She was a teacher that all the boys had a crush on. There was always talk that she was making out with one or another of them. And she got fired when she was found with one of them."

"Doyle, you don't know if this Eddie had anything to do with her. You're just stirring up trouble."

"She stirred up her own trouble." He chuckles. "Anyway, like I said, Eddie was a jock. Played football. He got a football scholarship to SMU."

I whistle. "I don't know anybody from around here ever played for SMU."

"Well, that's the thing. He didn't. Something went wrong. I never did hear what it was, but they withdrew the scholarship."

I excuse myself to go talk to a couple I saw at the hospital when I went to comfort Jenny the day Vera died. Martha and Lloyd Glenn tell me they've lived down the street from Vera for almost forty years. "I taught school with Vera for a few years, but I wasn't cut out for it the way she was. I retired a long time ago." Martha Glenn has ice blue eyes, a very pointed nose, and a severe look, so I expect there were students who were pretty relieved to escape having those eyes track them.

"You know her kids, too?"

"Oh, yes, our daughter Rhonda was Jenny's classmate, although they never were close. She came to the funeral today, though. She always liked Vera. Everybody did. Rhonda's over there." She points to a group of people Jenny's age. "She's the one with gray pantsuit. Her husband is next to her. He's a dentist."

"Did Rhonda know Jenny's brother, Eddie?"

"Of course she did. She had a crush on Eddie. But then, every girl did. Such a good-looking boy. And smart. The apple of Vera's eye." She's beaming, but then something catches at her thoughts and she glances at her husband. Their eyes meet and something unsettled passes between them. Her husband's lips are set in a line of disapproval. "Anyway . . ." She looks around for an escape.

"Did you know Howard Sandstone?"

"Yes, we did. We played bridge together when the kids were young. He was a nice man."

For the first time, her husband speaks up. "Shame he ran out on the family. Never would have expected it."

"Lloyd, we'd better be off," Martha says.

"Did Jenny and her brother get along?"

Again, that odd look between the Glenns. "You know how brothers and sisters are," Martha Glenn says briskly. "Now if you'll excuse us."

They bolt, leaving me to muse that no, I don't necessarily know how brothers and sisters are—especially Jenny and her brother Eddie. But I do know that there was something going on in that family.

As I'm walking out I spot Wilson Landreau, the man Jenny was arguing with the day I first came to see Vera. "Just the man I want to see," he says. "Can you give me a call, so we can get together and talk?" He hands me his card.

"Of course." I'm surprised, not so much at the request, but at the furtive way he glances around as if he doesn't want anyone to know we're talking.

CHAPTER 10

Until I see Loretta standing at my front door, I don't realize how much I've missed her. She bustles into my house full of chatter about her trip to Washington with the world's most perfect grandsons.

"We went to all the monuments and the Vietnam Memorial—I found Oliver Barkeley's name on it and got a picture of it for his sister. We spent a whole day at the *Smithsonian Air and Space Museum.* That is one big place! The boys loved seeing all the airplanes and space capsules." And then she brightens. "One thing I know you would have liked. You know my son's wife has some different ideas and she wanted to go to the Hirshborn Museum one day. I think that's the name."

"Hirsh*horn*?"

"That's the one, with all the modern art. I told her I'd go with her because none of the males would go and I could tell her feelings were hurt. But I liked it more than I thought I would. I guess I'm used to seeing some of the pictures here in your house . . ." She looks around vaguely. "And I brought you a book that shows a lot of the pictures because you said you'd never been there."

She talks a little more, but she winds down faster than usual. "You know how I love those boys, but they wear me out. It's going to take me a few days to get rested up."

"I don't mind saying I'm glad to see you."

We beam at each other until her cheeks get pink and then she says, "Tell me what's happened while I've been gone."

It takes me a few minutes to assemble my thoughts. I rustle up some coffee and she apologizes for not having any baked goods to bring. "I was too tired to get up and bake this morning. Time was, I'd never have been too tired for that. I don't like getting too old to keep up with things."

"Loretta, don't be silly. Anybody would need a day off after all that activity."

I tell her that Jenny lost her mother and that Ellen Forester's window got broken, but I don't go into the incidents with Jenny's horses. She'd worry that those events are too close to her house. And I'm not about to go into Vera Sandstone's request that I find her lost husband or about Jenny's feud with her brother.

I need to put in some time at headquarters. I've been asking too much of the two deputies—not that they complain. On the way to work, I stop by and pick up Rodell Skinner, who was the chief of police until his health broke down from too much drinking. To everyone's surprise, including mine, he has stayed on the wagon, and although he's never going to be healthy again, he has enough energy to come down and help out a couple of days a week. I've put him to work going through old files and cleaning out unnecessary paper. After all, it was his slipshod methods that led to boxes of unfinished reports, files containing notes that don't pertain to the case at hand, and misfiled items. He seems to think it's a fine way to spend his time, and when I'm there with him he keeps up a running commentary on old cases.

"Look here," he says, after he's been at it for fifteen minutes. "This is from one time when Carl White cornered a polecat in his fishing shack and called us to come out and catch it." He snorts. "I told that fool James Harley that he had to take care of it. Never figured he'd actually do it. Sure enough, the skunk reared up on James Harley and he couldn't come to work for a week. I think Carl had to burn down the shack." He laughs so hard he has tears running down his cheeks.

I can't help laughing with him, although my mind is half on the petty little things that have happened this week—plus the not so petty one of Truly Bennett being attacked. I rear back in my seat. "Rodell, let me run a few things by you."

"What have you got?" He wipes his eyes and sets the file aside.

I tell him what's been going on at Jenny's place.

He grunts. "Sounds like somebody has it in for her." He thinks for a second. "Isn't she in the DA's office?"

"That's right."

"I thought so. All this mischief might be caused by somebody she prosecuted and sent to prison. Maybe he's out now."

He's absolutely right. I had been so busy concentrating on the warning from Jenny's mamma that it hadn't occurred to me to think a little farther afield for the possible source of the trouble. "That could be. I'll look into it."

Rodell looks pleased with himself. I hadn't noticed when I picked him up this morning, but his skin has a yellow tint to it—not a good sign in somebody whose liver is pretty much shot.

"And you know Ellen Forester's store was vandalized?" I say.

"I heard somebody smashed the plate glass window. You think it's that husband of hers?"

"I don't know, but I wouldn't be a bit surprised."

I call Alvin Carter down at his daddy's marine store. He says he'll be glad to keep an eye on Jenny's horses, and can use the extra money. I don't want him to go in blind to the situation, so I tell him what happened to Truly. I tell me to keep a sharp eye out, and if there looks to be any trouble to call me.

With everything quiet, I leave Rodell "in charge" and head over to see how Truly Bennett is getting along. He lives in a little house on the other side of the tracks—the traditional area where blacks have always lived, although the houses have been spruced up over the years. Truly's wood house is painted a surprising bright green with yellow trim. It's at odds with Truly's sober nature to have such a brightly colored house.

He invites me in, and as always seems a little embarrassed to have me there, although I see no reason for him to be. I think the problem is that Truly was married for a few years and the furniture in the house was chosen by his wife, and it's a little fussy for his personality. She left him a dozen years ago, lighting out for Houston where she said she thought life would be more exciting. Truly said he didn't blame her, that he likes a quiet life. But I don't think they ever really divorced, and I wonder if he holds onto the furniture hoping that one day she'll come back.

I ask him how the shoulder is getting on and he tells me he'll be back in commission in no time, which I take with a grain of salt. "I'll get back to those horses as soon as I can. I don't like the idea that something might happen to them."

"You have to give that shoulder time to heal. Buzz Carter's boy needs some work, and he's good with horses, so I thought Jenny might hire him to help out."

"That sounds like a good idea," he says, and I see relief in his expression. "The shoulder's going to be fine, but I don't know how much good it would do me if whoever attacked me came back." He pauses, and I can see that he's got something more to say. "What I'll do, though, is keep the boy company. If you don't think he'd mind."

CHAPTER 11

Monday morning I call Jenny's friend Wilson Landreau, and we agree to meet at a coffee shop near the courthouse in Bobtail after work. I'm going behind Jenny's back by talking to him, but he said he had something important to tell me regarding Jenny. He's already there when I arrive. He looks as frazzled as every public defender I've ever known. They're always shorthanded, never lacking indigents to defend.

"I don't know what you want to talk about," I say, "but I don't mind telling you I'm worried about something you might be able to shed some light on." I describe the nasty little tricks someone has been playing at Jenny's place, ending up with the attack on Truly Bennett.

He pulls his tie loose and flings himself back in his chair. "Shed light? I can tell you who is most likely responsible. I tried to warn Jenny this might happen. But she's so stubborn, she wouldn't listen."

"Is that what you two were arguing about at the hospital?"

"It sure is."

"Tell me who you think is behind the attacks."

He sips his coffee, reaches over for a packet of sugar, tears it open, and pours it into the cup. "Ten years ago when Jenny had just started working in the DA's office, she prosecuted a man by the name of Scott Borland and got him sent away for manufacturing methamphetamine. Recently, his son Jett was in court. Somebody heard him threaten to get even with Jenny for sending his daddy to prison. Scott just got out on parole, and I wouldn't put it past the two of them to go after Jenny."

"You told her this? What was her reaction?"

"She thinks she can handle every damn thing herself. These are lowlifes, Mr. Craddock. I don't know whether the son has it in him to do serious harm, but his daddy is a whole different animal." He turns his coffee cup around and around in his hands as he talks.

"Letting the horses out was one thing, but like I told you, the situation has been escalating. It's time I got to the bottom of it."

"I hope you can catch Borland. But be careful. He's a bad number. He's a lethal combination of mean and stupid. I'm really worried that Jenny doesn't get how serious it is. When I try to talk to her about it, she blows me off." He drains the rest of his coffee and stares into the cup, his expression bleak.

I tell him that Jenny has at least hired a local man to watch the horses at night.

By now Landreau's face is full on flushed. "Jenny thinks I'm overreacting, and maybe I am, but I don't want anything to happen to her or to those horses she's so crazy about."

"That's two of us. She's a good friend to me. One more thing. You said the boy, Jett, was in court. I take it he wasn't convicted."

Landreau snorts. "Oh, he wasn't on trial. He sued one of his neighbors for killing his dog. Dog attacked the neighbor's daughter. Lucky the man was there and managed to kill the dog before it did any real damage. As it was, the girl had to have twenty stitches in her leg. But that didn't make any difference to Jett Borland. He sued the guy. Case got thrown out, which probably didn't improve his temper much."

"I'm glad we talked. It gives me something to go on. I'll try to get some fingerprints off the piece of pipe used to attack Truly Bennett. If the prints belong to either of the Borlands, I've got a case for getting them off the street."

"If it was the Borlands who attacked him, Bennett is lucky he lived to tell the tale. Both of them are white supremacists."

"You have any idea how I can find them?"

Landreau shakes his head. "But the lawmen from Bobtail will, and be sure to take one of them with you if you go looking for them."

"Can you send me over a copy of photos of the father and son so I can get a look at who I'm dealing with?"

"I brought some with me." He opens his briefcase and hands me two mug shots. Both Scott and Jett look like TV's idea of a bad guy. Scott's teeth are terrible, half of them rotted out, most likely from using meth. His hair is long and stringy, and cold eyes look out from under an overslung brow. Jett has the same chilly eyes and the same low brow, but at least for now his teeth are intact and his hair is only a little shaggy. Now I know what they look like.

The desk deputy at Bobtail Police Headquarters refers me to Wallace Lyndall, a hound dog–looking man over fifty. He's wearing black-rimmed glasses and a crew cut that makes him look like a TV character from the '60s. At first he's skeptical of my interest in the Borlands. He's pretty sure my plan to roust out father and son won't work for one reason or another. It's hard to tell whether he genuinely has a problem with the idea of questioning them, or if his personal style simply means saying no first and revising his stance later. But I make it clear that I'm going after them—with or without him.

It's hard to step into another jurisdiction to rein in someone who is up to no good. If the Borlands lived in Jarrett Creek, I'd most likely have known them my whole life—known their families, their cronies, their past, and what they are up to now. I might even have been able to predict their future with fair accuracy. This is the kind of information I'll have to get from Lyndall if I can light a fire under him.

Lyndall says he's too busy to go off with me this afternoon, so we arrange to meet tomorrow morning to approach the Borlands.

"I have something else I want to ask you," I tell him. "You've been here at the Bobtail PD a long time?"

"Over thirty years."

"Maybe you remember something about a man who walked out on his family? Howard Sandstone? His wife was a schoolteacher."

"That would be Vera Sandstone, who died last week?"

"That's right. I'm wondering if they ever filed a missing persons report."

He strokes his chin, pondering my question. "I don't remember the details, but it seems to me it wasn't his family that reported him missing—it was the guy he worked for. There was something funny about the whole thing, but I'm damned if I remember what happened. Let me look up the file and refresh my memory. I'll get back to you."

After I leave Lyndall, I drive by to scout out the Borland place. According to Lyndall's information, Borland has moved in with his son since leaving prison. Jett's house, up on cinder blocks, hasn't seen a coat of paint since it was built, and the windows are hung with venetian blinds, not one of which is straight. If they use the fireplace, they're courting asphyxiation, because half the chimney's bricks are missing. There are at least two unusable cars rusting in the long dirt driveway, and behind them is an old white Chevy that looks an awful lot like the one I saw sitting outside Jenny's house. I'm tempted to stop in and have a chat with them, but my smarter side prevails. Tomorrow will have to do.

As I drive slowly by the house, a pair of scroungy dogs come scrabbling out from under the porch and take out after my truck howling and barking, as if they've been stung in the backside. I wonder how we're going to get past them tomorrow.

I'm on my way home when I get a call from Bill Odum. "We've got a problem, Chief. One of Ellen Forester's neighbors called a half hour ago to say there's a commotion at her house. Zeke went to see what was going on, and he says it sounds like her ex-husband is tearing up her place."

"I'm only ten minutes away. I'll meet you there. And put in a call to Texas Rangers headquarters. Tell them we may have a hostage situation on our hands."

"I don't think it's gone that far." Odum sounds startled.

"He's caused enough trouble. It's time we put some muscle into letting him know we're not going to tolerate his harassment."

CHAPTER 12

When I drive up to Ellen Forester's house in my truck, Zeke Dibble is standing outside on the sidewalk next to one of our two patrol cars. "Highway patrol says they can't send anybody out unless we're sure somebody's being held hostage."

"That's okay. We'll take care of it."

Bill Odum arrives, and I wait for him to join us before I ask Zeke to fill us in.

Zeke hooks a thumb toward the house. "Neighbors next door say the ex drove up and jumped out of the car and banged on Mrs. Forester's door, yelling out for her. When she opened the door, he forced his way inside. Then they heard him hollering and heard some crashing sounds from inside the house. That's when they called down to the station. I talked to the neighbors when I got here and asked them to stay indoors."

"All right, let's go see if we can settle this amicably," I say. We all know it isn't likely. I had a standoff with Seth the first time I met him, when he came to order Gabe LoPresto to stop work on a house LoPresto was renovating for Ellen. The fact that it was Ellen's place didn't seem to keep Seth from horning in. And since then we've had two other confrontations. I'm not sure what he hopes to get out of creating an uproar. It's clear that Ellen has no intention of going back to him. If I thought it was love driving him, I'd feel sorry for him, but all I sense is a pure need for power over a woman who finally got up the courage to leave him.

Flanked by Zeke and Bill Odum, I knock on the door, not expecting an answer, but I hear footsteps and the door crashes open. Seth Forester is a big man, and his rage makes him look larger. His neck is bulging and his face crimson.

Behind me Bill Odum says, "Whew" under his breath.

"What do you want?" Forester thunders.

"I'd like to have a word with Ellen," I say in as calm a manner as I can, given that I'd like to yank the man out of the house and march him down the steps. Tarring and feathering always seemed like an extreme punishment to me, but at the moment it seems like a fair way to handle this man.

"A word with Ellen?" He mimics me.

"If it's not too much trouble. I'd like to make sure everything's okay."

"Everything is fine and dandy," he snarls. He starts to close the door. I may have several years on him, but my reaction time is still pretty quick. I slam my hand into the door. He's not expecting it, and it shoves him backward. "What the hell?"

I put my hand on my gun, which makes him notice that I'm armed. I seldom feel the need to have a gun, but this is one of those times. "Get Ellen out here," I say.

Forester twists his head to the side and yells, "Ellen! You've got company!"

Ellen approaches the door, but hangs back, eyeing her ex-husband. Her face is dead white.

Forester says, "Tell this phony lawman that everything is fine and that we don't need his help."

"Ellen, I'd like a word with you out here on the porch," I say before she can make some excuse. "Sir, I want you to step back."

"Ellen, tell him." There's no mistaking the threat in his voice.

She eases past him onto the porch. She looks like a whipped dog.

"Tell the truth," I say.

She swallows. "Thank you for coming." She looks at the man whom she divorced not that long ago, and something passes across her face. It's as if she is taking a few seconds to relive their history—the good as well as the bad. "Seth has been tearing things up and I want him out of here." Her voice is almost a whisper.

Forester's fists clench. "For Christ's sake! What is wrong with you? If you'd just answer my phone calls, I wouldn't have to come and find out what's going on in this godforsaken hole."

I turn to Zeke Dibble. "Take her to the street," I say.

"Ma'am," Dibble says, "it's best if you come with me."

"She's not going anywhere!" Before they've gotten three steps, Forester charges out of the house and grabs Zeke Dibble by the arm.

I haven't seen Dibble in action much, and I'm gratified when he slams his hand down across Seth Forester's arm. "Get your hands off me!"

I step behind Forester and grab his other arm and yank it behind him. It's a futile gesture. The man is bull-strong and he snatches it away. But by this time Bill Odum has stepped up. He puts one hand on his weapon and the other on Seth Forester's chest. "You need to get yourself under control," he says. I like the quiet authority in his voice. Odum told me that at the police academy they warned him that he was too interested in the psychology side of law enforcement, but his words have a better effect than a confrontational tone would have. Forester takes a step backward.

Neighbors are starting to come out of their houses. It's time to put a stop to this right now. "I don't know where you think your aggressive behavior is going to get you," I say, "but if you don't settle down right now it's going to get you a night in jail."

Forester mutters something I don't get, but I let it go. But then he repeats it, louder. "Just try taking me to jail, you two-bit hick."

By now Dibble has taken Ellen to the street. She's standing by the car, head down, arms hugged to herself. Nobody should have to put up with this humiliation. I yank the cuffs off my belt and say, "Put your hands behind your back."

"You've got to be kidding," Forester says.

"Don't count on it. I'm taking you in to give you the opportunity to rethink your situation."

"You are going to have yourself one hell of a lawsuit on your hands. And if I understand it, this town can't afford anything like that."

"We'll cross that bridge when we get to it," I say. My heart is pounding as I slip the cuffs onto him. I don't remember when I've been this angry.

No matter how much control Forester thinks he has over the situation, he realizes he's outnumbered and he lets himself be escorted into Odum's police car. Ellen looks distressed seeing what's happening, and I send her back into her house before she has a chance to protest. I don't think I can stand it if she starts defending this bully.

Dibble assures me that they won't have any trouble getting Forester into a cell. "With his hands cuffed behind his back, he isn't going to do much of anything."

As soon as they drive away, I head to the front door, which Ellen has left standing open. I call out to tell her that I'm coming inside. She's sitting in her living room on the sofa, bent over with her head in her hands. She looks up when she hears my footsteps. "He wasn't always this way," she says.

"People change." I'm in no mood to hear her make excuses for him.

Somewhere in the house there's a dog yapping frantically. I glance in that direction.

She jumps up. "Poor Frazier. I had to put him in the utility room while Seth was here. Seth hates him and the feeling is mutual. I'll go get him."

She returns carrying a medium-sized brown dog of uncertain breed. The dog is trembling in her arms and gives a half-hearted bark in my direction. "It's okay, Frazier," she says. "Good boy. Samuel won't hurt you." She sits down and puts the dog on the floor, where it huddles next to her leg panting, glaring at me.

"Rescue dog?" I say.

"Sort of. When my next-door neighbor died last year, I said I'd take the dog." She strokes its head. "Seth was furious. Believe it or not, that was the last straw. I thought if he can't even be kind to a poor dog, what hope is there for me?"

I don't reply for a minute as I survey the damage that's been done. There's a smashed lamp, a small end table lying on its side, and a broken cup and saucer on the carpet in a puddle of coffee. There are several photos lying on the floor next to an overturned chair. The coffee table is at an odd angle, as if it's been yanked around.

"What's going to happen to Seth?" she says. She's not looking at me but at the dog, who's still trembling.

"Look at what Seth has done," I say. "He forced his way in here against your will—that's assault—and then resisted arrest. I don't understand why you won't get a restraining order against him."

She rubs her forehead. "I just can't. My children would have a fit. They're barely speaking to me as it is."

"Where are your kids?"

"My daughter lives in New York, and my son lives in Houston. He's at the University of Houston getting his MBA."

"Have you told them the way he's been treating you?"

She shakes her head. "I didn't want to bring them into it. Like I said, he didn't behave like this in the past."

"How did they react to your divorce?"

Her voice is so quiet I can hardly hear her. "My daughter is furious, and my son Nathan thinks I've lost my mind."

I've been standing at the entrance to the room, not wanting to spook her, but now I walk over and right the upended chair. "Mind if I sit down?"

"Of course not." She starts to rise. "Can I get you something? Coffee?"

I gesture for her to stay seated. "Tell me if I'm wrong. Your kids were used to you always going along with your husband, always letting him have his way, never wanting to rock the boat."

She doesn't respond, so I continue. "And something made you take a hard look at things and decide you didn't want to keep doing that."

She nods.

"You're not the first person I know who made that decision." For a short time, when Jeanne was in her early fifties, I thought she was going to do the same. She told me she was restless and felt like she gave in to me too often and she wanted the freedom to do other things. We began to make some bargains and ended up with our marriage being stronger than ever, but that's not always what happens.

"You're right. Seth always put himself first. I felt my life slipping away, never doing what I really wanted to do." Now she does look at me with a tired smile. "I actually thought he'd understand. I knew we were simply going through the motions in our marriage. I thought he probably felt the same way." She gestures to the mess he's made. "You can see how wrong I was."

"Has he gotten violent before—I mean, since you told him you were leaving?"

She hesitates, pink flaring in her cheeks. "Once. He pushed me down. I think he was as shocked as I was."

She rises abruptly. "Anyway. The whole thing makes me feel so sordid. You can't imagine how embarrassed I am."

I get up, too. "I'll take you up on that coffee. You really do need to figure out how you're going to handle this. I can keep him in jail overnight, but unless you're willing to press charges, after that I'll have to turn him loose. Something tells me he's not ready to give up."

She throws her hands up to stop me. "No, I will most certainly not press charges."

I follow her into the kitchen, where she starts brewing a pot of drip coffee. "But the restraining order? Can I talk you into that?"

"I'll have to look into it before I make a decision."

I have to turn my attention to the high school prom next weekend. I don't remember it being such a big deal when I was in high school about a hundred years ago, but now the plans would rival a gubernatorial inauguration, with the pre-party and the prom and the after party.

This afternoon I have a meeting with the students in the gymnasium to warn them to behave themselves. The principal talked me into it. I wonder if the students can sense how half-hearted my efforts are at issuing the warnings. I know they're not listening anyway. No matter what I say, there will be a few students who sneak alcohol, and a few who refuse to adhere to the rules. But they can't get away with much. If the NSA took lessons from the school PTA ladies, they'd learn a thing or two about security.

CHAPTER 13

Before I leave for Bobtail to meet Lyndall the next morning I release Ellen's ex with a warning. He gives me a good bit of surly lip. I phone Ellen to tell her he's out and to nudge her one more time to look into a restraining order. But she's unmoved.

The Borland place is ominously quiet when Lyndall and I arrive. I expected the dogs to set up a fuss, but the dogs aren't around, and apparently no one else is either. Wallace Lyndall sounds almost satisfied when he says, "Those boys aren't here. If we're lucky, they've gone for good."

It's not likely, since the old clunker cars are still sitting in the yard. Only the beat-up Chevy is missing. I get a mental picture of Scott and Jett Borland in the front seat with their dogs hanging out the back windows, barreling down the highway looking for trouble.

I knock on the front door and call out to them, but there's no answer. Just for kicks I try to open the door, but it's locked. I trudge around the back of the house, Lyndall following me, grumbling to himself. The backyard is filled with trash; they seem to be big on takeout and favor McDonald's and Arby's. Pizza boxes, beer and soda cans, and empty whiskey bottles are piled up in a corner of the yard near the fence.

"Either of the Borlands married?" I say.

Lyndall has his hands on his hips, surveying the backyard as if he's thinking of cleaning up. "Scott Borland has a wife, but I don't know offhand where she's at. I'll have to see if I can find out. Jett, has a girl-friend who stays in an apartment in town. We might get some information out of her, I guess."

I notice a trail leading off beyond the back of the property through weeds and underbrush to a thicket of trees and bushes. If I were inclined to cook up some meth, I'd probably do it in a shack a good ways behind the house in a hidden area just like that one. But without a warrant, I'm not setting foot anywhere near the trail.

Back at Bobtail police headquarters, I ask Lyndall if he had a chance to look into the matter of Howard Sandstone's disappearance.

"Come on back to my desk," he says. "I have the file there."

It's a thin file. I take it to a vacant desk and read the notes. As Lyndall recalled, it was Sandstone's boss, Larry (Curly) Fogarty, who reported him missing. Sandstone was working as a carpenter on a crew with Fogarty, building a subdivision out west of town. The officer who took the report left notes about his follow-up interviews. The notes say that Sandstone called Fogarty the day before he disappeared and asked for a ride to work because his car was out of commission. Fogarty reported that Sandstone seemed upset and had something on his mind.

Fogarty also told the officer that there had been some talk of Sandstone having a flirtation with a local woman, and some people speculated that he had planned to run off with her. But apparently she was still around. The deputy then interviewed Vera Sandstone, who also said her husband had been upset and that she thought he'd gone off somewhere to cool down.

The notes continued, "I asked her if he'd ever gone off like that before, and she replied that he had not, but there'd been some trouble at home and he was angry. I knew she was referring to the son, who'd been in some trouble. She seemed to think her husband would come back when he'd had time to reflect. I asked if she knew whether her husband had been seeing another woman. She insisted that he was faithful."

There's a note dated a week later that says Mr. Sandstone's car went missing the same evening that he did and had not yet turned up. Mrs. Sandstone said she had contacted her husband's mother (father deceased) and his brother, but neither had heard from him. "Decision: Texas Highway Patrol will be on the lookout for Sandstone's car, but with no evidence of a crime being committed, there will be no further action from the Bobtail PD."

By now Lyndall is gone, so I ask at the front desk if it's possible to talk to the officer who took down the information in Howard Sandstone's file.

When I tell him the name of the officer, the deputy says, "He's long gone. He must have been on the cusp of retirement when he wrote that report. I never met him, but I think he died quite a while back."

So I have to make do with the cursory report that was done at the time. I can understand why the police didn't make too much of it, but I can't understand why Vera Sandstone didn't push them to find her husband. Does it have something to do with his first wife? There's no mention of her in any of the notes on his disappearance. From what I've seen in the file, I'm beginning to see my chances of finding Howard Sandstone recede. I'll try some national databases, but if he went to any trouble to hide, changed his name, for example, I don't see a lot of promise for tracking him down.

Before I leave the police station, I give Will Landreau a call and tell him we struck out locating the Borlands. "Maybe they've run out of steam anyway," I say. "From the look of the place, they're not the kind of people to focus much on a task."

"I hope you're right." He sounds distracted, and I start to tell him I'll be in touch when he says, "Craddock, can I ask you something?"

"Of course."

"How do you think Jenny is doing?"

"You were at her mamma's funeral. Did you talk to her?" I say.

"Not much. She had a lot of people to tend to."

"I don't know how well you know Jenny, but she and her mamma were pretty close. Stands to reason she's upset. I'd give her time. Any particular reason you're asking?"

He sighs. "Just work stuff. I'd hate for her work to slip." And then in a rush, he tells the real truth. "I guess I'm selfish. I want the old Jenny back."

I don't tell him, but from what I've seen I'm not sure the old Jenny is coming back anytime soon.

Jenny calls me later in the day and says she's spending the night at her house tonight and wants me to come over. When I arrive, bearing a pot of soup, we sit at her little dining table and talk like everything is back to normal. After a while we take the bottle of wine we were sharing into the living room and get comfortable.

"I am so glad to get back home. You know how I loved my mamma, but I believe she kept every damn thing any kid ever gave her—including the Teacher's Day cards. If I see one more card with a picture of an apple for the teacher on it, I'll set fire to her place."

"How much longer do you think it's going to take to finish?"

"It's going slower than I hoped. People keep dropping by. They want to chat. I don't have the heart to tell them that I would rather not talk—I want to get this over with."

"Why not leave it for a week or so until you've had a chance to settle down from losing your mamma?"

Her reaction is oddly curt. "I can't do that. I need to get it done fast." Her face has that strained look again, like I've crossed an invisible line.

"You planning to sell the place?"

"I haven't decided. Mamma owned it free and clear, so I don't have to make a decision right away." She jumps up and says, "Look at that. We've gone through a whole bottle of wine. I'll get another one."

I start to protest, but she scoots out of the room. I'm surprised the bottle is gone. It doesn't seem to me like I've drunk much more than a glass.

I wonder if I ought to tell Jenny that I've tried to find her daddy and my efforts have come to nothing, but she's been stirred up too much lately. I'll wait until things return to normal before I bring it up. There's no hurry.

It occurs to me later that it's curious that Jenny has inherited the house and its contents. Vera's neighbor said that Eddie was the apple of his mother's eye. So why didn't she leave any of it to him?

CHAPTER 14

The next morning I go over to the Jarrett Creek High School and meet with principal Jim Krueger to review plans for the end of the school year. Every year he wants to discuss the best way to handle the inevitable rowdy behavior that accompanies senior day, the prom, and then graduation day itself.

I'm only half paying attention. My mind keeps drifting back to Jenny. She was drinking a lot last night. Why does she get so wrought up at any mention of her brother? I haven't given any more thought to how Eddie knew Vera was in the hospital. Did Vera ask someone to call him? If she did, she must have had a relationship with him. She must not have had the same problem with him that Jenny does.

In the afternoon I run back over to Bobtail to the Borland place, but it still looks deserted—no dogs, no people, and no cars. On the way out of town I drive by Vera Sandstone's house and stop when I see Jenny's car in the driveway. Jenny answers the door in jeans and an old Dallas Cowboys T-shirt. "I am so glad to see you, I could cry," Jenny says. "Getting Mamma's stuff together is driving me crazy."

"Have you been working on this all day?" I gesture toward the boxes stacked in the living room. The house is starting to look bare—Jenny has taken the pictures off the walls and the knick-knacks off the shelves and tables.

"No, I went into work this morning. I've only been here since two o'clock."

"How much longer do you think it's going to take?"

"Another week at least. I keep getting sidetracked. I didn't know that Mamma used to write stories, and I keep finding them and then I stop to read them." Her eyes suddenly fill with tears. "I hear her voice in the stories. I don't know why she never tried to get them published. She was really good."

We talk a little longer, and when I get up to go, I say, "Did your mamma leave a will?"

Jenny looks surprised. "Samuel, I'm a lawyer. You actually think I'd let Mamma die without a will?"

"Some people won't listen to their kids," I say. What I really want to know is whether her brother is in the will.

"Mamma had a lot of sense," she says. "And she thought I was a good lawyer."

"So I assume there's no problem with you being able to dispense with this place the way you see fit."

Her eyes narrow. "Not a bit. Why would you think otherwise?"

"I don't want you to get all riled up, but I wondered if she left anything to your brother."

"You've been hanging around your friend Loretta too much. You're going to turn into an old gossip. I believe I've made it clear that my brother is not a subject that's up for discussion."

It's before five, so I stop at the Bobtail Police Department to take a look at the arrest record for Eddie Sandstone's assault charge. The record is straightforward: Eddie attacked a man at work in August of the year he graduated from high school—around the same time his daddy walked out on the family. Eddie was working for a builder and went after one of the men he was working with. The man had to have stitches after Eddie worked him over. There's no indication of what the altercation was about, only that the man eventually dropped the charges. I jot down his name, Otis Greevy.

The officer at the desk sends me back to Wallace Lyndall's office. Lyndall is getting ready to head home.

"Now what are you going to pull my chain about?" he says.

"The report about Howard Sandstone's disappearance mentioned that his son attacked a coworker. You remember it?" I show him the file.

He glances over it. "I remember it because I was new on the force. It didn't make any sense to me why Greevy didn't press charges. He had every right to. Eddie Sandstone hit him with a shovel and kicked him around before some fellows pulled him off. Was me, I would have had his hide."

"So it never went to court?"

"No. But the Sandstone boy paid the price anyway. He was supposed to get a scholarship to SMU and they rescinded it once he got into trouble."

Lyndall says Greevy still lives in town. "I don't know if he's retired or not. I don't remember how old he was, but he was several years older than Eddie Sandstone."

We turn our attention back to the subject of the Borlands. I tell him I went back to their place and still found no sign of them.

"I called Jett Borland's girlfriend, and she said she wasn't seeing him anymore and didn't know where he was. But wherever he is, he's up to no good, that's for damn sure," he says.

It's almost dark by the time I leave the Bobtail Police Department. I'm halfway home to Jarrett Creek when I see lights flashing and a few cars stopped by the side of the road. I slow down for a highway patrolman who is waving people past with a flashlight. There's a highway patrol car on the side of the road next to the wreck of an SUV that has run off into the ditch and is lying on its side. My windows are open, so I catch an acrid smell in the air, like something burning, though I don't see any flames. Another couple of cars are pulled off farther along the road, with people standing outside looking back at the accident.

I'm past the wreck when I realize that the car in the ditch looks like

Jenny Sandstone's. I make a squealing U-turn and then another one to pull in behind the patrol cars. As I open the door to my truck, I hear a siren approaching from the direction of Bobtail.

A body is lying on the ground near the SUV with a patrolman crouched next to it. When I get closer, I see that it's Jenny, and for a moment my stomach clenches. But then I see that her eyes are open and the patrolman is talking to her.

"Jenny, what the hell happened?" I say.

Another patrolman steps into my path. "Sir, I need to ask you to step back."

I identify myself, and he tells me his name is Bobby Cole. He pulls me aside. "She's hurt pretty bad, but she's able to talk. She says somebody tried to run her off the road."

The burnt smell is stronger here. I glance over at the SUV and see a fire extinguisher lying on the ground. "Her car was on fire?" I say.

He grimaces. "She doesn't know how lucky she is. Somebody called in the wreck on their cell phone and we happened to be two minutes away. Flames were just starting up and we managed to get the fire out fast. Normally we would have left her in the car until the ambulance got here, but we figured there was a chance the fire might start back up. That's why we went ahead and pulled her out."

I go over and crouch down on the other side from the patrolman who's tending to Jenny. She's got a goose egg–sized bump on her forehead, and her left arm is lying awkwardly across her torso. She's pale as death.

"You a friend?" the patrolman says.

"Yes." I lean over and put my hand on her shoulder. "Jenny, it's me, Samuel. The patrolman said somebody tried to run you off the road. Did you see who it was?"

She clutches my hand and groans. "Big black car, that's all I know. Saw it coming up fast in my rearview mirror." She shudders.

The ambulance comes blaring up and screeches to a halt. The siren dies with a moan. I hear the doors slam, and one of the drivers says, "Man, look at that car. Lucky it didn't roll over."

Jenny is still talking. Her voice is low, and I have to bend close to hear her. "I thought he was going around me, but he hit me from the side. Hard." She sighs and hums deep in her throat. "I saw that I was going off the road. I was scared if I tried to turn the wheel, I'd flip, so I steered toward the ditch."

"Smartest thing she could have done," the patrolman crouched across me says.

"Did you recognize the person who hit you?" I say.

"Didn't see the driver."

"Everybody move aside," one of the ambulance drivers says.

"No, I . . ." Jenny starts to say something.

"Ma'am, you need to stop talking. We're going to take care of you."

"No!" she says. "Horses."

"No need to put up a fuss," I say, squeezing her hand. "I'm going to the hospital with you and I'll call Alvin." And I'm going to talk to Zeke Dibble, too. I want him to go over to her place and check it out.

"I want to go home," she says. Tears are slipping down the sides of her face.

"If everything is all right, they'll send you right home from the hospital," I say, although it's clear that isn't going to happen.

I stand up so the EMTs can get her onto the stretcher. Another patrol car has arrived and two more patrolmen have gone up to talk to the people pulled onto the side of the road, to see if any of them saw the accident.

The patrolman who stayed by Jenny introduces himself as Arnold Mosier. Both he and Cole are in their thirties and could be mistaken for brothers. "We've called for a tow truck," Mosier says. "I don't know what else we can do unless there are witnesses."

I get a flashlight out of my truck and go over to look at the damage. There's a deep dent on the left rear bumper, but no scrapes along the side, so not likely to be any paint residue on the car that did this.

"Good thing she has an SUV," Cole says. "Probably saved her life. If she was in a small car, she'd have been toast."

Mosier is looking over at the SUV, frowning. "I don't understand why the airbag didn't deploy."

Cole says, "She wouldn't have been hurt so bad if the bag had opened. She might have a lawsuit against the car manufacturer or the airbag company."

All three of us stare at the wrecked vehicle. "Whoever did it is going to have a big dent in their fender," I say.

"We'll alert all the body shops, although . . ." His voice trails away. I know as well as he does that there are plenty of places where somebody can get a dented bumper repaired or replaced without anybody being suspicious of where the dent came from—or caring. The highway patrol can't canvas every little two-bit town that has a service station with a garage on the side.

I shine my light into Jenny's car to see if I ought to get anything out. Her briefcase has slid to the door on the down side, and there's no way I can get to it. I ask Mosier and Cole to retrieve it for me when the car gets pulled out of the ditch.

I follow the ambulance to the hospital in Bobtail. On the way, I'm going over what Jenny told me. She said it was a dark car that hit her, and it doesn't sound random. My first thought is that the Borlands have upped their war on her. But then I remember that the car I saw her brother Eddie get into when he left the hospital was a black town car. I don't know why he'd want to force Jenny off the road, possibly killing her. But I do know there is big trouble between the two of them. I wish I could have gotten more out of Vera. It's time I found out more about Eddie.

CHAPTER 15

The next morning, when Loretta brings me a big hunk of coffee cake, she's excited about some news.

"Hold up," I say. "Before you go off on a tangent, I need to tell you what happened last night." I give her most of the details of Jenny's accident, leaving out the part about her being run off the road. "They had to do emergency surgery on her spleen, but they said she should be okay to get out in a couple of days."

"I'll go over to the hospital right away."

"Wait a little while," I say. "I expect she's going to be sleeping late this morning."

"I'm glad they took her to the hospital if she had a bump on her head. People get those hematomas. That's what happened to that poor actress."

Until a few years ago, people got bumps on the head all the time without anybody getting all worked up over it. "She'll be okay," I say, tamping down the little twinge of worry that starts up. "Now tell me your news."

"You probably already know this, but for quite a while they've been planning to put up an outlet mall in Bobtail. Now they're finally going to do it."

"I don't know what you'll want to buy there that you can't buy right here in Jarrett Creek," I say.

"Samuel, you know good and well there's not a dress store here in town or anyplace to buy any kind of shoes."

"They've got shoes at Palmer's," I say, all innocent.

"I'm not even going to grace that with an answer."

Palmer's is a general store that caters to hunters and fishermen. They sell waders and hiking boots and moccasins. "I guess you know more about shopping than I do."

She looks at me with a critical eye. "No argument there. In fact, by the time the mall gets built, those pants of yours are going to be so worn out, you're going to need to go over there and get some new ones or risk giving people a show."

"I've got plenty of pants," I say. "But I happen to like these. They're comfortable. And I can get anything I want here in town. Where's this new shopping center going to be?"

"Out west of town. They're tearing down a subdivision to make room for it. Bobtail Ridge. Can you believe they're going to call the shopping center that, too?"

"What's wrong with that?"

"Ridge? The whole town of Bobtail is flat as a pancake. Not a ridge in sight. Some of the names they give those subdivisions are ridiculous. There ought to be a truth-in-naming law. There's one called Rio Linda over in San Antonio. It's as far from the river as you can get."

"They're tearing down a whole subdivision to build the shopping center? Seems like there'd be plenty of places to build it without tearing something down."

"You have to take that up with the city council. Somebody said the subdivision was rundown, but I don't know if that's why they chose that site. I don't care where they build it, as long as they build it."

She has heard the gossip about Ellen Forester's latest run-in with her ex and wants to know more. I tell her the bare bones.

"I don't see why a woman would put up with that kind of thing," she says. "If my husband had gotten out of line that way, he would have been seeing the inside of the doghouse."

I don't know that Loretta is as tough as she makes out to be, but I wish she could instill some of it into Ellen Forester.

When I get to police headquarters I return a couple of messages and then I call over to the hospital. They tell me that Jenny spent a good night and was asking for me.

I'm glad that Rodell Skinner is coming into the office today. I'm going to leave him in charge, which will make him feel good. I don't know how long I'm going to be able to count on him. I keep expecting him to decide that he'd rather go out sooner with a bottle in his hand than later, and sober. It's a damn shame because sober, he's got some sense—something you wouldn't have known if you saw him with a case of beer under his belt.

He comes shambling in before eleven and eases himself into his chair. This morning his color is pretty good—not quite as yellow as it was earlier in the week. His voice has become high and querulous with illness. "Samuel, don't you have someplace to be?" he says. He still has a strong territorial instinct for the job as chief.

"As a matter of fact, I do." I tell him what happened last night.

"That's a damn shame. Just losing her mamma and then ending up in the hospital. You think it might be related to that business with her horses?"

"I don't know, but I'm going to find out."

Jenny's eyes are closed when I walk into her room, but she hears my footsteps and lifts her head. "Well, this is a fine pickle," she says. Her voice is scratchy.

"You may not like it," I say. "But I've been thinking it might be the best thing that happened. You're safer here than you're likely to be anywhere else until I find out who's after you."

The swelling over her left eye has gone down, but it's left an ugly purple bruise. "Now don't you start," she grumbles. "I've already had Will Landreau over here giving me chapter and verse about the danger I'm in. And speaking of Will, I have a little question for you."

"You're wondering how he heard you were in an accident?"

"You wouldn't interfere in my personal life, would you?"

"I figured your office needed to know where you were."

"Will and I are not in the same office. If you don't recall, he's a defender and I'm a prosecutor. And you just happened to have his phone number close at hand?"

She may have had emergency surgery last night, but it didn't slow down her thinking. As far as she knows, there's no way I should have Will's phone number. Will and I met on the sly to talk about the Borlands. "I remembered his name, and the two of you seemed friendly, so that's who I asked for when I called the courthouse. He's a nice guy."

The fire in her eyes tells me she'd like to challenge my lie, but her sigh tells me she doesn't have the strength at the moment. "I feel like hell," she says. "But I've had some more thoughts about who did this."

"Good. What have you got?"

"I guess I ought to tell you what Will Landreau and I were arguing about the day you saw us in the hospital."

I already know because Will told me, but I'm curious to know how Jenny is going to spin it. She tells me pretty much the same thing Will did, with a few details of the trial that put Scott Borland away. "His son is as hotheaded as he is, and I guess with his daddy out of prison, they decided it's time to put a scare into me."

It's a relief to have the business with the Borlands out in the open. I don't tell her I've already been on their trail. Plenty of time for her to find out when I track them down.

When I ask Wallace Lyndall how I can find Scott Borland's wife, he rears back in his chair and squints up at me. "Must not be a lot going on in Jarrett Creek. You seem to have plenty of time to be poking your nose into business best left to Bobtail."

"I've got plenty of backup," I tell him. He doesn't really want to handle the Borland matter, but he doesn't want me to do it either. Jealous of his territory. I tell him about Jenny's accident. "I don't know if they had anything to do with it, but I want to find out. The Borlands are in your patch, but most of the mischief they've done is in mine. So I'd at least like to have a chance to talk to the Borland woman and see if she has any idea where they are."

He ponders for a second, can't find a hole in my request, and sits forward and starts digging through the folders on his desk. "Here's what I've got." He hands me a sheet of paper with some scribbles on it that include "Donna Mae Borland" and an address and phone number.

"I'm happy for you to go with me if you'd like," I say.

"Knock yourself out," he says. He takes his glasses off and rubs the bridge of his nose. "If you get anything out of her, I owe you lunch."

The address is in a trailer park on the outskirts of Bobtail. Scott Borland's wife lives in a small Airstream, old but in fairly good shape. A Pontiac convertible with a patched top is parked out front. Standing sentinel at the bottom of the two-step porch there's a long-dead geranium in a terra cotta pot. I have to knock on the front door a couple of times before I hear someone inside say, "Hold on, I'm coming as fast as I can."

The woman who opens the door is hefty but seems easy in her body. She's dressed in a robe of some kind of slithery material, green with purple flowers. Her hair is dull blonde and frowsy, and her face is puffy in a way that makes me think I woke her up. "What do you want?"

"Are you Donna Mae Borland?"

"Yes, but I don't owe anybody a damn dime and don't plan on buying anything that will change the situation."

"I'm the chief of police over in Jarrett Creek and I'm looking for your husband."

She snorts. "Good luck with that." She reaches in her dressing gown and comes out with a pack of cigarettes and a lighter. She lights the cigarette and blows smoke out the side of her mouth.

"When was the last time you saw him?"

She takes another drag. "Three nights ago. He came by where I was working to remind me he was out of prison. I told him whoop-di-doo and he had a beer and left. I haven't seen him since."

"You have any idea where he might have gone?"

She yawns, and with her free hand she fluffs up her hair. "Don't know, don't care. I have me a new man and as far as I'm concerned, my marriage with Scott Borland is over."

"Is he likely to go along with that?"

She looks surprised at the question. "Not a lot he can do about it." She seems to be enjoying the chat. She's leaned up against the door, relaxed.

"How about your son, Jett? You know where I can find him?"

She brings herself upright. "I'll tell you anything you want to know about Scott, but I've got nothing to say to you about Jett. He's a good boy. Never gave me any trouble."

"Where does he work?"

She plucks something off the end of her tongue with her forefinger and thumb and flicks it off to the side of me. "Like I said, I've got nothing to say about him."

"When was the last time you saw him?"

"You're a persistent man, aren't you?"

"Got to be. Especially when somebody doesn't want to tell me what I need to know."

She starts to close the door.

"Wait. Where do you work? Maybe I'll stop by for a beer."

"I've been working at the Smokin' Pistol for thirty years. It's about a half mile down the road. Don't expect anything on the house just because you're a cop, though."

CHAPTER 16

I call headquarters to see how Rodell is faring, and Zeke Dibble answers the phone. "What are you doing there?" I say.

"Rodell wasn't feeling all that good and he called and asked me if I could come in. I wasn't doing anything. My wife was after me to work in the garden with her, so I was happy for the excuse. I've got myself a good book to read and some iced tea from the café, and I'm having a nice quiet afternoon. What can I do for you?"

"Just checking in." I tell Zeke to call me if he needs me.

I want to find out more background on Eddie Sandstone before I talk to him in person. He seemed to have been a well-liked kid in high school, but obviously something happened to get him into trouble.

The best place for me to start finding information about his history is the high school. Eddie is two years older than Jenny, which puts him in his late forties. That means any teacher he had back then would be at best close to retirement. Still, it's a place to start. If Eddie had a scholarship to SMU, some teachers would likely remember him. I'll start with the football coach and work from there.

Bobtail High School was built back in the '50s, but because it was built of local stone, it looks ageless. Over the years, as the town has grown, they've added to it, but the main entrance remains as a reminder of how architecture can define the way a building is used. Walking up to the massive front door, you feel the importance of education. At least I do—I suspect the students have too many other things on their minds to pay any attention.

"I need some information on a student who would have been

here somewhere around thirty years ago," I tell the bright-eyed young woman behind the front desk.

"I'm going to turn you over to Mollie," she says. "She's been here longer than anybody. If she doesn't know the answer, she'll know where to find it."

She leads me down the hall to an office of admissions and into the presence of a stern-looking woman of at least seventy with steel-gray hair and the posture of a drill sergeant, Mollie Cleaver. But she turns out to have a warm smile and gives keen attention to my request. "I'm going to look up the records for Edward Sandstone. You know his mother Vera taught here for many years. She passed on recently, God rest her soul."

"I had the pleasure of meeting her a time or two," I say.

"Now with regard to her son," Mollie says, and a frown puckers her forehead. "The specifics are long gone from memory, so let's dig out his transcript and the yearbooks and maybe we'll find the name of somebody who can tell you what you need to know."

It's not likely that there will be any mention of the assault charge against Eddie in his school records, because it happened after he left high school. What I want to know is if Eddie ever got in trouble in high school as well.

Mollie sits down in front of a big computer screen and starts tapping into it. After a few minutes she says, "Here we are," and turns the screen toward me.

"You've got all these records computerized?"

"I certainly do. I'm not one of those technophobes. I love computers. People need to keep up with the times. As soon as we got the computers in here, I took a course over at the junior college and learned how to set up the files, and then I got students to help me with it."

I look at the screen and see that Eddie Sandstone's grades were pretty good. Not good enough to be valedictorian, but if SMU recruited him to play football they wouldn't have had to fudge his records.

"These are his grades," I say, "but do you have anything that details his conduct—any trouble he might have gotten into, that sort of thing?"

"We decided to only keep that kind of information for ten years, so you're out of luck with that. So let's look at those yearbooks and see who his teachers were. Teachers remember strange things about students. Somebody is bound to remember something."

Eddie's picture is on every other page of the yearbook—in the student council and the yearbook staff and the Spanish club. And he's an athlete—on the football team in the fall and the baseball team in the spring, lettering in both sports. He's Homecoming King and Prom King and Most Likely to Succeed. In all his photos, he shows a cocky, dazzling smile that declares he's got the world by the tail. Jenny told me that high school was hard for her—she was never a popular girl, being taller and heftier than her counterparts. It must have been especially hard having her brother be the big man on campus.

I pause looking over the yearbook. "Handsome, talented, popular, smart . . . so why isn't he the governor?"

Mollie Cleaver laughs. "Some people peak too early. They walk out of here thinking life is theirs for the taking, and the first time they're faced with the real world, they don't know how to handle it. They go off to college full of plans and dreams, and they come home baffled by the fact that in college they met a hundred kids just like them."

"Can you point out to me which of Eddie's teachers might be likely to remember him?"

She thumbs through some pages and comes to the football section and frowns. "The coach back then was Cougar Johnson. He died of a heart attack a few years ago. Maybe an assistant coach." Her fingers trace the photos. "Here. Stubby Clark. He's moved up in the world. Coaches at the junior college, though why they think they need a football team is beyond me." She writes his name down in neat, firm cursive and then looks through the books some more.

"Oh, yes there's one more." She looks at me with a raised eyebrow. "This one will know any little thing that happened with the boys." She taps a photo of a sultry-looking woman with pouty lips and dark, lustrous hair. "That's Careen Hudson. The typing teacher. You can see by her looks why the boys fell all over themselves for her. She got a lot of the athletes in her class, too, because she was an easy grader. She was only seven years older than they were and didn't have the sense of a goose. She got herself fired for making out with a seventeen-year-old boy in the backseat of her Chevy—right here on school grounds."

This is the woman Rowena and her husband talked about at the reception after Vera Sandstone's funeral. "You ever hear any rumors that there was anything between her and Eddie?"

"Not that I recall, but that doesn't mean there wasn't."

"You know where I might find her?"

"I've got to hand it to her—for all the scandal she caused, she stayed right here and rode it out. For a while she opened up a dress shop, but I think being around women all the time didn't suit her. For the last twenty years she's been working for the County Fair Association—I think she gets plenty of action there."

I thank her for giving me two good leads.

"If you talk to Careen, you be careful. Last I heard she had ditched husband number three and was on the prowl." She pauses, mischief in her eyes, "But then again, I think she goes for younger men." Her yelp of laughter follows me down the corridor.

I call over to the college, but they tell me Stubby Clark is gone for the day, so I'll have to talk to him later in the week.

I'm going back by the hospital to see Jenny before I leave town, but I've got one more stop to make. Wallace Lyndall gave me the address for Jett Borland's girlfriend, Janice Gerson. She's a clerk at a grocery store, and I called and found out she's off today at five o'clock. I wait until she's had time to get home and settle in before I ring her doorbell at six o'clock. She lives in a duplex in a marginal neighborhood.

She answers the door carrying a little girl on her hip. The girl, maybe three years old, has been crying and is sucking her thumb, and Janice Gerson looks frazzled. "Oh," she says. "I thought you were the pizza guy."

"Pizza!" the little girl whines and buries her face in her mamma's neck.

"I'm Samuel Craddock, chief of police over in Jarrett Creek, and I'm looking for Jett Borland."

"You're outta luck. Jett's in Abilene." Janice is pretty, with short brown hair and soulful brown eyes. She's wearing jeans and a baggy gray T-shirt and sandals.

"You his girlfriend?"

She grimaces. "Sometimes."

"You know when he'll be back?"

"Supposed to be back last night, but I haven't heard anything from him."

"Mommy! Pizza!" The girl has a healthy set of lungs, and Janice Gerson flinches and pulls away from her.

"Kimberley, that's too loud," she says. "You hurt my ears."

The girl hits her mother half-heartedly, but instead of reacting angrily, Janice rolls her eyes at me.

"I'm sorry, why do you want to talk to Jett?"

"There are a couple of questions I need to ask."

"This is about Scott, isn't it? Scott has only been out of prison a couple of weeks and it sounds like he's already managed to get Jett into trouble."

"I don't know whether he has or not. That's what I'm trying to find out."

She shifts her daughter to her other hip. "Kimberley, you're getting so big it's hard for me to carry you. You're a big girl."

At those words, Kimberley is emboldened to look at me. "You've got a hat," she says, pointing at the hat I'm holding in my hand.

"I do. A well-used hat."

Janice grins at me. "A hat that's seen better days."

"I'm not a big shopper."

This time she laughs. "A cop with a sense of humor. A rare bird."

"I don't want to keep you. Do you happen to know why he went to Abilene?"

"There was a 'business opportunity' that Scott was excited about. Jett went with him to try to keep him out of trouble. Not that that has worked too well in the past."

"When did they leave?"

She bites her lip, thinking. "Five days ago. I told Jett to stay out of his dad's business, but he's loyal."

I hear a car pull to the curb and turn to see a pizza delivery car. The guy jumps out and runs up to the house, pizza in hand. "Sorry about the delay," he says. "That'll be eighteen seventy-five."

Janice looks at me as if she's hoping I'll take the hint and leave, but I'm going to try to stay long enough to get my questions answered. "Okay, wait," she says. She disappears inside and comes back with twenty dollars. She hands it to the guy. "Keep the change."

I take the pizza box and say, "Let me carry that in for you."

"Okay, Slick, come on in," she says.

I follow her into the kitchen and put the box down on the counter. She tries to set her daughter down onto the floor, but Kimberley clings tighter. "No!"

"Let me do it," I say. I open the pizza box. Janice pulls a door open and points to the plates. I get out a couple of plates and put them on the table, and Janice pulls out a chair and sits down.

"Here you go, Pumpkin," she says. "Might as well get a plate for yourself, too," she says to me. "Looks like you plan to stay."

"Thanks, but that's okay. I'll be out of here soon. I need to clear up one more thing."

"Suit yourself. You mind getting me a Coke out of the refrigerator and some milk for Kimberley?"

I do as requested and then sit down and watch her feed pieces of pizza to her daughter and herself.

"Do you know what kind of business Scott Borland was looking into?"

She shakes her head. "Not a clue. He's always got some big scheme going."

"Going back into the meth business?"

She flushes and pushes her hair back from her neck. "I couldn't tell you."

Kimberley wiggles down off her lap, and Janice heaves a sigh of relief. "Go find your doll," she says. Her daughter wanders off into the living room.

"Tough being a single parent."

"Sometimes. My mamma takes care of her during the day, so it's not so bad. And she's a good baby."

"Is she Jett's?"

"No, but I was with him so long that she thinks he's her daddy. He still comes by to see her." She looks embarrassed. My guess is he comes around and sweet-talks her and she's lonesome taking care of this baby by herself and so she spends time with him.

There's a crash from the living room, and Kimberley sets up a wail. "Uh-oh, bedtime." Janice jumps up and heads for the living room. I follow her. Kimberley is sitting on the floor wailing, having pushed a vase onto its side on the coffee table. It had a single flower in it, and water from the vase is dripping onto the floor. "Nothing to cry about," Janice says. "Let me get a rag and you can help me mop it up."

"I'd appreciate it if you tell Jett I was here."

She seems like a nice girl. I don't know why she'd be mixed up with somebody like Jett Borland.

I stop back by the hospital to fill Jenny in on the conversation I had with Janice Gerson. The bruise from the bump on her head has spread out so that her whole forehead and one eye are shades of purple and yellow. "Bottom line," I say, "we can't find Borland at the moment, but we'll keep checking back at his place."

Jenny sits up a little higher, wincing as she does so. Just then the door opens and a familiar face peeks around the corner.

"Monica!" Jenny says.

The nurse I couldn't seem to get along with when Jenny's mother was in the hospital bustles over to the bed and gives Jenny a hug. "I heard you were in here, and I came to see you as soon as I got done with my rounds." She looks at me and her face clouds up. "Oh, it's you again. Trying to cause trouble with Jenny now that you've finished with her mamma?"

"Monica, stop that!" Jenny starts to laugh and then groans. "Ow, don't make me laugh. That hurts. Listen, Samuel is a good friend of mine, and you have to be nice to him."

"If you say so. Now, honey, if there's anything that isn't right in here, you let me know. I'm not on this ward; I'm upstairs. But you send somebody to find Monica and I'll set everybody straight."

"I will. But if I have any say in it, I'll be out of here tomorrow."

Monica cocks an eyebrow at Jenny. "You'll do what the doctor says! I know people like you. You think you don't need to follow the rules like everybody else. And the next thing you know, you're back here with an infection or pulled stitches. You stay put until the doctor says otherwise." Monica turns her attention to me. "If you're such a good friend, you'll make sure she follows orders."

"Count on it," I say.

Monica glances at her watch. "All right, I've got to get back." She's almost to the door when she pauses and says, "Did the man who came to visit your mamma get everything squared away with the paper he wanted her to sign?"

Jenny looks confused, but before I can hear the explanation, my cell phone rings. Monica glares at me, but I have to answer it because it's Zeke Dibble.

"You on your way home?" Dibble says. "Jim Krueger's after you. Apparently he has a prom rebellion on his hands."

CHAPTER 17

"The kids are giving me trouble," Jim Krueger says. He mops beads of perspiration from his forehead, dislodging a long thread of hair from his comb-over so that it springs up like a question mark.

"I'm not surprised." I could have told him the kids were likely to rebel at some point. Every year the rules for the prom get tighter. First it was more chaperones, until it seemed like there were more chaperones than students. Then the doors of the gym were guarded during the dance so that the kids couldn't go in and out—not a bad thing, because it cut down on the drinking outdoors between dances and the girls didn't have to put up with boys who could barely stand up, much less dance or drive home. Then it was tightening the reins on after-prom parties.

This year someone's bright idea is to keep the kids in the gym all night. The plan was to have party games and a casino with fake money, ending up with breakfast. But the Baptists put up a fuss about the casino, and the organizers ended up with a bunch of games that sounded like they were more appropriate for children than teenagers.

"Several of the kids signed a petition saying they aren't going to attend unless the rules are relaxed," Krueger says. "Trouble is I can't figure out who's behind it. And the parents who planned all this are demanding that I find out which kids are behind it and expel them."

He looks so bleak that I can't help laughing. "Jim, I wouldn't have your job for a million bucks."

"That doesn't help me much. Any ideas? I hate to think of the kids tearing around all over town after the prom getting into mischief."

"Let me ask you something. When you were in high school, did the parents get this involved in the prom?"

Jim stares and blinks for a few minutes. He starts to nod. "I see your point. You're right. Back when I was in school, the prom committee was the senior girls and as far as I can remember the school had the devil of a time finding parents even willing to chaperone—much less spend the night here supervising. But times have changed." He scoots forward to prop his elbows on his desk. "Trouble is, it's a little late to be telling parents they can't be involved. Honestly, Samuel, it's like they think it's their prom instead of the kids.'"

It's times like this I wish Jeanne were still alive. She would have known what to do. So all I can do is try to think what she would have suggested. The key is in what Krueger said about people thinking this is their prom. They need to be given something to do that's more appealing than holding kid's games for their almost-grown high schoolers. "Who is the most well-liked family in the senior class?"

"What do you mean?"

"Who would parents go to for advice if they had a problem with one of their kids?"

"I suppose that would be Emily and Jake Ford." He gives a mirthless laugh and shakes his head. "If you ask me, Emily is sometimes a little far-out, but she's the first one anyone mentions if there's anything to be done."

"Is she one of the parents planning the prom?"

He shakes his head slowly. "She bowed out. She said she thought they were going overboard."

"Can you call her and get her in here?"

"It's almost six o'clock. She's probably cooking supper."

"Let's try her anyway. Tell her there are problems with the prom."

Emily says she'll be right down, and fifteen minutes later she arrives, puffing into the office like she's run all the way.

"You caught me doing my workout on my exercise machine," she says. "I hate it, so I was happy to leave. Although I made myself run here so at least I'd get some exercise." She pulls her T-shirt away from her chest and flaps it. "I probably smell like a goat." She laughs. I don't know her at all except to nod to, but I like her right away. She'll do fine for my purposes. "What's going on that has to get done right this minute?"

Krueger explains that the kids are digging their heels in. She sighs and shakes her head. "I tried to tell them they weren't dealing with third graders, but Mary Lou Jennings has always been a helicopter parent."

That isn't a term I've heard before, but I figure I know pretty much what it means without her having to explain it. "The trouble is," I say, "what do we do now? I think we have to have something that appeals to those parents that they'd rather do than hang around the gym all night."

"Hmm." I can see the wheels turning. "Something kind of unusual and that makes them feel ritzy." She looks at me in a calculating way, and I start to worry that she's going to involve me in some way. "I hear you know something about wine. How about a wine tasting? I could run over to San Antonio this week and buy some wine and fancy cheese. And I'd tell them that you're going to be there to give a little tutorial about the wine."

"Oh, no. Wait a minute," I say. "I need to be on duty."

"You only have to be at the party long enough to say a few words. Thirty minutes? Okay, twenty minutes. It can't be that hard. But if parents know you'll be there, they'll be more inclined to come."

"Why is that?" Jim Krueger says, before I have a chance to ask.

"Samuel is the chief of police. They'll figure if it's okay with him, it's got to be okay to sample a little wine. And besides, you've got to admit it's a little unusual. Kind of like a talking dog . . ." She grins.

"I know, I know, it doesn't matter what I say."

She's all business and writes down my suggestions for a few different kinds of wines. I tell her to ask the advice of the store where she buys it. "Tell them you have a budget. Speaking of budget, how is this going to get paid for?" I turn to Jim Krueger.

"Money's no problem," Emily says. "I'll charge the parents. That way they'll think it's worth more. And if I need any extra money, Jim's going to have to find it in his budget."

Krueger grumbles a little but admits that it's better than having the kids refuse to go to the prom. "Now the thing is," Krueger says, "what are we going to do about the rules for the kids? I hate to give in to their petition. That's not a good precedent."

"Why not?" Emily says. "It's the end of the school year. By next year nobody will remember what happened this year."

"I like your style," I say. "You ever thought about running for public office?"

"Got too much sense for that," she says. She jumps up. "Is it all settled then? Because I've got to get home. My daughter's about to have a nervous breakdown because she suddenly doesn't like her dress. Sometimes I think we ought to drop the whole idea of a prom!"

CHAPTER 18

I stop in for breakfast at Town Café the next morning, and everybody is full of a story that shakes all the other news right off the map. Gabe LoPresto's building company has won the bid against some big outfits to build the new outlet mall that Loretta told me about. That must be what had him so excited last time I saw him. Gabe hasn't shown up yet, and everybody's waiting to hear the full story.

Town Café is nothing to look at—a Quonset hut with the inside finished in knotty pine. The walls are decorated with a couple of deer heads, photos of every Jarrett Creek sports team from the last twenty years, neon beer signs, and year-round Christmas tree lights strung along the front counter. But it's the local gathering spot because the food is good.

"LoPresto's probably over at Palmer's trying to find a bigger hat," one of the men says. Everybody laughs, but we're proud of Gabe.

Finally LoPresto comes busting in the door with a big grin on his face, wearing a snappy black Western-style business suit with his best snakeskin boots and his good hat. He deserves to be pleased with himself. He may be a braggart, but his company has a good reputation and his getting the contract is going to put a lot of local people to work after a period of trying financial times for the town.

"Gabe, I'm buying you breakfast," Harley Lunsford says. We all look at him with wonder. He's never been known to offer a dollar when a dime would do as well. But then he says, "Better yet, you buy—you can afford it now."

LoPresto laughs along with us. We pump him for information, and he's happy to tell us how he outwitted "the big boys." He came up with an efficient plan for tearing down the old subdivision, which meant he could underbid the other companies. He tells us that he's going to be looking for subcontractors from all over the place. "If anybody knows of carpenters looking for work, tell them I'm going to be hiring. First, though, I'm looking for anybody who can do grunt work. We've got a lot of tearing down to do and permits to get before we even put a spade into the ground." He stands up. "You know, Samuel, you may not have to hang on as chief much longer. If the economy picks up around here, we could be in a position to hire a new one."

After he takes off, I sit around and drink another cup of coffee and wonder why his comment about hiring a new chief doesn't thrill me as much as it ought to.

The word is that Careen Hudson, the ex-teacher who had a fondness for young high school boys is spending every day this week at the fairgrounds in Bobtail showing vendors around and taking applications for those who want to work the state fair in early September. I go over to the fairgrounds to see if I can have a word with her. It's in a big field out east of town.

The grounds look a lot bigger without all the concessions, rides, and crowds. There are several permanent structures on the grounds—the ticket booths, now shut up tight; a huge barn where the livestock part of the fair is held; a big arena with concrete bleachers for the rodeo; and entertainment stages.

I head down to one end where I see cars parked in front of a couple of small wooden buildings. Over the entrance to one is a brass plate that says "Bobtail County Fair Headquarters." It's eleven in the morning. I came at this time, figuring Careen Hudson would be taking a lunch break and she might have time for me.

Several people are waiting in the outer office. I go over to a desk that holds four stacks of papers—information and applications for vendors and general fair jobs. Hearing my footsteps, a man who looks barely twenty years old comes from around a screened-off area. He's tall and muscular, with a dark head of curls, intense blue eyes, and a strong chin. "Vendor or general work?" he says.

"Neither. I'm here to see Careen Hudson."

"She's tied up—all these people are waiting to see her." He tilts his chin in the direction of the waiting supplicants.

"It's a police matter," I say. "Couple of questions I need to ask her. I can wait."

He frowns, and I see he doesn't quite know how to handle this wrinkle in the day's business. If I were to guess, he was hired because of his looks rather than for his brains. "You have a card?" he says.

He takes the card and starts toward another door, but the door opens and Careen Hudson steps out. The men in the waiting room come to attention. It's been thirty years since she was a teacher, but time has been good to her. In her school picture she had full lips, dark eyes, and long, lustrous hair. Her hair is shorter, the eyes have a few lines around them, and she may have a few more pounds than she'd like, but she looks good. And she is dressed to take advantage of her assets. She's wearing high heels and a short skirt that shows off shapely legs, a red blouse with enough of the top buttons left undone to give a peek at fine breasts, and a gold necklace that stops an inch short of nestling between them. This is a woman to be reckoned with.

Her assistant hurries over and hands her my card and says a few words to her. She looks at her watch and says something to him.

He comes back and says, "Careen is going to try to fit two more applicants in and then she'll see you while she eats her lunch at her desk."

The assistant calls the next applicant in, a burly man whose face has gone bright red at the prospect of being in the same room with the bombshell.

Thirty minutes later I'm ushered into the office. Careen is sitting at a wooden desk in a straight-backed chair and she gestures for me to sit in the same kind of chair across the desk from her. It's hot in the office and she is fanning herself. When I sit down she picks up a tissue and blots her nose and forehead. "Every year I promise myself I'm going to get an air-conditioner for this office." Her voice is low and has a trace of humor in it.

"Why don't you?"

"I'm too cheap. The fair barely makes ends meet as it is, and since I only use this office a few weeks out of the year, I can't justify the expense. That was before I hit the change of life." She gives me a knowing wink, and I can't help laughing. "Good, at least you've got a sense of humor," she says. "Some of these poor people are so desperate for a job that they wouldn't know a joke if it pounded them on the head." She lifts the vee of the blouse away from her and fans herself, and I find myself wishing for the first time in many a year that I was twenty years younger and looking for a challenging woman. "Now what kind of questions can I answer for you?"

"I'm trying to find out if you remember a kid you had as a student back when you were teaching."

The humor leaves her face. "If you mean that incident that got me fired, I don't have anything more to add."

"I don't mean that," I say. "This is about a boy by the name of Eddie Sandstone. Somebody said you were one of his teachers and might remember him."

She lifts an eyebrow at me. "What I remember may not be very helpful to you. Eddie was a very attractive young man. I was only a few years older than him, and let me tell you, he was one hunk I would like to have gotten to know a little better. Cocky as hell, but I like boys that way." She shifts in her seat and fans her chest again. I imagine what it must have been like for adolescent boys sitting in a classroom with her.

"I heard he had a temper," I say.

She pauses, speculating, and I wouldn't be surprised if she liked that in a man, too, but if she does, she keeps it to herself. "I heard that, too. And there was something else. I'm trying to remember exactly what it was. Something that happened with his sister that upset her."

"You have any idea what it was?"

She shakes her head. "You know how kids are. They'll blab every little thing about stupid stuff—but when something important happens, they clam up. And quite frankly I wasn't all that interested in the drama that high school girls get up to."

"Any idea who might know something about it?"

She pouts her lips. "Is he in some kind of trouble?"

"He's not in any trouble that I know of. But I'm curious to know why you'd think so."

She shrugs. "He was one of those kids who likes to be the big cheese, and he had a way of butting heads with people. I suspect he hasn't changed all that much. He had a couple of good friends back then, but I can't even remember their names."

I thank her for her trouble and start to rise, but she gestures for me to sit back down. "I don't have to get back to work just yet. Why don't you tell me a little bit about yourself? How long have you been chief in Jarrett Creek?" She leans forward, propping her arms on her desk and offering a little more view. I'm sorely tempted, but the reality is she's not my type, and more to the point, I doubt I'm hers either—she just wants the practice.

Otis Greevy is only ten years older than Eddie Sandstone, but his face is as lined as an alligator. His light-brown eyes are sunken back in his head, only their friendly look saving him from looking reptilian. "What can I do for you?"

"I'd like a word with you concerning something that happened a good while back."

"Come on in. I don't have long. My wife is out and when she gets back we have to go see a man about a dog." Seeing the look on my face, he gives a snort of laughter. "No, I mean that for real." He leads me into the living room. "Our dog died a couple of months ago, and my wife has her heart set on a little cocker spaniel. I'd rather have a real dog myself—a nice hound or a Labrador retriever or something like that. But she's the boss. Set down there. Can I get you some iced tea?"

"Sounds good."

He's back quickly with the tea. "You take lemon?"

"No. This is fine."

As soon as I take a sip of it, I regret not asking for the lemon because it's too sweet.

"What questions do you think I have an answer to?"

"This goes back a ways. Apparently you had a little dust-up with Eddie Sandstone, and I'd like you to tell me about the incident."

Otis Greevy tugs at the collar of his shirt as if it's suddenly too tight. "That is going back a long time. What in the world do you want to bring up that old business for?"

"I don't want to pry if it's something you'd rather not discuss." Words designed to make sure he'll talk to me.

"No, it's not a problem. Just seemed like a lot of water under the bridge since then. I haven't seen Sandstone in a heck of a long time."

"Can you tell me what led to him attacking you?"

"Well, it's not something I'm proud of. I guess you'd have to say we were both at fault." Looking embarrassed, he clears his throat and drinks some tea.

"We was all workin' under Curly Fogarty as carpenters and whatnot. Building a bunch of new houses. I was a carpenter—still am—and I worked alongside Eddie Sandstone's daddy. All of a sudden one day his daddy didn't show up for work. I didn't think much about it at first, but we had more work than we could do, so after a few days of him not coming in I asked Eddie where his daddy was. Eddie was sort of a gofer. You know? Go fer this, go fer that?" He laughs at his stale joke.

"What did Eddie say?"

"He said he didn't know where his daddy was." Greevy sighs. "That's where I made my mistake. I thought I was pretty funny back then. Good sense of humor. Like to make everybody laugh." He looks to me for confirmation.

"I hear you," I say.

"I said, 'Eddie, has your daddy run off with Alice Blackman?'" Alice sang in the choir with Howard and she was a good-looking woman. Somebody had told me he had a crush on her. I didn't take it seriously, but I guess Eddie did. He picked up a shovel and knocked me upside the head with it." Greevy has a good head of hair and he moves a bit of it aside and leans forward for me to take a look. "I've still got the scar. Bled like a pig. Had to have a bunch of stitches."

"But you didn't press charges?"

"I was going to. It's not right hitting me with something. If he'd used his fist, that would be one thing, but using a weapon? No, sir. But then his mamma came around to talk to me. She said Eddie had had a hard time of it since his daddy left and could I see my way clear to drop the charges. She was worried that her son would lose his scholarship with an assault conviction on his record. She was a sweet lady, and by that time the wind was out of my sails and I told her sure. Didn't do any good though. He lost the scholarship anyway."

"Did anybody else have trouble with Sandstone?"

"Not at the job site they didn't. He quit at the end of the week and went to work on somebody's farm. No great loss, if you ask me."

I hear a back door open and the rustle of grocery sacks, and a cheery voice says, "I'm home! Let's go get us a dog!" A short, chunky little woman with snappy blue eyes comes barreling into the room and stops short when she sees me. "I'm so sorry. I didn't know we had company."

I stand up. "I was just leaving. I won't keep you from your business. Thank you for the iced tea."

"Hold up," Greevy says, rising. "Elaine, would you give us a minute?"

"I sure will. I've got to put the groceries away."

As soon as she walks out Greevy says, "Why are you asking about Howard after all these years? It was a funny business that he walked out like that. Have you had word of him or something?"

"I don't know if you knew it, but Vera Sandstone died last week. She had asked me to find her husband and I'm following through on that."

"I see. I can tell you I don't know anything about that."

"The woman in the choir he supposedly was interested in," I say. "Alice, you said her name was? Is she still around?"

"There wasn't anything to those rumors. She stayed around here. Although, some said maybe he felt like he had to get out of town before he made a fool of himself over her."

"I wouldn't mind talking to her, to see if she has any idea where he might have gone."

"Let me ask Elaine. She'll know." He disappears into the kitchen and comes back with her. She's wiping her hands on a tea towel.

"Alice? She's still around. I don't think she sings in the choir anymore though. She had breast cancer and she dropped out of choir after that."

Greevy's cheeks pink up. Some men can't even hear the word "breast" without getting all flustered.

Stubby Clark looks like he's likely to follow his former boss to an early grave. He's as wide as he is tall and huffs and puffs as we walk across the field to his office. It's late afternoon, and he's been looking over his crop of football players for next fall. He has had them doing sprints, and I don't envy them. In late April it gets over ninety in the afternoon. Needless to say, Stubby isn't going to show them how it's done. He tells his assistant that he'll be back in a half hour. I have a feeling he's happy to get out of the sun. His face is a dangerous shade of red.

"I'm going to ask you to go back a good while," I say. "I'm interested in a boy you coached back when you were just getting started, Eddie Sandstone."

I've borrowed a yearbook from Mollie Cleaver and I open it to the pages that show the football seniors. He barely glances at it, and I notice that he stiffens ever so slightly before he sits back in his chair and folds his hands over his belly. "What kind of interest do you have in him?"

"I just need to contact him. His mamma passed away." A vague explanation will be enough. Anything to get him talking.

"I heard that Vera passed. But I haven't really kept up with her son."

"He was a pretty good football player?"

He looks at Eddie's picture and then off into space, then back again. There's a subtle change in his face as he remembers something. "Pretty good." He's frowning.

"Good enough to get a scholarship to SMU, I understand."

He nods again, sits back, and says, "If they could have tamped down that mean streak, they might have made something of him."

"Mean streak? Everybody I've talked to seemed to think he was pretty popular."

"Yeah, he was popular, all right, as long as nobody crossed him. But a few times people did, and he had a way of getting back at them. And then he ended up attacking somebody. I don't remember the details, but he lost that scholarship." I'm intrigued by the look of satisfaction that settles on Clark's face. "I warned the folks at SMU that he might give them some trouble, but they had a crying need for a middle linebacker and they said those boys were always a little mean." He snorts.

"But I could have told them even as young as I was that there's mean on the field and then there's just plain mean."

"For example?" If I'm not mistaken he's harboring a grudge against Eddie Sandstone, and I've stirred up some uncomfortable memories. Exactly the kind of thing I was trying to pry loose.

"He'd play pranks on his teammates for no good reason and then act all innocent. Stuff like making out with somebody's girlfriend and then bragging about it in front of everybody. And if the guy got upset, he'd claim he thought they were broken up or some such nonsense."

"That was asking for trouble."

"Yeah, except he had his little group of friends, and if anybody acted like they were going to mess with him they closed ranks. I don't mind telling you I didn't like him."

"Stubby" Clark. A short, wide man with a nickname that must have been easy for a kid like Eddie Sandstone to make fun of. From the pictures in the yearbook, Stubby was smaller than most of the boys he coached. And thirty years ago, starting out as an assistant coach, he'd have been sensitive to gibes from the players.

A father who disappeared and a popular son with promise who went off the rails after that. The more I dig into the matter, the more I wonder what happened to make Jenny despise her brother, and if it all has something to do with his daddy leaving home. Something happened around that time, and for Jenny's sake, I want to know what it was.

CHAPTER 19

When I go down to the pasture behind my house to see to my cows the next morning, I take the time to give myself a good, stern talking to. Jenny's on the mend—from her mamma's death and from her accident. It's time I sit her down and insist on finding out what's behind her problems with her brother. It may be nothing but old grudges, but it also may be something serious enough to have made him try to run her car off the road. A while back I lost a friend because I didn't take the danger to her seriously, and I'm not going to let that happen again. The problem is I dread the confrontation. Jenny is not a person to push around. She's determined to fend for herself—how that came about I don't know, but it's deeply ingrained.

As if reading my mind, the phone rings. It's Jenny. "You planning on coming to the hospital today?"

"I was just fixin' to call you. You want me to come over now?"

"Yes, but I need you to come in some kind of conveyance besides that truck of yours so you can take me home. No way I can climb into the truck."

"They're letting you out? That's good news."

She tells me they'll release her at noon. I call to see if the highway patrol is finished with her car, but they say they need to keep it a little longer, so I go down to headquarters and clean out one of our two squad cars. It's not a luxury vehicle, but it'll work well enough for bringing Jenny home.

I expected Jenny to be excited to come home, but in her hospital room she's subdued. I worry that she's in pain, but she says she's feeling fine and speaks so curtly that I figure it might be better to give her a little room to be surly. It's always an ordeal getting out of the hospital. It's hurry up and wait time. They act like they want you out right away, but then when you're ready they make you wait to sign papers and then talk to the head nurse and anybody else they can think of to get into the action. And then they have to scare up a wheelchair because God forbid that you walk out on your own, even though as soon as you get home you'll be on your own.

When we finally get into the car and on our way, Jenny still hasn't said much. But as soon as I turn out of the parking lot, she says, "Do you mind if we go by Mamma's house on the way home?"

"You sure you feel up to it?"

"I need to go by there," she says. "Unless you have somewhere you have to be."

"No, I cleared the deck. I'm at your service."

There's no question that Jenny is tense. The air feels charged around us. The only comment she makes as we drive to the house is to complain about the odor of the squad car. "You ought to have it cleaned," she grumbles.

"I'll get right on it," I say, trying to put a little smart aleck in my voice, but if she picks up on it she doesn't respond.

When I park in front, she sits still for several seconds, as if mentally steeling herself for the ordeal of climbing out of the car.

"You want me to go in and check on things so you don't have to get out?"

Her only reply is to open the car door and ease her legs out onto the sidewalk.

"Wait a minute. Let me come around and help you," I say. I fling my door open, but by the time I get around to her side, she's pulled herself upright and is standing with her hands on the side of the car, panting.

I wait while she catches her breath and then walk beside her to the house. She's so pale that I'm worried she'll faint. At the door, she suddenly looks at me, her eyes stricken. "I forgot I need a key."

"Is it in your bag? I'll get it."

I know better than to scrabble around in a woman's purse, so I bring it to her. She finds the key right away and slips it into the lock and opens the door. And then she surprises me by calling out, "Hello?"

For a second, I wonder if she's having a bad spell and has forgotten that her mamma is gone. But then I see the grim look on her face. For some reason, she thinks somebody is in here. "Who do you think is here?" I say.

She ignores me and walks gingerly through the living room back into the kitchen. I follow her, my eyes darting this way and that, looking for signs that somebody has been in the house. To me the place looks like it did the last time I was here. In the kitchen nothing seems to be disturbed. Jenny stands for a couple of minutes looking from the counters to the little table and to the back door.

"You want me to check the bedrooms?" I say.

"I doubt you'd notice if anything was out of place," she says. At least I've gotten that much out of her.

We walk through the rest of the house, and she seems to relax with each room we go into. And then, just as we get back to the living room, someone pushes the front door open wide.

In steps Eddie Sandstone.

"You!" Jenny snarls. "Get out of here!" She steps over to the sofa and grabs the back of it in a death grip.

"Jenny, don't be that way. Mamma wouldn't want you to be nasty to me. She'd want us to make up." Up close, Eddie Sandstone doesn't look much like a demon. He's only two years older than Jenny, but from the lines on his face, it appears that the years haven't been all that kind. He's wearing jeans and a Western-style shirt faded from its original black to a washed-out gray.

"You don't know what Mamma wanted," Jenny says. "Now get out."

He flushes as he struggles with his temper. "Jenny, I hate to tell you, but it turns out you don't have a right to throw me out."

"I most certainly do. Mamma left this place and everything in it to me."

"That may be the way it was a while back, but before she died she changed her mind." He fishes in the back pocket of his jeans and comes out with a folded paper that he opens up and thrusts at Jenny. "I went to talk to her while she was in the hospital and she agreed that it wasn't fair for you to inherit everything. You can have the contents of the house—but the house is mine."

Jenny doesn't make a move to touch the paper. "I heard you pulled something like this. What did you do to her to make her sign that?"

"Come on, Jenny I didn't do anything." His tone is injured. "You know it wasn't fair for her to leave you everything. When I told her how much it hurt my feelings, she was real contrite and said since you had a house, maybe it wouldn't be such a bad thing if she left the house to me."

Jenny snatches at the paper and looks at it. "You know I'm going to fight this in court," she says. "Mamma wasn't fit to be signing anything like this."

"She seemed perfectly competent to me." Eddie points to the document. "And to the nurse who signed as a witness."

Jenny's shoulders sag in defeat as she reads the document. I recall the nurse, Monica, asking Jenny if the man who came to the hospital to see her mother got what he wanted. I wonder which nurse signed the document. "We'll see," she says.

Eddie looks Jenny up and down. "What happened to you? You've got a big bruise on your face."

"None of your business."

He shrugs. "That's okay. But it looks like you're healing from something. If you need time to pack up everything, don't worry. I'm not in any hurry. You take all the time you need getting stuff out of here. I won't need it for a couple of months. It'll take that long for me to wrap up things in Temple anyway."

"You're planning to move in here?" she asks.

He hesitates. "I haven't decided exactly what I'm going to do. I may decide to live here, or rent it out, or even sell it. I'll keep you posted, though."

"I'll be out of here before the month is over," she says. "And I don't need to know your plans." She's leaning heavily on the back of the sofa, and I can tell she's shaky.

"Jenny, I ought to get you home," I say.

Eddie turns his attention to me and extends his hand. "I don't believe we've been introduced. I'm Jenny's brother, Eddie. I imagine she hasn't mentioned me." He smiles ruefully. "Jenny is one to hold grudge. Are you Jenny's boyfriend?"

I shake his hand. "I'm Samuel Craddock, Jenny's friend and neighbor." Jenny looks daggers at me, but I have no reason to be rude to her brother. "Jenny was in an accident a couple of days ago and I just picked her up from the hospital. I think I'd better take her on home."

"Accident? What kind of accident?"

"Maybe she can tell you another time."

"Or maybe I'll tell you about it when hell freezes over," Jenny says.

"Fine." For the first time since he walked in, a cloud crosses his face. "I'll be seeing you," he says, and strides out the door.

When Jenny and I walk out the door, he's standing next to his car, looking at the house. I'm holding onto Jenny's arm and I feel her flinch. The car is a little white Toyota that looks too small for him. Not the dark car I saw him in at the hospital.

"This your car?" I say.

"No, it belongs to my ex-wife. I borrowed it while mine's in the shop."

My antenna goes up, wondering if that black car might be in the shop to have a big dent removed from running Jenny off the road. But he's given me no reason to suspect him of that. In fact, he's been downright cordial.

Jenny doesn't have any fight left in her. She's pale and shaking. I adjust her seat back so she's reclining and can rest. I try to talk to her on the way home, but she's gone somewhere I can't reach. I keep remembering that the coach, Stubby Clark, said Eddie was cruel. I saw no evidence of that today. But I'm on Jenny's side, and whatever he did has to have been pretty bad for her to carry such a grudge against him.

CHAPTER 20

There's no way I have a chance to get close to Jenny for a few days. Once Loretta finds out that Jenny's home from the hospital, she takes over, declaring, "She doesn't need to be by herself except when she wants to rest."

Although I know Jenny will complain that people are hovering too much, I think it will be good for her, especially after the shock she got from her brother's announcement. She's had too many hard things happen lately.

I've been neglecting my duties as chief of police, so I spend a couple of days catching up on paperwork and going to see people who need a follow-up. Bill Odum is on duty on Thursday and he seems to like taking care of the day-to-day business of police work, so I take off for the two-hour drive to Temple. I want to have a private chat with Eddie Sandstone. I hope he can give me some indication of what happened to the family around the time his daddy disappeared, and what led to his being shut out by Jenny.

At ten o'clock I pull up in front of the address I have for him, which turns out to be a dreary, two-story brick and wood apartment building without much in the way of amenities. It's built in an "L" shape and might even have been a motel at one time. It hasn't been painted in a while, and the green trim is flaking. The carport doesn't have many cars in it at this time of day, but the ones that are there look as shabby as the building.

The address I have for Eddie doesn't include an apartment number, so I don't know which one he lives in. I see a small sign that says "manager" pointing to the back of the building. Around back I find an office closed up tight, with a handwritten note on the door giving a phone number in case of questions. I dial the number and am not especially surprised to find that it's disconnected. I'm trying to figure out what to do next when I spy a maintenance man wheeling a garbage bin into a big enclosed area.

"Excuse me," I say. "Can you tell me how I can find the manager?"

The man is a light-skinned black man around fifty years old, wearing blue coveralls and a bandana around his neck. He parks the garbage bin and squints at me. "I guess that would be me," he says.

I introduce myself. "I'm looking for a man by the name of Eddie Sandstone. Can you tell me which apartment is his?"

"He doesn't live here, but he visits his wife a good bit."

"Do you know where I can find her?"

He jerks his thumb toward the building. "Apartment 8. Name is Joyce. She's a nice lady."

I mount the wooden stairs up to the second floor. Joyce Sandstone opens her door dressed in a T-shirt, knee-length shorts, and no makeup. She's a skinny woman with a pasty complexion. Her dull blonde hair is held back by a rubber band. She's holding a cleaning rag in her hand. "If you're one of those Jehovah's Witness people, forget it. I'm not interested." She starts to close the door.

"Whoa," I say. "Mrs. Sandstone. I'm chief of police in Jarrett Creek. I'm looking for your husband."

"Jarrett Creek? Where is that?"

"It's over by Bobtail, where Eddie grew up."

"Why are you looking for him?"

"I want to have a word with him. This is the address I have for him, but the man I talked to downstairs said Eddie doesn't live here. Is that right?"

She peers over the railing, frowning, and then looks back at me. "Me and Eddie aren't living together at the moment."

"Can you give me his address and phone number?"

She hesitates. "Has he done something?"

"I need to talk to him, that's all."

She can't seem to come up with an objection, so she gives me his phone number and address, which I enter into my cell phone.

"How long have you two been married?"

"A couple years."

"When did you split up?"

"I don't know that we're split up. We're trying a trial separation."

"Yeah?" Sometimes just looking like you're interested will get you more information.

"Eddie's not the easiest person to get along with."

"Really. In what way?"

"I told him he has anger management issues." She smirks. "That's the newest term for a bad temper."

"Is he violent?"

She screws up her face. "Not exactly. But he's been in a bad mood for a while, and I got tired of feeling like he was on the verge of getting violent. You know what I mean?" Suddenly she looks guilty. "I'm not telling you something that will get him in trouble, am I?"

"No, nothing like that."

She looks behind her. "As long as we're talking, you might as well come on in here and get some coffee and I can sit down. This is my only day off this week and I'm trying to clean this place up."

Over sizeable mugs of good coffee, she tells me that she met Eddie when he was in the hospital after he broke his foot on the job. "I've never been good at picking men." She's already stirred three teaspoons of sugar into her coffee, and she adds another one, not really paying attention to what she's doing. "Eddie is a brooder . . . I always go for the brooding ones, for all the good it does me." She takes a sip and frowns. I can't believe what she's done to a perfectly good cup of coffee.

"You said recently he'd been in a bad mood. Anything in particular upset him?"

"I wouldn't know. He keeps things to himself. Always has. It didn't bother me so much when we were first together, but I don't know if he's gotten worse or if I'm more impatient. I told him he ought to see a therapist to help him perk up. You know, not always be thinking somebody's out to get him or out to put something over on him."

"Is he paranoid?"

"I wouldn't go that far. Just suspicious."

"He ever talk about his sister?"

"Oh, boy, don't get me started on that sister of his. I think she's the source of his problems. He said she never liked him and was always out to get him, and that she eventually turned his mamma against him."

That's a different slant on things. "Did you know his mamma died recently?"

"Yeah, he told me. Called me one night and told me she passed. He was pretty cut up about it. Eddie almost didn't go the funeral because he said his sister might pitch a fit. Now I ask you, what kind of sister doesn't want her own brother at their mamma's funeral?"

"Did he say why she didn't want him there?"

"No, just that she wouldn't like it."

"Did you ever meet either of them—Jenny or Vera?"

She shakes her head. "I wouldn't have minded meeting his mamma, but he said there was no sense in it because she was under his sister's spell. And as for the sister, I figured it was best if I didn't meet her, because I'd have been likely to give her a piece of my mind."

"How did Eddie find out his mamma was sick?"

She gives me a blank look. "I don't know. Maybe she had somebody call from the hospital."

"Eddie was married once before, wasn't he?"

"Yes, and would you believe it, me and his first wife are friends. She lives down at the end of the row here." She inclines her head to the end of the apartments.

"You two okay living so close to one another?"

She smirks. "Everybody always says that. Marlene is good people. Me and her get along fine. We work together at the hospital. She's an LPN, and I work in the dining room. For a while after we met, I didn't even know that her and Eddie had been married. We got to talking one day and figured it out. We had a good laugh over it."

"I wouldn't mind talking to her."

Joyce calls Marlene for me, but she says she's working late. I'll have to come back later in the week if I want to talk to her. From my car, I call Eddie to set up a meeting with him, but the phone goes straight to his messages.

When I get home in the late afternoon, I call Loretta to see how things went with Jenny.

"She seems awful depressed to me. I don't blame her. First her mamma dies and then she gets injured with somebody forcing her off the road."

I plan to go over and see Jenny, but first I check in at headquarters. Bill Odum says things have been okay. "But Jim Krueger wants you to call him. He says there are more prom issues."

Krueger tells me the idea of the wine party for the parents was well received. "They decided to shut the prom down at two a.m. So those kids who said they were going to boycott have decided to come. But now we have the problem of what kind of mischief they'll get up to after two o'clock in the morning."

"Jim, leave that to the police. We'll be out at the usual spots. We'll get through it again this year."

By the usual spots I mean the dam road and a couple of country roads that attract kids who have had too much to drink and think it's a fine idea to show off their ability to drive. We don't arrest them; we take their keys and drive everybody home.

When I get home from work, I eat a bite of dinner, giving Jenny a chance to recover from a day's worth of company before I call and ask if I can drop by. She says to come on over. Her voice sounds funny. When

I walk in the front door, I find her lying on the sofa in her living room with an almost empty bottle of wine on the coffee table nearby.

"You sure it's a good idea to be drinking that much if you're on pain meds?" I ask.

She snorts. "Now don't you start, too. I've had it with people telling me what to do. If those ladies who were here today were doctors, there wouldn't be any sick people left. They know how to cure everything, including a missing spleen."

I had planned to talk to her about what happened with her brother yesterday, but with as much as she's had to drink, I don't know that it's a good idea. "Mind if I join you?"

"If you bring another bottle."

Ignoring that, I go and get a wineglass out of her cabinet and pour the last of the bottle of wine for myself. I sit down, not looking at her because I expect she's glaring at me.

"I'm serious," she says. "I want you to bring out another bottle of wine. That bottle was only half full and I need some more."

"If it was only half full, how come the cork and corkscrew were out on the cabinet?"

"Just bring me another bottle of wine and stop making a federal case out of it."

"I'm not going to let you kill yourself simply because you're mad at your brother."

"I don't want to talk about that."

"Neither do I. You're too drunk to talk about it with any kind of sense."

"I'm not drunk. And even if I were stone-cold sober, I'm still not going to talk about Eddie." She pulls herself upright, wincing.

I get up. "Do you need me to help you get to bed?"

"I can make it on my own."

"Have you talked to Alvin Carter? I told him he should be riding your horses since you're not going to be able to for a while."

Her face flushes. "I appreciate what you've done to keep my horses safe, but don't use that as ammunition against me."

"Jenny, that wasn't my intention. I'm just trying to change the subject."

"Sorry," she mutters. She heaves herself to her feet and sways unsteadily. I edge closer, ready to catch her if she starts to fall. She glares at me. "Walk with me down the hall, if you will."

It's the only admission I'm going to get that she could use the help. I take her arm and lead her down to her bedroom. She sits on the edge of the bed. "I'll be all right now. I've got everything right here."

I nod at the phone. "You've got the phone right there, too. Call me if you need anything."

CHAPTER 21

"I swear, every year it gets worse. Everybody is going crazy because of the prom." Loretta is standing in my kitchen with her hands on her hips, looking exasperated. Ever since she got back from her trip with her son, nothing that goes on in town seems to suit her.

"It's a small town, Loretta. You have to expect kids to get worked up. There's not much to do around here."

"You can say that again. But it's gotten ridiculous. Girls tearing up the road between here and Bobtail, here and San Antonio, and here and Houston, looking for the perfect dress—a dress they'll never wear again and won't remember a year from now."

"You were complaining yourself that you couldn't find anything to wear around here. In a couple of years that mall will be in and the girls will go there."

Loretta gives me a withering look. "You don't buy prom dresses at an outlet mall."

I've just taken a bite of the coffee cake she brought over, and I have to wait until I've swallowed it before I can reply. "And why not?"

"Prom dresses have to be special. The things you buy at an outlet mall are overstocks and last year's stuff. No girl wants that."

Loretta usually makes a fuss over how much girls spend on their clothes, but I think I'd better not bring that up. Nor do I bring up that the few times I've been at the high school the last couple of weeks it seems like the boys are hanging around on the school grounds after school looking like the world around them has suddenly tilted, leaving them off balance. The girls have gone crazy, and the boys don't know how to react. Any man could tell them that there's no help for it. It's going to be that way for a few years to come, until they get some experience behind them.

Remembering Jenny's complaint that she was always an ugly duckling in high school, I say, "Are there any girls you know who are wanting for a date?"

She blinks at me like I've asked her for the key to hieroglyphics. "What in the world has gotten into you? What kind of a question is that?"

"I saw something on TV about girls who feel like wallflowers in high school, and it affects them for years to come," I say.

"Then that program you saw was outdated. Things have changed. These days half the girls go to the prom in a group instead of with dates. If you want my opinion, I think it's better that way."

"What about the ones left out of the groups?"

"Well, I don't know." Her tone is exasperated. But then she frowns. "That's not entirely true. I did hear that the little McGregor girl was having some trouble. She's not popular with the girls or the boys, and her mamma said she was upset because she didn't have anybody to go to the prom with."

"Seems a shame. What do you do about something like that?"

"There's no reason you should know any of this, but Judy Holt, the English teacher—all the girls love her—got a couple of the girls together and talked to them about it, and they said they didn't even know Carrie McGregor wanted to go to the prom and they'd be glad to include her." She lifts an eyebrow. "Does that make you feel any better?"

"I don't know why you should take that tone with me. What's wrong with me taking an interest?"

She throws her hands up. "Nothing's wrong with it. I never heard you talk like that is all."

I've barely sat down at my desk at work when Wallace Lyndall calls me up. "Scott Borland is back in town. I went by there this morning before work and the car was in the yard and the door was open. I didn't bother them."

"Thanks for keeping me posted. I'll go on over there in a while."

"You want me to go with you?"

I tell him I'll stop by and pick him up on my way, but that it will be an hour before I can get to Bobtail. First I have to soothe Jim Krueger's rattled nerves one more time. Now it seems that a few of the hard-shelled Baptists are up in arms because of the wine-tasting event. They say that if the kids know their parents are drinking wine, they'll want to do it, too. As if they miraculously wouldn't have any interest in alcohol if their parents didn't lead the way.

I call Loretta and ask her if she has any bright ideas. She's not much of a drinker, and doesn't like it if people drink too much, but she's not a nut on the subject. "I hate to say it, but they're right," she says. "What-ever possessed Emily Ford to have a wine tasting anyway—especially the night of the prom?"

She's exasperated when I tell her it was sort of my idea. "There's no help for it, then. Somebody needs to tell the Baptists that it's not every-body else's jobs to keep their kids from drinking."

I call Emily Ford and she laughs at the problem. "I don't know who's behind all this complaining, but they might be interested to know that Patsy Thompson was one of the first people to sign up. She's a big Baptist, but she seems to think that if Jesus drank wine, she can, too. Anyway, it's too late. They're just going to have to gripe." Every time I have a conversation with Emily Ford, I like her better.

Jim Krueger isn't comforted by what I have to say, but he agrees with me that it's too late to change anything now.

"And it's only teachers chaperoning the kids?" I say.

"It was supposed to be, but a couple of the parents insisted that they still wanted to have a hand in it, and I gave in. Lord, I'm tired of fighting these battles every year."

"Better you than me," I say.

The door of the Borland's house is still standing open, and Scott Borland himself is sitting on the steps outside with his shirt off, drinking a beer. Several empty cans are scattered at his feet. It's not quite eleven o'clock, which seems a little early to be drinking beer. When Wallace Lyndall and I get out of my squad car and walk over to him, he stays put, scratching his hairy belly.

"Morning, Scott," Lyndall says.

He tips his beer can at Lyndall. "And to you, too, Officer. What brings you out here?"

Lyndall introduces me. "Chief Craddock has a little mystery on his hands and thought maybe you could shed light on it."

"I'm more than happy to help you lawmen solve your problems," Borland says. He seems relaxed for a man who's guilty of something.

"You know a lawyer by the name of Jenny Sandstone?" I ask.

"Know her! I not only know her, I hate her guts. Why do you ask?"

"There've been a couple of incidents at her place that I thought you might know something about."

Borland sets his beer down, stands up, belches, and makes his way down the two steps, watching his feet carefully, as if they might make a false move. Some men who have spent ten years in prison use the time to beef up their muscles and come out looking like somebody out of an Arnold Schwarzenegger movie. But Scott Borland's muscles are slack. He's not heavy, but his belly and chest sag, and his arms look scrawny. Up close, his beery breath could knock you down. "You're asking about something that went on at Jenny Sandstone's house? I was hoping you would ask me something I knew something about. Or had some interest in."

"You interested in snakes?" I say.

"Not especially." His eyes get a glint of mischief. "Although there's something about a rattlesnake that I like. They have pretty markings. You ever noticed that?"

"You by any chance get up close and personal with a timber rattler lately?"

He strokes his belly, looking pensive. "I don't believe I'm familiar with the look of that rattlesnake. I'm more thinking of the diamond-back. If I recall my snake lore, however, I believe we don't get timber rattlers around here. You'd most likely find that kind up around Nacogdoches."

I'm pretty sure he's having a little fun at our expense, but that's okay. I wasn't expecting him to admit to anything today. The idea is more to warn him that I have an eye on him. "Any chance your boy Jett has had occasion to go up to east Texas recently?"

"You know, I just got out of prison and I can't really vouch for what that boy might have been up to while I was gone. Why don't we ask him?" He turns his head toward the house and yells, "Jett! Come on out here. Somebody I want you to meet."

"Hold on a minute," a voice yells back.

"He'll be out directly," Borland says. He tilts his face toward the sun "I'm surely enjoying this fine weather. I can't get enough of the sun since I walked out of prison. I'm going to have to get me some of that suntan lotion. Wouldn't want to ruin my skin." He gets a good laugh out of that one.

Jett doesn't look much like his daddy. His hair is dark and his eyes are black pools that seem to suck up the light. "Cops?" he says to his dad. "You brought me out here to meet cops?"

"These fellows are mighty nice," Scott Borland says. "You know, I've had occasion to meet some awfully unfriendly police, but these two are as polite as they can be. I believe it's because they're older gentlemen. I didn't think you'd mind answering their questions. It won't take much of your time, and then they can be on their way."

Jett sneers. "I get what you're saying. Sure. What can I do for you?"

I say, "Somebody has been threatening the horses that belong to one of my neighbors, Jenny Sandstone, who happens to be acquainted with your dad."

"Somebody overheard you threatening to get even with her for putting your dad away," Lyndall puts in.

Jett snickers. "Threatening horses? Why would I do something like that?" Then his voice turns cold. "No, if I was going to make good on any threats, I wouldn't bother with horses. I'd go straight for that nasty lady lawyer who made a monkey out of my daddy's defense lawyer. She cheated every which way. Daddy never should have been convicted of those crimes. He was innocent."

"I'm sure he was," Lyndall says. "So you're claiming you didn't mess with the horses in any way?"

"You're damn right I'm claiming that. And nobody can prove any different."

"How about ramming her car with yours? Did you do that?"

Scott Borland has been contemplating the yard, but at those words, his head snaps up. "Was Ms. Sandstone hurt? Bad, I hope?"

"She was hurt. She'll be okay."

"Well, damn. Jett, if that was you, I'll give you a medal," Scott says. "Fess up, now." He tosses his empty beer can out into the yard.

Jett punches his daddy on the arm, smirking. "You old fool. You're going to get me in trouble if you don't look out."

Scott ruffles his son's hair. "Like father, like son." As if they're getting into trouble is special. And then his eyes go dark. "What makes you think you can come here and accuse me and my son of anything?"

"I'm pretty sure I saw your car out in front Jenny's place, for one thing."

"Jett, did you go to that lady lawyer's house? Did you take her some flowers?"

I've had enough of their comedy routine. "I want you to know, I've got my eye on you. If I catch you anywhere near Jenny Sandstone's place, I'll arrest you."

"You can't just arrest me for lawfully being outside her place."

"Believe me, I'll think of some good reason."

Scott starts to say something, and I raise my voice. "Don't give me any b.s. about it being a free country. My guess is, your activities won't stand up much to any scrutiny, so if I were you I'd give up on the idea of messing with Jenny."

"Oh. Knight in shining armor!" Scott says. "We'll most certainly take heed to your warning."

When we drive away, Lyndall says, "People like that make me tired."

"You have much problem with meth here in Bobtail?"

"More than we used to, but not as much as some."

Which doesn't tell me a whole lot. I keep wondering when it's going to crop up in my neck of the woods. Probably already has and I just don't know it.

I'm on my way out of town when my cell phone rings. I pull over when I see that it's an unfamiliar number.

"This is Eddie Sandstone. Am I talking to the man I met with my sister Jenny last week?"

"Yes. This is Samuel Craddock."

"I understand you had a conversation with my wife."

"I was hoping to find you at home, but since you weren't there, she and I had a nice chat."

"If you have anything to say to me, I'd appreciate it if you'd leave her out of it."

"Where are you calling from?"

"I'm on a job. But I can drive down to Bobtail and meet you? Tonight maybe?"

"Unfortunately, I've got business tonight. Can we meet tomorrow around lunchtime? I can come to Temple."

"No need. I'll meet you at my mamma's house."

"Do you have a key?"

He hesitates. "Get Jenny to come with you and I'll get a key from her. I didn't want to bother her with that yesterday."

"That isn't going to work. Jenny is still recovering from her accident and she isn't up to the drive. I'll get a key from her and meet you there."

"You can tell her for me that she can't avoid me forever. We're going to have to meet one way or the other."

"I'll see you at noon."

CHAPTER 22

Ten years ago, I don't think a wine party would have been possible in this community. Could be TV or the Internet, but our little town seems to be easing into the modern age. Some of the men aren't too excited about wine—I'm sure they'd rather be at a beer tasting—but the idea was to get these parents out of their kids' hair, and that part is a success.

I leave the party early, and by midnight I'm sitting outside the high school gym with Bill Odum, my chief deputy, watching for kids who might try sneaking out of the gym. If they do, our job is to escort them home and let their parents take care of the rest. Bill tries to get me to go on home, but if I'm going to be chief, I intend to be chief all the way. The prom doesn't end until two o'clock, and I practically have to prop my eyes open by then.

I'm barely settled into bed when I hear a car driving slowly down the street, stop, and then doors being closed quietly. I don't know why it takes my attention. I'm sure cars come by all the time when I'm sound asleep. Maybe I'm still keyed up and not able to drop off to sleep the way I usually do. But whatever the reason, I slip out of bed and go into the living room to peek out the shades. What I see puzzles me.

Two young boys are walking toward Jenny's side gate. They slip along the side of the house, and then I lose sight of them. I hustle to the window closest to the gate and hear them muttering. I put my ear to the window in time to hear one say, "I don't like this. That old police chief lives next door. If he hears us, we're toast."

"He's not going to hear anything. Old people can't hear, and besides he was at the gym until the dance let out. He's asleep by now."

135

"How do you know he was at the gym?"

"I saw him there."

I hear clanking noises and then scuffling. I wish I could see what's going on, but it sounds like one of them has climbed over the gate leading to Jenny's backyard. There's more scuffling, and I hear one of them say, "Grab my hand." And then I hear a thump, like someone jumping to the ground. I don't know what these boys are up to, but I imagine it has something to do with the mischief that's been going on with Jenny's horses. Maybe Scott Borland isn't the culprit after all. I can easily picture boys cutting a lock and letting the horses out onto the street. But where would young boys get a snake like that rattler? And why would they take a pipe to Truly Bennett? And the biggest question is, what do the boys have against Jenny—or her horses, for that matter?

What they don't know is that Alvin Carter is sleeping in the barn and is surely going to catch them sneaking in. I throw some clothes on and head out my back door and down to the gate between my pasture and Jenny's. My cows stir as I go through the pasture. They're huddled up near the fence, a few of them lying down.

I slip through the gate between our properties and start up the back of Jenny's pasture, straining to hear the boys. I hear the creak of the barn door opening. I hope Alvin stays quiet until I get there.

Suddenly I hear the soft whinny of one of the horses, and then a scramble of footsteps. "Oh, shit!" one of the boys says in a loud whisper.

Then I see a beam of light from the open door, and Alvin says, "Stop right there unless you want to get a buttful of buckshot."

"Run!" one of the boys says.

I'm close enough now to see the play of their shadows. "I wouldn't," I say. "I'm right outside the door and you're not going anywhere."

The shadows freeze. "Chief Craddock?" Alvin says.

"Yep." I step inside and flip on the light. Alvin is holding a shotgun at his side, and the two boys are standing in front of him looking like rabbits trying to figure out which way to run. They're high school boys, both slim and lanky. The taller one has a thatch of dark hair and a jutting chin. The other one is chunkier and looks soft in every way.

"Buster Mitchell! What the hell are you two boys doing here?" Alvin says.

"None of your business," the dark-haired kid says. Of the two, I'd say he's the ringleader. His eyes are darting this way and that, full of calculation. He hasn't given up on the idea of being able to get past me. The other one's shoulders have slumped and he looks scared. He runs a hand through his wheat-colored hair. "I told you!" he says to the dark-haired boy.

"Hush, Jimmy," the dark-haired one says.

"You know these boys?" I say to Alvin.

"I know that one," he points to the dark-haired one. "Buster's from Bobtail. His daddy has a fishing shack out at the lake. He rents a boat from my daddy sometimes, and the kid has come with him once or twice."

"We weren't doing nothing," Buster says to me.

"I don't want to hear it," I say. "I'm tired and I'm not in any mood to hear your excuses."

"If you're tired, you can let us go. We won't come back."

"I'm not that tired," I say. "Jimmy, what's your last name?"

"I'm not telling," he says.

"Suit yourself. We'll clear it all up in the morning." I walk over to an empty stall, open the door, and look inside. It will fit my purposes. "Get in there," I say.

Buster looks like he's ready to protest, but Alvin says, "You ever been hit with buckshot? It won't do you any permanent harm, but you won't like it. Do as the chief says and get in the stall."

They stumble into the stall, and I close both the doors. The two of them peer out through the slats on the front. "Keep an eye on them while I find a lock." I go into the tack room and find a big padlock and a board and take them back in to secure the stall.

"You can't keep us in here," Buster says.

"Sure I can. In the morning I'll find out what I need to know, and then you can go."

"What if we need a toilet or something?"

"There's a bucket in the corner and plenty of straw for comfort. Lie down there and sleep until the morning. Then we'll sort this out."

"I'm thirsty," Jimmy whines.

I spy a hose coiled up at one end of the barn attached to a faucet head. I feed the hose in between the slats. "Here you go. Room service."

"You got us in a fine mess," Jimmy says to his partner in crime.

"Don't be a sissy," Buster says. "My daddy will have this old guy's hide."

Alvin laughs. "I wouldn't count on it, Buster. Your daddy's not going to like finding out you were sneaking in here."

I hear sniffling and I know the smaller one is tuning up for a cry.

"Alvin, you going to be all right? These boys may whine for a while, but you ought to be able to get some sleep."

"I'll be fine. You go on back to bed."

It seems clear to me that these boys didn't come up with whatever they planned on their own. I'll find out tomorrow who put them up to it.

Before I turn in, I call the Bobtail Police Department and tell them I've got the boys tucked away in a safe place in case their parents are looking for them.

CHAPTER 23

I'm never one for sleeping late, although after being up until three o'clock this morning, I wish I could force myself to sleep past seven. But that's what time I'm up. I can't help thinking of what I heard some youngster say, "Party now. Sleep when you're dead." I'll have to go with that for today, although the party part of the equation doesn't sound appealing at the moment.

I call Loretta and ask her if she can bring some extra sweet rolls this morning, figuring it won't hurt to show a little mercy to the boys in the barn. When she comes by, I tell her I can't explain what the extras are for because I'm in a hurry, but that I'll fill her in later.

"You look tired," she says.

"I may be tired, but I'm satisfied," I say. "I'll sleep tonight."

Not only are the boys not stirring in the barn, but Alvin Carter is lying on his sleeping bag snoring like he doesn't have a care in the world. The boys are piled up on the straw, Buster sprawled out like he's been pushed over and is lying where he fell, and Jimmy curled into a ball. "Rise and shine," I say.

Alvin snorts and half rises, shaking his head. "Damn, Chief Craddock, you interrupted a pretty good dream."

I laugh. "You can go back to sleep if you want to. It's these boys I'm after."

He scrambles off the sleeping bag and stretches. "No, once I'm awake that's the end of it. Besides, I don't want to miss the action."

The boys aren't so quick to rouse, and when they finally stand up, they're as surly as bears. Before I unlock the door to the stall they're in, I go over and close the barn door so they don't get a notion to run away.

I open the paper sack I've brought with me and bring out cups and the thermos of coffee and sweet rolls. "You can use the toilet in the tack room," I say, "and then come back here and help yourself to breakfast."

Both boys follow the instructions. As I figured, they aren't any more able to resist the lure of Loretta's sweet rolls than any of the rest of us.

When Buster has polished off two of the rolls, he says, "We're entitled to a phone call."

"You're entitled to squat," I say. "You're entitled to keep still and answer my questions."

"I'm going to sue you," Buster says.

"Go right ahead. But first, tell me what you boys were up to last night."

"Not until I get my lawyer."

"Okay, Jimmy, it looks like Buster isn't going to talk. Tell me, how much did the man who put you up to this say he was going to pay you?"

"He said . . . ow!" He flinches away as Buster punches him in the side.

"I tell you what. If you two come clean about who put you up to this, and what they wanted you to do, you can walk out of here and never hear another word about it. If you don't, I'll be taking you to the jail and let you sit around and think about it while I call your folks and tell them I found you breaking and entering."

"We didn't break nothing," Jimmy whines.

Buster glances at Jimmy but moves his attention right back to me. He's assessing the chances that he'll come out of this with the upper hand and realizing that whoever put him up to this is not going to bail him out or even acknowledge the boys.

"Son of a bitch," he says. I don't take the words personally. He means the situation, not me.

"What is it you two were supposed to do here?" I say.

Jimmy would make a terrible criminal. He glances at Buster's pocket, so I know exactly where to look.

"Buster, empty out your pockets."

"No way."

"Here or at the station in front of your folks. Your choice."

He swears again and pulls a plastic sandwich bag out of his jeans pocket. In it are a handful of big pills. He throws the bag on the floor.

"What the hell?" Alvin Carter says. "Pick that up and hand it over."

"Doesn't matter." I reach down and pick it up. "What are these?"

"I don't know," Buster says.

"Then why do you have them?"

Jimmy has been shifting from one foot to the other. I can see he's had it with keeping things to himself. "Buster, tell him!"

"Damn! There goes five hundred bucks."

"Somebody was going to pay you five hundred dollars to give pills to Jenny Sandstone's horses?"

Jimmy nods.

Alvin looks like he could punch these boys and never feel a thing.

"Come here." I beckon to the two boys.

Mahogany and Blackie have been watching the proceedings as if they were thinking of going to law school. I take the boys over to the two horses. "Look at these horses."

Buster grumbles deep in his throat.

"Why would you want to hurt them? They can't fight back. They don't know what you'd be doing to them."

"It's just a horse," Buster says with a sneer.

"A horse is worth a lot more than your sorry hide," Alvin says.

"So who put you up to it?" I say.

"A guy I know. Jett Borland."

"How do you know him?"

"I don't see how that's any of your business."

"You're right. It's going to be the business of the Bobtail Police Department somewhere down the line when you and Jett Borland are cooking up methamphetamine together and you get caught."

"Meth!" Jimmy looks at Buster like he's suddenly covered in cockroaches.

"I don't know what you're talking about. All I know is he asked me to do him a favor and said he'd give me $500. He said Jenny Sandstone sent his daddy to prison and he wanted to get back at her."

"Did he also have you open the gate and let the horses out a couple weeks ago?"

"Maybe."

"And bring a big old timber rattler in here?"

Buster's horror at those words has to be genuine. He turns pale. "Not me. Not a chance. Don't get me anywhere near a snake. No sir, not for any amount of money."

Borland must have done that little trick himself.

"But you did let the horses out?"

"I didn't figure that would do any harm. Jett said it was supposed to be a warning."

"I'm going to take you boys down to the station and put together a statement for you to sign."

"Now wait a minute," Buster says. He's sweating now. The idea of the snake spooked him, and now he's losing control of the situation. "If Borland finds out I ratted on him, he'll kill me."

"You mean that seriously? You're really scared he'll kill you?"

He squirms. "I just know he's not going to like it and . . ."

"Don't worry. He's already in enough trouble as it is. I just need your signature as insurance. I'll try not to have to use your statement."

I start to herd them out the door, and then I stop. "Let me ask you one more thing. Did you by any chance smash a window on Main Street the other night?"

"What the heck would we do that for?"

"You tell me."

"If somebody says we did that, they're lying," Buster says.

CHAPTER 24

"Akey? What do you want a key to Mamma's house for?"

"Don't ask questions. I'm in a hurry. I'll tell you later."

Jenny must get the drift of my mood, because she struggles to her feet, goes to her purse, and hands me a key. "I could go with you."

"No, you can't. I'll be back later and I'll explain everything."

Eddie Sandstone is waiting for me when I drive up to his mother's house.

"Come on in," he says when I open the door, as if he were the one wielding the key.

"We don't have to stay long," I say. "I have a couple of questions I want to ask you."

"At least I can offer you a cup of coffee," he says.

I can't argue with that. We end up sitting in the kitchen over dainty cups of coffee. Eddie complains that his mother didn't have "real mugs, just these skimpy little teacups."

"What is it you want to know?" he says.

"For starters, I wouldn't mind knowing what happened between you and Jenny to make her so dead-set against you."

He tips his coffee cup back and forth, watching the coffee slosh. "I could say that's between Jenny and me, but she seems to like you, and quite frankly it would be awfully nice if somebody could work out things between us."

"I can't promise anything, but I would like to help Jenny if I can."

He nods and thinks for a minute before he looks up at me. "It's simple, but not a pretty picture. Jenny was always jealous of me—plain, flat-out jealous. I had the good fortune to be a guy who got along with people in high school. Was pretty good at football and baseball, was in a lot of clubs, and made good grades. Poor Jenny couldn't seem to buy a break. She was smart, but she was a mess. What do they call it? A wallflower. Didn't know how to dress or fix herself up. Hardly had any friends. All she ever did was study. I tried to ease the way for her, introducing her to friends and whatnot, but it never took hold. She resented the hell out of me."

"So you're saying she still holds a grudge because you were popular in high school and she wasn't?" I don't try to hide my skepticism.

He shrugs and opens his hands as if to offer me to make my own assessment. "That's the only explanation I have."

"And she agrees with you that that's the problem?"

"She won't talk to me. Our mamma said it was best if I let Jenny come to me. I guess she never realized how stubborn Jenny is."

Something tells me there's a lot more to the story, but I'm not sure how to get to it. "Why did you move to Temple?"

He shrugs. "Job opportunities were better there. I make a good living in Temple."

"Somebody told me you were supposed to get a football scholarship to SMU. What happened with that?" I know the basic answer, but I want to hear his version.

His smile tightens. "That was a sad situation. I take full responsibility for my actions, but I still think SMU made a big mistake not looking at all the facts."

"What did they overlook?"

He leans forward, forearms on his knees, cradling the cup of coffee in his hands. "Nobody ever asked me why I hit Otis Greevy. If they'd known the whole story, they might have excused me for hitting him."

"And what would that story be?"

He puts his cup down and shakes his head. "We don't need to go over old territory. It's long since past."

"I'd like to hear it."

He sighs. "Greevy said something nasty about my daddy."

"What did he say?"

"I don't know if Jenny ever told you, but our daddy walked out on us in the summer the year I graduated from high school, and everybody in town knew it. Greevy was working as a carpenter on the same crew as Daddy and me." His lip curls. "Greevy was a smart-ass. One day he made a joke he thought was funny. Said he guessed my daddy got himself hooked up with another woman. I didn't like him talking that way. My daddy wasn't like that, and besides, it didn't reflect well on my mamma, so I hit him." He holds his hands up in surrender. "I admit I hit him harder than I should have. He had every right to call the police. Like I said, I take full responsibility. But you see what I mean about SMU not getting the full story? If they'd looked into it, they would have understood. In the end, Greevy dropped the charges, so even he knew that I had every reason for hitting him."

The way he spins it, he sounds justified, if not innocent—but he neglected to mention that he hit Greevy with a shovel, not his fists.

"What do you think happened to your daddy? Why did he leave?"

He toys with his empty coffee cup. "I wish I knew. Not a day goes by I don't wonder where he ended up."

"Right after your mamma had her stroke, she asked me if I might be able to find him. Have you had any contact with him over the years?"

"No sir. Believe me, if I had, my mamma would have been the first to know."

"You have any idea where he might have gone? Did he ever mention wanting to travel somewhere? Did he have dreams of the big city? Or some other country?"

He chuckles and shakes his head. "You know how kids are. They don't pay much attention to their parents as people." He gets up abruptly and takes his coffee cup to the sink and washes it out.

"Was he ever in the service?"

"Not that I know of. Maybe there's some information in Mamma's stuff. If Jenny will let you go through it."

"Where was he from originally?"

"He grew up on a farm forty miles east of here. Middle of nowhere."

I know that territory and can't imagine what they would have farmed there. It's as poor as land can get. "One more thing. You ever hear that your daddy was married before?"

He's as startled as Jenny was. "No way. What gave you that idea?"

"Something your mamma said when she asked me to look for him."

He walks over to the window overlooking the backyard and peers out. "You actually think you might be able to find my daddy?" he says, without turning to look at me.

"You never know. There are all kinds of ways to look for people through the Internet that didn't exist until the last ten years or so. It doesn't sound to me like anybody ever made a big effort to find him, and I can be persistent when I go after something."

He turns back around, glaring at me. "If you're wondering why Mamma didn't look for him, it's because she thought he'd be back. By the time we realized he was gone for good, I don't think she knew how to look. She didn't have a lot of time to spend on it. She had to make a living, and she wanted to help me with college expenses, and Jenny was still at home. . . ."

"Did you consider going to SMU and going out for football without the scholarship?"

"That was way too expensive. I went to Bobtail Junior College. Didn't graduate, though. It was a waste of my time. My daddy didn't have a college education, and he did all right, so I figured I could, too."

I take my cup to the sink. "I'll be calling if you if I think of anything else you might remember about your daddy leaving."

"Feel free."

"I have one more question for you. What kind of car do you usually drive?"

"It's a black town car. I like something with a little room in it. I also have a pickup that I use for work."

"The car that forced Jenny off the road the other night was a big, black car. You have anything to do with that?"

"What do you mean? You think that was me?" He takes a couple of steps toward me, and I'd swear he was threatening me. "You ought to be out looking for some drunk driver instead of picking on me. Why would I do anything to hurt my sister?"

"I don't know, but it sounds like you have a bit of a temper, and the two of you have had problems."

"I think you're trying to stir things up." Before I can reply, he says, "And you stirred up my wife, too. Like I told you on the phone yesterday, I don't see any need for you to bother my wife. We're trying to work things out between us and you don't need to upset her."

"I didn't have any intention of doing that. She didn't seem to mind talking to me."

All the anger seems to go out of him, leaving him deflated. "She's a nice person. You can see why I don't want to lose her. Sorry if I overreacted."

We part amiably enough, although Eddie isn't happy that I won't leave him the key Jenny gave me. "Never mind, I'll get it from her. She's going to have to turn the house over to me sooner or later."

I stop by Bobtail Police Headquarters, but Wallace Lyndall is out on a call. I get him on his cell and tell him I've got news about the Borland situation. He says he'll meet me back here in an hour.

With an hour to kill—not enough time to go back to Jarrett Creek and get anything done—I go over to the hospital. There's a loose end I want to tie up. I track down Vera Sandstone's nurse, Monica, and ask if she has a few minutes to talk to me.

"You've been nothing but trouble since the minute you showed up here," she scolds. "What is it you want?"

"I want to talk to you about Vera Sandstone's son, Eddie."

She goes still and I watch her make a decision. "Go on down to the waiting room at the end of the hall. I have a couple of things I have to do first, but then I'll come and talk to you."

There's no one else in the waiting room, which is a dreary room with no outside windows. Someone waiting here for news that somebody is coming out of surgery would probably rather be anywhere than this room. It's stuffy and quiet, which is why I'm almost asleep when Monica comes back. I stand up, and my neck has a crick in it from my head slumping sideways.

"I've got a full ward, so we have to be quick," Monica says, frowning at me. "What is it you wanted to know about Vera's son?"

"I'll come right to the point. Was she afraid of him?"

She studies me, thinking. "I don't know. I thought there was something wrong between them, although it didn't occur to me that she would be scared of him. He seemed sweet to her. But she was definitely glad when he left the day he visited."

"He was only here once?"

"Once when I was on duty. But he came back the day before she died, when I was off duty."

"How did you hear that?"

"He upset the little nurse who was on that night. He wanted her to sign as a witness to something, and she didn't know whether she should. She's a young nurse. She said Vera told her it was okay, and I told her she didn't do anything wrong, if she signed with Vera's consent."

"Can you tell me her name? I'd like to ask her a couple of questions."

Monica sighs. "I'll tell you her name, but don't push her too hard. She's skittish as a kitten, and we have a shortage of nurses as it is. We can't afford to lose her."

I find out that the nurse, Betsy Ferris, will be coming on at 4:00 this evening. "I'd like to get her number at home," I say to the woman I talk to behind the nurses' desk. "I'd rather not bother her at work."

For once today, I'm lucky and she's home and says she'll talk to me if I can come right now, but that she has to pick up her little girl from a play date in an hour.

She lives in a nice brick house in a new subdivision called Tuscan Hills. There are no hills here, and the only bow to Tuscany is that every one of the houses has an arch over the doorway. It makes me think of Bobtail Ridge, the subdivision that's being torn down. Not a ridge in sight.

A tiny woman, barely over five feet tall with a pixie grin, Betsy Ferris tells me they moved into their house a year ago when the place was new. "My husband is a dentist. We wanted to live close to his office so he could bike to work. He's big on saving the environment." She beams at me like she couldn't be prouder of him.

She shows me into a pristine living room with mostly beige and white furniture. The only art on the walls is a commercial print of a painting by Modigliani, which kind of surprises me because his work hasn't been in style for a long time. She perches on the edge of a chair that dwarfs her, looking like a hummingbird that has come to rest. I sit in a matching chair facing her.

"I want to find out a few details about something that happened a couple of weeks ago. You had a patient by the name of Vera Sandstone."

"What a sweet lady she was. I was sorry when she passed away."

"Her son asked you to witness a document that he got her to sign?"

Her cheery face closes up. "I hope I didn't do the wrong thing. Vera said it was okay with her."

"No, no, no problem with that. I'm more interested in Mrs. Sandstone's state of mind when she was talking to her son."

"State of mind?"

"Was she happy? Or did she seem troubled at all?"

Betsy cocks her head at me. "You want to know something? That's why it bothered me to sign that paper. I got the feeling she felt trapped."

"Trapped?"

"Like she didn't want to sign it, but she couldn't think of a way out. That's the best way I can say it. The way she looked at her son was like she wished there was some way to get away from him. Not scared, exactly, but more like she didn't like him much. Does that make sense?"

I nod. "You're a good observer."

She flushes. "I want to help people. I thought maybe Mrs. Sandstone didn't want to sign that paper, and that's really why I said I didn't know whether I should. But she said to go ahead. So I did."

"Did you talk to her afterward?"

She shakes her head. "It got busy after that and I didn't have time to stop and talk. I was off work the next day. When I came back to work, they told me she had died."

"Did you hear her son talking to her about signing the paper?"

"No, he was there when I came in."

"What kind of mood was he in?"

"He was smiling. He seemed like a nice enough man. He was holding her hand and telling her how much he loved her. That kind of thing."

"But she wasn't happy with him there."

"It was unusual. You know, some of my patients don't have anybody who comes to see them. So you'd think she would have been thrilled that he was being so nice to her. But she seemed nervous, like you get when you're not sure what somebody's going to do next."

"I'll be damned," Wallace Lyndall says when I describe last night's run-in with the boys sneaking into Jenny's barn.

"They said Jett Borland promised to pay them if they slipped the horses some pills."

"Looks like now we've got something on them."

"I've got the vet testing the pills to see what they are," I say. "The problem is, I'd like to avoid having the boys identify Borland. I don't want him or his daddy to know they ratted on him if we can avoid it."

"We might need their testimony."

"Let's wait and see what comes up. At least the boys confirmed that Jett was involved in the attacks on the horses. And the Borlands aren't likely to stay out of trouble. We'll nail them before too long."

"Sounds like a couple of kids need watching, too."

I think of the blond boy's fear and distress when they got caught. I suspect his life of crime is over. "One of them does anyway."

CHAPTER 25

I'm no sooner in the door when Loretta calls me on the phone. "Can you come down to my house? I've got something to tell you."

"Let me get some dinner first. I've had a long day and no time for lunch."

"I've got enough for two. Come on down."

I'm glad I don't have to cook, even if I had only planned to warm up some chili, but I'd like not to *have* to have a conversation. After last night I want nothing more than to eat a bite and crawl into bed. Still, it's unusual for Loretta to call me in the evening. She likes to eat early and watch her TV programs. She must have something important on her mind. I tell her I'll come on down.

As soon as I walk into Loretta's house I'm glad I decided to take her up on the meal. "Whatever you're cooking smells good," I say.

We eat at her kitchen table. She dishes up chicken and dumplings with green beans. "While we eat, why don't you tell me what you've been up to," she says. She asks for my version of how the prom went. "I've heard the opinion of everybody else and I'm worn out from all the complaining."

I'm surprised. "Seems to me it went off pretty well."

"The prom itself did. But you probably didn't hear that a bunch of the girls had a slumber party over at little Tricia Ford's house and the boys sneaked in with beer. Now everybody is blaming Emily and Jake Ford for having that wine party and making the kids think it was okay to drink."

"As far as I know, nobody called us down at the station. What happened to the boys?"

"The Fords called Diane Hanscomb—her boy was one of the ones who snuck in—and had her and her husband come over and take the kids home . . . girls and boys both."

"Well, now the kids know it's not okay with the Fords to drink at their house."

She laughs. "You must not know Diane Hanscomb. She was furious that she had to haul the kids around in the wee hours of the morning, and she hasn't stopped complaining yet."

Without naming names I tell her that I caught two boys getting into mischief. "They were from Bobtail, so I was over there straightening things out today."

"What did they do?"

"They were trying to sneak into Jenny Sandstone's barn and slip a drug to her horses." I haven't told her about the other incidents because I didn't want her to get scared, but now I think it's time to spread the word in the community. It will help keep the horses and Jenny safe if people are alert that there've been problems at her place. "That's not the first incident." I tell her about the others.

She jumps when I tell her about the snake. "Ugh! I can put up with a little garden snake, but not rattlers. You think the boys put the rattlesnake in the barn?"

"They said they didn't. One of them was deathly afraid of snakes and said he'd never do anything like that."

Loretta has a calculating look in her eye. "All this that you're telling me makes some sense."

"Makes sense of what?"

Loretta gets up and clears our dishes. "You want a little dish of ice cream?"

"If you're having one."

"I only have vanilla. That's the only kind I like."

"I'll take a taste of vanilla. But tell me what you called me down here for. I'm not going to last too much longer. Between not getting any sleep last night and this big dinner you've fed me, I'm ready to get to bed."

She gets the tub of Blue Bell Ice Cream out of the freezer and pulls two bowls out, moving deliberately. "Clara White went to see Jenny this afternoon to take her some dinner, and she told me that Jenny was acting like she was drunk."

Suddenly I lose my appetite for the ice cream. "She was probably exaggerating."

"Maybe. But Clara's not real judgmental. She's more live and let live. She told me she didn't know quite what to do. She was afraid Jenny was going to fall down. She knew I was friendly with Jenny and wondered if I'd go talk to her. I thought it was best to leave it to you."

"Might have been that she's in pain and took some medication and maybe took too much."

She sets the bowls of ice cream down on the table. "The thing is, Clara said she went into Jenny's kitchen, and there was an open bottle of Jack Daniel's right on the counter, and that Jenny had a glass that looked and smelled like whiskey. I wonder if you ought to go talk to her. If she's taking pain medication and drinking, that's a bad idea."

Loretta likes a good bit of gossip and is interested in people's business, but I've never known her to be mean. I know she's telling me this out of concern for Jenny, not because she wants to be malicious.

"I appreciate you telling me this. If you don't mind, I'm going to eat and run. I think I'd like to stop by and make sure everything is all right next door."

"Good. I know Jenny has had a hard time the last couple of weeks and somebody needs to keep an eye on her."

I'm so tired I could lie down on the sidewalk, but I head straight for Jenny's. I've never known her to drink hard liquor. I don't know everything about her, and maybe she has a regular habit of drinking a cocktail when she comes home. But I remember two nights ago when I was there and she had put away at least a bottle of wine. It makes me queasy to think of her heading for the bottle to solve her misery. I don't have much patience for drunks, having had a daddy and a brother who killed themselves with drink, and having seen the way alcohol has destroyed Rodell's health. But something is eating at Jenny, and I can't turn my back on that.

I ring the doorbell and get no answer. It's only 7:30, still light out, so I doubt Jenny has gone to bed. If she has, she won't thank me for getting her up. But I'm not going to let that get in the way of insisting that she answer her door. After the second ring, eventually the door opens, but there's no one there.

"Jenny?"

"Come on in." She's standing behind the door. Her voice is slurred.

"I've been gone all day and didn't have a chance to talk to you last night so I wanted to check in and say hello." I feel like a fool, with my voice sounding as cheerful as a high school cheerleader with the team behind ten points.

She doesn't reply, so I step in. She's drunk. There's no getting around it. She's standing up, but she's swaying and squinting at me like she's having trouble focusing. Her hair is all frowzed out as if she's been pulling at it, and she has food stains on the front of her T-shirt.

"Here now!" I say. "You're not feeling too good. Let's get you off your feet."

"I'm drunk," she says, and gives a soft belch that sends a cloud of alcohol fumes my way. "And happy to be."

"I still think it's probably best to get you seated. It won't do your stitches any good if you fall down." My heart is beating hard. I don't like to deal with people who are drunk—especially people I care for.

"Huh!" Her bark of laughter has an ugly sound to it. "You sound like Little Mary Sunshine," she says.

"I don't feel like that," I say. "I wish you'd tell me what makes you think it will do you any good to be drunk at 7:30 at night. Let's go into your living room and sit down."

She lets me take her elbow, but then she wheels away toward the kitchen. "I need to get me another drink."

"Let me get you situated, and then I'll get you a drink," I say.

She peers at me, her head weaving. "I know you. You say you'll get me a drink, but then when you get me sat down, you'll think of some excuse not to."

"If I promise to get you a drink, will you let me get you into the living room?"

"A stiff drink. Not some sissy drink."

"Whatever you want."

I guide her into the living room and keep a firm hold on her as she sinks onto the sofa. Her head flops against the back so she's staring at the ceiling. "Oh, it's like being on a carnival ride."

"I imagine it is. What's your favorite ride?"

She starts laughing, and the sound is unpleasant. "Like I said, I knew you'd try to weasel out of it. You promised though. Bring me a drink. Please. Pretty please."

"What do you want? Wine?"

"No, hell no! Whiskey. It's on the counter."

"Mind if I get one, too?"

"Help yourself."

I go into the kitchen and make a lot of noise, opening and closing cabinets, opening and closing the refrigerator, dropping ice cubes into glasses. And then I wait. After five minutes I walk back into the living room. Jenny has sagged sideways on the sofa. I go back in the kitchen and pour some water over one of the glasses of ice and bring it back in and sit down on the easy chair across from her. I don't know if she's taken pain medication, but if she has, I worry that it won't mix well with the alcohol. I'll stick around until I'm sure she's okay.

An hour into my vigil, Jenny wakes with a start and babbles something unintelligible, but then drops back to sleep. Somewhere along the line I realize that I'm in over my head with Jenny. She needs a therapist to help her through whatever has thrown her for a loop. I can imagine her response if I suggest such a thing. I drift off to sleep for a bit and then wake up.

Around ten o'clock I begin to think over my conversation with Eddie Sandstone today. He seems like a nice enough guy, but there's something I don't like about him. I haven't been around him enough to pin down what it is. But that doesn't mean he's lying when he says his spat with Jenny is because of her being jealous. His estranged wife said much the same thing, although I suppose whatever she understands of Jenny is through what Eddie said.

I get up and head outside. To stretch my legs, I go down to the barn to check on the horses. I surprise Alvin Carter propped up against the wall facing where the horses are quiet in their stalls. "What are you reading?"

Carter looks guilty. "Something stupid. I found it in the tack room and thought I'd see what all the fuss is about." He holds up the book. He's reading a tattered copy of a thriller that was wildly popular years ago. I wonder what it was doing in the tack room.

We talk of this and that for a few minutes. He tells me he's decided to go back to college, and we kick it around a little bit, me encouraging his decision.

Jenny's still passed out, but her pulse is strong. Back when my daddy drank, I always worried that he'd pass out and not wake up. My mamma didn't seem to take it seriously. I wonder whether I ought to wake Jenny and make her get into her bed, but instead I drape a blanket over her and prop her up on pillows.

As I get up to go, I notice a box shoved off to one side of the living room. There are letters scattered around the floor next to the box. I go over to put them back in the box and see they are all torn halfway across.

I pick up two of the halves and piece them together. It's a short letter to Vera from Eddie, saying he's fine and was glad to hear from her, that he is busy with work and he'll write more next time. Curious, I pick up a few more. They are all from Eddie and have the same kind of impersonal tone. There are dozens of these letters in the box. The return address on them is Temple. Why would Eddie be writing letters to his mother when he could as easily have picked up the phone? Or driven to see her in a couple of hours?

I dig down to find some of the oldest ones. Maybe they will tell me more about the family's problems. At the bottom I find a partial answer. A letter written a dozen years ago says, "I'm going to keep writing to you. I don't think it's fair that you took Jenny's side against me. You don't know the whole story. If you knew, you'd understand." Vera's nurse told me that she thought Vera didn't like Eddie very much. If that's the case, I wonder why Vera kept the letters, and why Jenny tore them up—why not just pitch them out?

When I get home it's hard for me to get to sleep. To listen to Eddie, you'd think he was the wronged party. But Vera Sandstone was a sensible woman. Why would she keep such an uneasy distance from her son unless she had a good reason? She changed her mind and left him her house at the last minute, but if the nurse's description is right, it sounds like he intimidated her in some way to make that happen.

CHAPTER 26

After two nights of too little sleep, the next morning I feel like I'm the one who was drunk last night. I feel sore all over and like my eyes aren't working the way they ought to. Coffee. I usually wait until after I see to my cows before I brew up a pot, but this morning I need it first thing. It's later than usual when I get down to the pasture, and I give the cows less attention than I usually do. Surely it's my imagination that they glare after me resentfully when I head back up to the house.

When Loretta comes by after church, she's tactful and doesn't tell me I look like something my cat dragged in. "Did you go by Jenny's last night?"

"I did. She'll be okay."

"What can I do? Should I go by and see her? Should I tell people to stay away?"

"I'd say maybe people should let her alone for a while. She's got some things to work out."

"I still might take her something."

I consider how Jenny's going to feel this morning and say, "Wait until tomorrow."

Loretta has no sooner left than I get a call from Ellen Forester. "I tried to locate you yesterday, but they said you were out and about and I didn't want to bother you. Can you come by the studio this morning?"

I tell her I will and realize I'm looking forward to seeing her. I hope she's calling to tell me she's decided to get that restraining order. But either way, I'm glad to see her. She's the only person in town who really understands why I enjoy my art so much. We don't have the same taste, but she at least knows how art can feed the spirit. With that in

161

mind, while I finish up my coffee and a piece of buttered toast, I walk over to the mantel and rest my eyes on the painting that draws me this morning—a landscape with quiet colors that somehow captures the idea of early morning in a gray time of year, a little desolate but soothing nevertheless.

Without my really thinking about it, I've decided that Monday I need to go to Temple to talk to Eddie Sandstone's first wife. He won't like it, but I'm doing it anyway. Maybe he told her what happened to bust up the family.

Before I leave, I need to do clean-up detail from the prom. Sure enough, when I get to the station, there are half a dozen calls from people complaining that something happened over the weekend that they attribute to "those rowdy high school kids." There are some I'm sure are legitimate—a missing lawn gnome; someone's trees draped in toilet paper; a picket fence spray-painted in school colors; and an old, abandoned outhouse tipped over. I call Jim Krueger and tell him to hunt for culprits and get them to make amends. Sometimes kids do own up to their mischief—a fence gets miraculously repainted, a gnome reappears, and the t.p. gets taken down. However, I'd guess that the outhouse isn't going to be put back upright.

Other complaints I have to deal with one at a time. Bernice Lindauer is pretty sure somebody moved her car, and I call to find out if the car is okay (yes) and if she knows who moved it (no). Bernice is growing forgetful. I call her son, and he sighs and tells me that she knew he was taking it to be serviced—she forgot. Then there's Ben Graham, who calls to tell me that someone sideswiped his car Friday night. I tell him I'll look into it, although I have no intention of doing so. His car got sideswiped five years ago. He received the insurance money for it but never had it fixed and keeps trying to call it in as a new incident to get more insurance money.

The only one I take seriously is a call from Brenda Sears. She says somebody broke in and stole her cell phone and money out of her wallet. I go over to take a report. She finally breaks down and says she's scared that her grown son stole the things—that she thinks he's got a drug problem and stole the money to buy drugs. "He knew I'd taken money out of the bank to pay for some work I had done on the house. When I found out the money was gone, I confronted him and he got mad and said he was going down to Galveston to get a job." She's crying a little bit. "He said he didn't want to be around if I was going to accuse him of stealing."

"You call me the minute he comes back and I'll come over and have a talk with him." I have no doubt he'll be back as soon as he uses up the $300 he stole.

It's almost noon by the time I get to Ellen's art gallery, and her morning class is ending. Her students are packing up to leave. They've been working on watercolors, and some of the pieces are nice to look at. Ellen is a good teacher. The students are a mix of men and women, all seniors, and all seeming to be in a good mood. I wasn't sure when Ellen opened the gallery and workshop that she could make a go of it. I'm surprised at the number of people who want to try their hand at art.

I hang back until everyone leaves. It's not until I see Ellen close up that I notice a bruise on her cheekbone below her right eye. "How'd you get that?"

She waves me away. "I know it's a cliché to say I walked into a door, but I promise I really did."

"You'd tell me if your ex-husband hit you, wouldn't you?"

"He didn't. But listen, that's not why I asked you to stop by. I want to show you something."

She beckons me to follow her to the work area where people leave their work to sit until the next class. She picks up a watercolor done on a nine-by-twelve paper and holds it up for me to see. "One of my students in a beginning class did this," she says.

"Doesn't look like any beginner I ever saw." It's a simple composition of a pitcher and a couple of lemons. I glance at the other works done from the same still life and see that most of them, although reasonably accurate, are stilted and tense. The one she's holding up has a free, relaxed feel to it. Instead of sticking exactly to the subject and painting it in the middle of the paper, small and painstakingly accurate, like a beginner, this painter has filled the whole page with it and added a bit of drapery at the back, suggesting a table.

"Looks like somebody has talent. Maybe they've had some other classes."

"She swears she hasn't."

I don't understand why she's showing me this. "It's nice," I say.

"Your friend Loretta did this."

"Loretta?" I'm dumbfounded. "When?"

"She got back from her trip to Washington and she called and said she thought she'd like to try a class. This beginner class had already started, but I told her to come ahead. I was as surprised as you are when I saw what she came up with. I know you're a friend of hers and I wanted to share this with you. I love to discover when somebody has talent they didn't know they had."

I laugh.

"What's funny?"

"Loretta never has had the least interest in my art. I wouldn't have thought she'd have it in her to even attempt a painting, much less do such nice work."

Ellen beams. "She said she wanted to try it out. She said she's too busy to do much with it, but she thought it would be fun. I wouldn't be surprised if she starts forgetting about making her rounds with those sinful treats and starts putting time in painting."

"Sinful treats? You don't look like you're tempted."

Color rises to her cheeks quickly. "Well, I am."

It's a couple of days before I get to Temple, determined to talk to Eddie's first wife, even if I have to wait for her to get off work. But she's home, and she's a surprise. She's several years older than Eddie and fifty pounds overweight. Her shorts and skimpy tank top are meant for someone a good bit smaller. Rolls of belly fat pooch out the tank top, and the shorts have her tree-trunk legs in a death grip. Her brown hair, streaked with gray, tumbles to her shoulders as if she has a fantasy of still being a fetching young woman. She's holding a cigarette down by her side.

I introduce myself and tell her I'd like to ask her some questions about Eddie.

She takes a drag on the cigarette. "Why don't you ask Eddie?"

"I've had a conversation with him. I wanted to get your take on a couple of things."

"Joyce told me you were here last week and that Eddie wasn't too happy that she talked to you." She chews on the side of her lip.

"You're not married anymore, so what difference does it make if he's happy about it?"

She shrugs. "Not a damn bit of difference. I can take care of myself. But I can't add anything to what Joyce said." Her apartment is on the second floor, and she sticks her head out the door, glancing left and right as if she's worried somebody will overhear.

"Maybe we should talk inside," I say.

"Can't do it. My house is a mess."

I suspect the real reason is so she can tell Eddie she didn't invite me in. They may not be married anymore, but he's still got a hold on her. "That's all right. I won't keep you long anyway. Tell me, when did you and Eddie get married?"

She looks up at the overhang of her apartment as if the date might be written up there. "It was around four or five years after he left college."

"How'd you meet him?"

She snorts. "How does anybody meet anybody? We met at a bar.

I'll say this about Eddie. He knows how to turn on the charm." She lifts her eyebrows in a suggestive way.

"How long have you been divorced?"

She shrugs and takes another drag, blowing the smoke up toward the sky. "Ten years give or take. We're still friends, though. Eddie's all right as long you don't have to put up with his b.s. twenty-four seven."

"When you say b.s., what do you mean exactly?"

She takes one last puff of the cigarette, steps over to the rail, and throws it over the side to the pavement below. When she comes back, she leans against the door with her arms crossed. "I mean he has kind of a quick temper. He gets these moods where you feel like you're walking on eggs around him."

"Did he ever hit you?"

"Oh, hell no! He knows I would have done a Lorena Bobbitt on him." She smirks.

"His temper ever cause him problems on the job?"

She ponders her answer. "Doesn't help any. It's hard enough to make a living in the building business. All you have to do is look at somebody funny and next thing you know, you're fired."

"I thought he was an independent contractor."

"He is. He wouldn't be able to stand working for anybody else. But even with your own business, you have to suck up to the general contractor to get hired, and then you have to make sure not to piss him off."

"Is Eddie working now?"

"He sure is. Things are looking up in the building trade and Joyce said Eddie's got plenty of work. She said he's trying to get a contract on a big mall project in Bobtail."

"Why would he want to go all the way over there to work?"

"Hold on a minute." She disappears inside and comes back with a fresh cigarette and leans against the doorjamb again. She's relaxed a little since we started talking. "I asked Eddie the same thing. I know he's from Bobtail, but it seemed like a long way to go when he can work right here. Turns out he helped build that subdivision they're tearing down to put up the mall. He said he happened to know the houses were shoddy to begin with and it'll give him satisfaction to see them come down." She laughs.

"How did he know they were building the mall?"

"I don't know. I expect the same way he finds out about any job, through the grapevine."

"You know Eddie's mamma passed away a short time ago?"

"Yeah, I knew his mamma passed. Far as I'm concerned that's no big whoop. She always treated Eddie like dirt. Broke his heart. I think that's one reason he's so moody all the time."

"His mamma left him her house, so maybe he plans to move back there."

She raises her eyebrows. "First time I heard of that. But I'd be surprised if he plans to move back. He never had much good to say about the town." She glances down the hallway again, and I know she's getting restless to be rid of me.

"Did Eddie ever talk about his daddy?"

She frowns. "Just that he walked out on the family."

"Did he tell you he was supposed to get a football scholarship to SMU?"

"Oh, yeah. To hear him tell it, that was his one big chance and he blew it. Not that it was his fault. He was still a kid, and he was upset because his daddy had abandoned them."

"He ever try to get in touch with his daddy that you know of?"

"It wasn't a topic of conversation."

"Did you ever meet his mamma or his sister?"

"No way. He didn't have anything to do with them. They had some kind of falling-out and he said I was better off not meeting them."

"You know what they fought about?"

"Not really. Eddie said his mamma didn't approve of his first wife because she was a Mexican."

"He was married before you?"

She smirks. "Like I said, Eddie could turn on the charm. Problem is, it doesn't last. His first wife ran out on him."

"Did you ever meet her?"

"No, she wasn't around." Marlene straightens up and takes a step back. "I think we're about done here."

"What do you mean she wasn't around?"

"She was gone. Eddie told me he was off in Austin and when he got back she had left him a note saying she was leaving him and heading out to west Texas. Never saw her again." She eases back into her apartment, preparing to close the door.

"If he didn't know where she was, how did he get a divorce so he could marry you?"

"He got an annulment." She snickers. "At least he said he did. Hey, maybe I'm a bigamist and didn't even know it. I'm sorry, I can't talk to you anymore."

I thank her for her time, but I'm talking to a closed door.

Driving home, I try to read between the lines of what Marlene told me. Despite her bravado, I think she's a little afraid of Eddie. The more I heard what she had to say, the more I think Eddie is the kind of guy who always feels like people are picking on him and blames others for his problems.

I'm almost home when my cell phone rings. It's Jenny.

"You feeling any better?" I say.

"Not particularly. But I figured since I hadn't heard from you today, I'd better call and find out if you're still speaking to me."

"Of course I am. I've had a busy day is all, and I didn't want to disturb you too early."

"Where are you?"

"I'm almost home. I'll stop by a little later."

"You don't have to. In fact, it's probably not a good idea. I'm probably going to spend tonight the same way I did last night."

"You mean with a bottle?"

"Yeah, that's what I mean. Drunk."

"Doesn't sound like much of a plan to me. Try to lay off a little. I'd like to talk to you and I can't come over right now."

"I'm not promising anything."

CHAPTER 27

I get home in time to feed Zelda, who is barely speaking to me these days except to tell me she's half starved. I consider taking food over to Jenny, but she still has a refrigerator full of casseroles. I argue with myself about whether to take over a bottle of wine. I don't want to encourage Jenny's affair with the bottle, but at the same time, I usually do bring wine. I'd like to look like things are normal, even if they aren't. "Zelda, I'm thinking you ought to come with me," I say as I'm walking out the door. She doesn't think much of the idea and stays right where she is on her favorite chair.

Jenny has already started on the Jack Daniels. I open the bottle of wine and take two glasses out to the living room, hoping I can ease her into wine instead of the hard stuff. There is a wealth of Jell-O salad and casseroles in the refrigerator, but I rummage around and find some Jarlsberg cheese and a box of crackers.

When I bring out the plate of snacks and the wine, she says, "Cheese and crackers and wine! That's more like it. If I eat one more pimiento cheese sandwich or noodle casserole, I'm going to lose it."

"That bruise on your face is a fetching shade of yellow," I say. "Looks like you've been in a bar fight."

"Don't try to butter me up with compliments." I'm glad to find out that she's got some sense of humor back. We talk a little and drink a glass of wine, and then I decide it's time to leap. "Jenny, I've got something to say, and I'm going to come right out with it. It's about your brother."

Her face and body freeze. Her lips form a thin line, and I can tell she's doing all she can to resist lashing out at me.

"Hear me out. I don't need to know the particulars of why you had a falling-out with him. That's your business. But I do need to know a few things."

The doorbell rings, and we both look at the door as if we're the only two people left alive and we're suddenly confronted with the idea that someone else may be around. "Shall we ignore it?" I say.

"No. I think it's Will. He told me he wanted to drop by and I told him not to, but I expect he came anyway."

"I'll get the door."

It is Will Landreau, his face almost hidden by an imposing potted plant. He peers around it, and when he sees me he takes a step back. "Have I got the right house?"

"Yes, this is Jenny's place. I'm over here having a chat with the patient. Come on in."

I take the plant from him so that he doesn't have to negotiate greeting Jenny and wrestling with it at the same time.

"Will, that's awfully nice of you," Jenny says, eyeing the plant, a dieffenbachia with shiny leaves, as if it might have hidden thorns.

Will's eyes dart from Jenny to the plant and back. "I didn't think that this might be more trouble than it's worth," he said.

"No, it's pretty. Very thoughtful." I've never heard Jenny speak in such a conciliatory voice. She doesn't have any plants in her house, but I don't know if it's because she doesn't want to take care of them or if she is afraid she'll kill them. "Sit down over here." She pats the sofa near her. "Samuel, do you mind getting Will a glass so I can pour him some wine?"

His hands spring up in front of him. "Nothing for me, thanks. I've got a lot of work to do tonight. I only came by to see how your recovery is going."

The three of us try hard to make it a pleasant twenty minutes of conversation, but it's obvious that Jenny feels the effects of the booze she downed earlier. Will seems puzzled that she's slurring her speech. He keeps giving her speculative looks.

By the time Will leaves I know that Jenny has drunk too much for me to go back to the question of her brother. As jumpy as she is regarding him, I expect I'll only have one chance to bring up the subject again before she shuts me down for good. I'd better choose the time wisely.

I'm yawning more or less nonstop, and Jenny insists that I go on home. "I'll be fine. Waking up with a nasty hangover isn't the way I'd like my life to go. The reason I drank too much last night is that I had a sort of shock."

I remember the box with the torn letters around it. "What kind of shock?"

She leans over and pours herself another glass of wine, looking like she's on automatic pilot. "If I told you, it probably wouldn't mean much to you."

"Let's test it out."

She takes a sip of wine, and I'm glad that at least it isn't a gulp. "My mamma told me . . ." she cocks her head and squints up at the ceiling as if looking for cobwebs. "No, that isn't true. I don't think she ever actually told me outright. . . . I got the impression that she had not stayed in touch with Eddie. I don't mean that she didn't know where he was, but I thought they weren't on speaking terms. And then I found all these letters he sent her and it shook me up, thinking she had let me believe one thing when something else was actually going on. I mean the fact that she kept the letters. See, I told you it wouldn't mean much."

"Did you read the letters?"

"A few. I couldn't stand to read them. He's such a whiner."

"What was he whining about?"

She thinks for a few seconds. "He complained that she would barely answer his letters—that she was polite, but nothing more."

"That should make you feel better, knowing she kept him at arm's length."

"I guess. But why did she keep the letters?"

Same question I asked myself. I ease back down onto the sofa. "I'd like to know why you and your mamma were on the outs with Eddie."

She doesn't reply, but she also doesn't bite my head off, so I plunge ahead. "I've done a little nosing around and I know Eddie was arrested for assault the summer after he graduated from high school. He seems to have a clean slate since then, but a few people I talked to told me he had a mean streak."

"You don't know the half of it." Her voice is strangled. She reaches for her glass of wine and gulps the rest of it down. Here we go again.

"No, I don't know the half of it. That's why I'm asking you to fill me in. Did you know he's been living over in Temple for a long time?"

"Why would I know that? With the possible exception of you, everybody who knows me knows the less I hear about Eddie the better."

I ignore the barb. "He's been gone for thirty years, and suddenly he shows up when your mamma is sick. Do you have any idea how he found out she was in the hospital?"

"I don't know!" Jenny practically shouts. "I don't know anything about him. I don't know who his friends are or why he showed up." She draws a deep breath and speaks a little more calmly. "There are plenty of busybodies who might have wanted to stir things up and let him know Mamma was in the hospital, but no one mentioned it to me."

She stomps off into the kitchen and comes back with the bottle of Jack Daniels. She pours a slug into the glass she was drinking out of before. The ice has melted now, but she seems not to notice. She tosses back the drink and slams the glass down on the table.

"Is there any possibility that Eddie was responsible for trying to run you off the road the other night?"

"There's a possibility, but I don't know why he'd want to. He got what he wanted when Mamma left the house to him."

I could tell her that for some people "more" is never enough—they aren't satisfied until they have it all.

She gets up again and this time disappears for a few minutes. When she comes back, she's put on a sweatshirt. It isn't cold, so this has to do with her own internal temperature. She sits down and picks up her glass again. "I don't know why you're so interested in Eddie, but I want you to stop asking me about him. I don't know how he found out Mamma was sick, and I don't want to know. As far as I'm concerned, the faster I get that house turned over to him, the better. And then I never want to see him again."

"If you feel that way, why don't you hire somebody to move all the stuff left in the house and put it in storage? You talked earlier about having Nate Holloway from next door do it. I could arrange to rent a storage space for you in one of those places outside town. Or the stuff could go in your garage."

She nods her head, staring off into space. "Then I wouldn't have to go there anymore."

"You sure you want to do that? You don't want to go there one more time to say good-bye?"

Her expression is desolate. "When Eddie walked in on me the other day, he tainted that house. Just like he tainted anything he ever touched. I said good-bye to Mamma, and that's all I needed to do. The house isn't the same without her there."

CHAPTER 28

"**E**llen Forester showed me your watercolor painting." I've invited Loretta in for coffee the next morning when she brings me coffee cake, and we're sitting at my kitchen table. I haven't turned on the air-conditioning yet, and it's the coolest room in the house.

Loretta makes a sound of exasperation. "Why did she do that? All I'm doing is dabbling."

"She thinks you're pretty good."

Loretta's hands flutter over her cup of coffee. "That's nice of her, but she shouldn't be showing it off." She chews at her lip and looks at me. "What did you think?"

"I liked the painting a lot. You've got some talent."

"Lot of good it does me. I'm a little bit old to start on a new career as a famous artist. And don't tell me about Grandma Moses. I'm not *that* old."

"I wanted you to know I liked your picture, that's all. No need to get all dramatic about it."

She smiles and seems to be at a loss for words, a rarity for Loretta. "I forgot to tell you," she says, suddenly sober. "Did you hear about Rodell?"

"No! What?"

"He had a heart attack last night. They took him to Scott and White Hospital in Temple."

As if triggered by her words, my phone rings. It's Bill Odum, giving me the same news. He says he went to work early and the call was on the answering machine.

"Wonder why nobody phoned me at home?" I say.

"It was late," Odum says. "The call came in after midnight."

"I'll call over to the hospital and see if there's anything I can do."

Loretta tells me that she heard Rodell woke up feeling bad and told his wife he thought he ought to go to the hospital.

"Does anybody know his condition this morning?"

She shakes her head. "I haven't heard. Funny how the two of you got friendly after he got sick."

"He's a pretty smart guy. He'd have been a good police chief if he hadn't ruined himself with alcohol. I'm glad he has stayed off the booze." Hearing myself talk, I feel nervous for Jenny. I won't be able to take it if she continues to drink herself into a stupor every night, no matter how much I want to be a friend to her.

The two-hour drive to the hospital in Temple feels more like five hours. Rodell's wife, Patty, is sitting in the hallway outside of Rodell's room. It looks like she's been up all night. She was bitter over the fact that I took on the job of chief of police when Rodell was incapacitated, but now she jumps up and greets me like a long-lost friend. "Thank you so much for coming, Samuel. Rodell will be so glad to see you. He's already going stir-crazy and he hasn't even been in the hospital twelve hours."

"How is he? Was it a bad heart attack?"

She looks sad and her bottom lip starts to tremble. She shakes herself like she's got feathers on her that need settling. "They say it's not bad, but . . . Samuel, you know perfectly well he's not going to get much better."

"Let's leave all that speculating to the doctors. Won't do any good to make up the future."

"I know you're right." She looks at her watch. "I'm waiting for my sister to get here. I'll feel better once I have her with me."

"How about the kids? Are they coming?"

"They said they'll be here this afternoon." Suddenly she throws up her hands and wails, "Why in the world did he have to get into that drinking?"

I put my arm around her shoulders and say, "Listen, you've got to look ahead and not behind. You can't change the past and it's a waste of energy to think you can."

She takes a deep, shuddering breath. "You're right."

"Can I go in and see him?"

She looks at the door of his room. "Yes, go on in. Gabe LoPresto is in there and I figured I'd give them a minute to gab, and it would give me a chance to catch my breath. Since you're here I'm going down to have a bite of breakfast, if you don't mind."

I tell her I'll hang around until she comes back. If he's up to it, I want to talk to Rodell about Scott Borland and son. I push open the door and go into the room. There are two beds. The first one holds a wizened old man hooked up to a lot of gear. His eyes track me as I walk past his bed.

A curtain is pulled across between the two beds. I step around it. LoPresto is standing, holding his hat in his hands, and looking down at Rodell. LoPresto is a hearty guy most of the time, but he's not in that kind of mood right now, and I can see why. I don't know why I thought Rodell would look the same. I was wrong. His face is sunken into itself, his cheeks and eye sockets hollow. His skin has lost all hint of color. The truth is, he looks worse than the man in the first bed.

"Hey, Rodell, you've got yourself in a fix," I say.

Rodell makes a sound deep in his throat.

LoPresto lights up as he sees me. "Well, look who's here!" He sticks his hand out to shake mine. A look passes between the two of us. We're both unnerved by the man lying in the bed. It's strange that I feel miserable at the idea of Rodell going downhill. He was never anything but aggravating. A drunk. Mean. Surly. But in the past few months since he's been sober, I've seen a different man—one that was hidden under a stagnant pool of alcohol. I'm not only feeling regret for seeing the man sinking; I regret the man he could have been.

"How you feeling?" I say.

"I'm hanging in there," Rodell says. "A beer would taste good right about now."

"Rodell, it isn't even ten o'clock," LoPresto says. "Maybe after lunch."

"Not likely," he says. "I feel like that guy in the joke. You know the one?"

"I know," LoPresto says. "The one whose wife feeds him bran muffins all the time and when he's on his deathbed he wishes he'd eaten whatever he pleased?"

Rodell chuckles and then coughs. It's a painful sound. "That's the one."

LoPresto looks at his watch. "Samuel, I'm glad you came, so I can slip out. Did you see Patty?"

"She went down to get some breakfast. I told her I'd keep an eye on the patient until she got back so he doesn't get it in his mind to light out of here. How are things going with the project in Bobtail?"

"I tell you what, I'm mighty proud of that, but it's like getting a tiger by the tail. I hope I didn't bite off more than I can chew. Those guys are rarin' to go. They had already paid off most of the families out there and we're starting to bulldoze the empty houses."

"I expect they think that every minute that mall isn't built is a minute they're not making money. Gabe, you're gonna do fine."

"I hope so. Rodell, I'll come see you when you get home." LoPresto puts his hat on and eases past me.

When he's gone, I pull up a chair next to Rodell's bed and say, "You feel up to hearing what's been going on?"

"Better than laying here wondering who all will come to my funeral."

"I expect you'll have a pretty good crowd." And my guess is they're all going to lift a glass in his honor.

I tell him my tale of catching the two boys sneaking into Jenny's barn the night of the prom and their connection to Scott and Jett Borland.

"Borland? I remember when Scott Borland got sent to the penitentiary in Huntsville."

"You do? How come you remember him?"

"I was friends with the sheriff at the time and it was one of the few times he said somebody scared him. He told me Borland was a bad guy. Your friend Jenny must have been pretty young to be handling that case."

"She was doing that stint as assistant DA that a lot of lawyers go through. But I guess with her it stuck. She said she likes seeing to it that bad people go to prison."

"Only problem is, that can come back to bite her." He frowns and shifts around in the bed.

"You doing okay? Can I get you anything?"

"Just feeling weak. I hate it."

"I want to run something by you." I tell him about the altercation between Ellen Forester and her ex-husband. "I'm beginning to think something has got to be done."

"By God, it's past time something was done. You can't let that kind of thing go on. Next thing, he'll be knocking her around. You've got to put a stop to it." His agitation sets up a deep, guttural cough. When he's done coughing, he looks wrung out.

I tell him about the prom and the parents hovering too much over their kids. It's not very interesting, and by the time I'm done, his eyes are closed. Maybe it was soothing to hear me drone on about everyday problems in Jarrett Creek. He's certainly no stranger to that.

After a while Patty comes tiptoeing in. When she sees that Rodell is asleep, she motions for me to come out in the hallway.

Her eyes tear up as soon as she starts to talk. "I know I haven't been very nice to you, Samuel, but I want you to know I appreciate how much you've helped Rodell since he came home. Going down to the station and working a couple of mornings a week is all he looks forward to."

"Patty, Rodell has been helpful. He knows the place. And he knows people and how they get into things. I just wish . . ."

"I know what you wish. Same thing I do. That he hadn't gotten so far into the bottle."

"Water under the bridge." I pat her arm.

CHAPTER 29

I've still got Jenny's key to her mamma's house, and as soon as I leave the hospital I head over there. It's noon by the time I arrive. I've had plenty of time to think over my conversation with Marlene, Eddie's second wife. She claimed that Vera Sandstone's spat with Eddie stemmed from her prejudice toward Eddie's first wife. True, prejudice was more widespread back then, but knowing Vera, it's hard for me to imagine her being upset that Eddie married a Hispanic girl. Maybe there was something else about the girl that created problems between Vera and Eddie. I want to find out more about the girl. Going to Vera's house to arrange for moving the goods out is exactly the opportunity I need. Maybe I'll get lucky and find what I'm looking for.

I'm relieved that Eddie Sandstone's car isn't in the driveway. I'd like to take care of business without having to answer to him. But then I realize Vera's car isn't there either. I don't remember Jenny telling me that she did anything with the car, and I wonder where it is. I'm standing in the driveway when a young man comes out of the house next door.

I wave him over. "Are you Nate Holloway by any chance?"

He says he is. He speaks with a certain reticence.

"You're just the man I wanted to see." I tell him who I am and ask if he knows where Vera's car is.

"Jenny asked me if I'd take it in to have it serviced so she can sell it. And I did."

"That answers one question. Can I ask you if you've seen her brother Eddie around? You know what he looks like?"

His expression darkens. "Yeah, I know him. I was out taking care of the yard the other day and he came around and told me if I expected to get paid for doing it, I could think again."

That explains his hesitation with me. "You don't need to worry. Jenny will take care of your expenses."

"Nobody needs to pay me for anything. Mrs. Sandstone saved me from going down a bad road, and I'll always be grateful to her."

"Jenny will want to compensate you anyway. She appreciates everything you've done."

"That's up to her. Eddie told me he inherited the house and he's moving in and there's no need for me to come around anymore." His face is flushed at the memory of Eddie's rudeness. "I don't mind saying it's going to be a change having somebody like him living in this house."

"Have you seen him around here a lot?"

"Just that one day. He was trying all the doors to see if any of them were unlocked. I didn't know who he was, so I wanted to be sure it wasn't somebody trying to break in. I came over and asked who he was. When he found out I lived next door, he asked me if I had a key to the place, but I didn't."

"Did he say what he wanted inside for?"

"No, and I didn't ask."

"Look, Jenny needs help getting all the boxes moved out of here, and I'm looking to hire someone. You interested?"

"As long as I don't have to deal with her brother I am. Does she want the furniture moved, too?"

"Let me call her and find out."

I put in a call to Jenny and ask her if she still wants to go through with having someone else move things out of the house.

"Yes, I do. Ever since we talked about it last night, I've felt better. It was hanging over my head."

"What about the furniture?"

She thinks for a minute. "Take everything. I'm not leaving a thing for that son of a bitch."

When I hang up, I say to Holloway, "Furniture, too. You'll need to get someone to help you."

"Say no more. I know a fellow with a truck. How soon do you want it done?"

I tell him the sooner the better and ask him if he can arrange to rent a storage space, too. He heads home to start making arrangements, and I go inside to see if I can find what I'm after.

The house is stuffy inside, despite the air-conditioning still being on. Odd how fast an unlived-in house begins to go stale. I survey the three bedrooms and then the garage to take stock of how many boxes I have to go through to find what I'm after.

It's possible that Vera kept no record of Eddie's first marriage, but I doubt it. The problem is, whatever information she might have kept is at least twenty-five years old, and there's no telling where it's stashed. I could get the information from the courthouse, but I want to see what mementos Vera kept about the wedding, if anything.

In one of the rooms is a desk that hasn't been cleaned out, and I take a cursory look through the drawers in case Vera kept old records there. All I find is current information. In the closet I find several boxes on a shelf. I pull them out and open the one that was farthest back on the floor of the closet. It contains tax returns from twenty years back. There's no need to keep tax returns more than seven years, but like everybody else, Vera Sandstone stuck them in a box and never opened the box again.

It takes me almost an hour to go through each of the boxes from the closet, and none of them has any personal information about Eddie. I'm going to have to be smarter about my search. I go out into the garage, thinking it's possible she stored her oldest stuff there. I'm relieved when I see that the boxes are labeled—Jenny's toys, Jenny's grades one through three. And then there are boxes for Eddie's things—yearbooks, school projects, trophies. Under them is a box simply labeled "Eddie." I move the other boxes off it and open it up.

It's full of photographs from childhood through high school, some of them in shoeboxes—mostly pictures of Eddie with friends. Tucked onto the side of the box is a shoebox, and when I open it I'm sure I'll find what I'm looking for. There's a tassel from his graduation mortarboard, some letters from SMU, and then a small manila envelope. Inside is a clipping from the *Bobtail Weekly News* showing a picture of a young girl in a light-colored suit and a hat with a veil. She's a pretty girl with a sweet smile. It announces that Eddie Sandstone and Estelle Cruz were married right after Estelle graduated from Bobtail High, and that Eddie attended Bobtail Junior College.

As I'm putting the box back, I see another one, marked "H." Howard. The things Vera kept from her husband are poignant. Their framed wedding picture shows two raw young people grinning as if life will never be anything but good. She kept the marriage certificate and a newspaper clipping about the wedding. And there are photos with just the two of them, before the children were born. A little cracked leather pouch contains an old driver's license from when Howard was eighteen, an old checkbook with his name on it, and a high school transcript.

No other box is marked with his name or initials. I don't remember seeing any men's clothes in Vera's closet, and when I put the box back I check the bedroom closets to make sure. I wonder when Vera decided her husband wasn't coming back and it was time to pitch out the things he left behind. I wonder if he took any clothes with him. Maybe he took a suitcase, and she knew all along he had planned to leave and wanted to keep the information from her two kids as long as she could.

As I drive off, I think about the wedding photo of Estelle Cruz. That long ago it would have been highly unusual for a young Hispanic woman to walk out on her husband. The only thing I could think of that would persuade her to do so would be if she went back to her family, or if she ran off with another man.

Right after Eddie Sandstone graduated from high school, his daddy ran out on the family. And two years later Eddie's wife did the same thing. Losing one person is unfortunate. Losing two starts to look like a pattern.

And that's when it hits me. I don't know why it has taken me so long, but I suddenly realize that I've been wrong all along about what Vera Sandstone meant when she asked me to find "his" first wife. She didn't mean Howard's first wife. There was no such person. She was talking about Eddie's first wife, Estelle. A pang runs through me. What is it that Vera had in mind?

Gabe LoPresto said I could find him most of the time at Bobtail Ridge these days with the surveyors. I drive over and as soon as I take the freeway ramp off and turn into the subdivision, I immediately see why the city council chose this site for their mall. First of all, it's right off the freeway. Any mall worth the money put into it needs to be easy to get to. Second, it's surrounded by fields, which means there's room to expand.

Also, like Loretta said, the housing development has not fared well. Whoever built it clearly used the cheapest materials he could get; most of the houses sag in one way or another—porches dipping in the middle, roofs looking like they are ready to slip off onto the ground, windows gone out of true.

I find the surveyors, and they tell me that LoPresto has gone off on a coffee break and will be back before too long.

I drive through the streets of the subdivision and find a buzz of activity going on. On every block there are two or three houses with garage doors open and cardboard boxes stacked inside. In a couple of driveways there are moving trucks parked, ramps down, with movers conveying boxes into the vehicles. Many of the houses are already vacant. At the end of one of the streets I stop and get out to look around.

Beyond the subdivision lies a huge open space with several tractors parked on it. I assume the area has been bought up for the mall. I note that the trailer park where Scott Borland's wife lives is on the other side of the open space. It reminds me that I need to talk to the vet about what those pills were that Jett Borland intended for the horses.

I drive back out through the big rock pillars that promised such grandeur back when Bobtail Ridge was built and make my way along the frontage road until I find a place where I can get a hamburger and a cup of coffee.

When I get back, Gabe LoPresto is talking to four other men. He breaks off and invites me over. I'd previously told him that I wanted to meet the contractor who built Bobtail Ridge. "Let me introduce you to Rich O'Connor. Rich, for some reason, Samuel, has a burning desire to talk to you."

Rich O'Connor is over sixty but sturdy and with a sharp-eyed look. I have a feeling he doesn't miss much.

"So you built this?" I wave my arms to indicate the houses in front of us.

"Hate to admit it. Doesn't look like much. I knew it wouldn't stand up. The son-of-a-gun developer nickeled and dimed us every which way. I told him these houses would fall down around people's ears, but he said not to worry. I guess he's right. Folks here have gotten a nice buyout. They can't wait to get out of here."

"You remember a man who worked for you by the name of Howard Sandstone?"

"Sure I remember Howard." He smiles and then checks himself. "Damnedest thing. He was a steady fellow. I never would have figured him for somebody who would walk off the job and never say word one about it. But that's exactly what he did. Why are you asking?"

"Something came up that made me curious. His family never heard anything either after he left. You say he was a steady worker?"

"Up until then, yes. In this business you find out who you can count on, and he was one of them."

"Did anybody ever suspect foul play?"

O'Connor hooks his hands in his back pockets and shakes his head slowly. "I never heard anything like that. Fact is, there was some talk about him maybe having a woman on the side and maybe he ran off with her."

"Who was she?"

He laughs. "Some of the talk got pretty wild. Somebody said he thought Howard was interested in one of the women in the church choir, and then somebody else said there was some woman who played fast and loose that he'd hooked up with. Couldn't have been the choir lady, because as far as I know she never left town."

"He had a son working for you, too. Eddie Sandstone. Do you remember him?"

"I do, vaguely."

One of the men who was talking to O'Connor when I got here perks up. "Edward Sandstone? He applied to work on the demolition here. Supposed to start right away."

"You sure?"

"Yeah. Sandstone is a building material. Funny that he's in the building trade. That's why I remember it."

"I mean you're sure it was demolition he was applying for? He's got a sheetrock business up in Temple."

The man laughs. "Yeah, he told me that. He's applying for the sheetrock job, too. But he said he helped build this place and he also wants to help tear it down."

"Did Eddie talk about his dad after he disappeared?" I ask O'Connor.

"Now you're asking a question I wouldn't know the answer to. Eddie might have talked some about his daddy, but he wouldn't have been talking to me. I didn't get involved much with the day-to-day activity. The head carpenter hired him because he was Howard's son. He mostly did grunt work."

"Head carpenter. Man by the name of Fogarty?" I remember the name from the file I read about Howard Sandstone's disappearance. Fogarty is the man who reported him missing.

"Yeah, Curly Fogarty. Gabe, have you talked to Curly about working with you?"

"I haven't gotten that far."

"Let me give you Curly's information," O'Connor says to me. "He's probably on a job, but tell him I sent you by."

I call Curly Fogarty, and he says he'll be leaving the job he's working on now in an hour and I can meet him at his house.

Fogarty lives between Bobtail and Jarrett Creek, on a nice piece of land with several trees and a small creek running through the front yard. "This is a handsome place," I say, when he comes to the front door. He gets his nickname honestly, with a thick head of curly gray hair that would please a poodle.

"Built it myself. My wife says it's getting a little big for us with the kids gone, but I told her they're going to have to take me out of here feet first. I'm not building another house, and I wouldn't be satisfied with anybody else's work. I told her if she has to leave, I'll get me a new wife." He laughs heartily.

"I heard that," a voice says from somewhere in another room. "One of these days you're going to regret it."

He grins at me. His wife appears around the door. She's a plump little dumpling, a contrast to his lean build. But it's clear the way they look at each other that they've got a solid marriage. For a second I feel the pinch of Jeanne being gone. "This is my wife Linda," Fogarty says and tells her who I am.

"Let me get you two a beer," she says. "Go on out on the back deck."

"Yes, boss," he says and winks at me.

The back deck is on the shady side of the house. The backyard dips down to a gentle slope with lots of trees. "Beautiful property," I say.

Fogarty is a talker, and while we wait for the beer he tells me how he came to buy this piece of land and how long it took him to build the house. Usually I'd be impatient to get on with questioning him, but I've had a hard few days and I'm glad to let him chatter.

Eventually we have beer and tortilla chips on the table between us, and Fogarty asks what I can do for him.

"Hope your memory works well." I ask him if he remembers Howard Sandstone and his son Eddie.

"Of course I remember them. I remember one of them with a little more fondness than the other. Howard was a hardworking man, a decent man. His son was a little more problematic. Kid had a good line of b.s. but didn't always back it up with his actions."

"What do you mean exactly?"

"Well, Eddie would tell you how hard he was going to work, but then he'd leave a little early or call in sick or give somebody a little trouble. His dad on the other hand could be counted on. At least until he skipped out."

"You were Howard Sandstone's foreman and you reported him missing."

"I did, because it didn't seem like him. But to tell the truth, I was one of the few that wasn't totally surprised when he disappeared." He takes a sip of his beer, sets it down, and hunches forward with his hands on his knees. "The morning he left he called and asked me for a ride to work. He said his car was out of commission. When I picked him up he seemed agitated. I assumed he was annoyed because of the car and I told him I didn't mind picking him up, not to be upset about it. He said that wasn't what he was upset about. It was a family thing."

"He didn't tell you what it was about?"

Curly grimaces. "I don't like to pry in people's business. You work around people all day and you hear things, but I keep out of it."

"You never heard anything from him after he left?"

He shakes his head.

"You remember anything else?"

He takes a sip of beer and eats a chip while he considers. "There was one thing, although it doesn't amount to much. I asked if his son needed a ride to work that morning, too, and he said Eddie was driving his own car. I thought at the time it was odd that he wouldn't bring his daddy, but I let it slide. With Howard saying he was upset about a family matter, I figured they might have had a falling-out or something."

"Did you take Howard home that night, too?"

"Yep, took him home, too. I seem to recall he was a little calmer by then. Hard physical work will do that, you know."

"How come you remember all the details?"

"Because I had worked with Howard a long time and I counted on him in particular. It was during a week when we were pouring concrete. There were four or five slabs and they have to be handled right—the forms have to be removed at the right time. Too soon and the 'crete can sag. Too late, and it's hard to get the forms off without damaging it. Howard was good at judging the timing, and I left it to him to take care of it. Without him, I had to go over and handle it myself. I wasn't too happy about that."

CHAPTER 30

Midmorning the next day I hear from Wallace Lyndall. "You know I told you it wouldn't be long before we got something on Scott Borland?"

"Yeah?"

"The fingerprints on that pipe used to attack your man Bennett came back a match."

"Why would anybody be that stupid?"

"As you know, criminals aren't necessarily the PhD type. I'm going out there to make the arrest. You want to join me?"

A half hour later I park in the lot behind the Bobtail Police Department and find Lyndall waiting in his squad car for me.

The Borland place looks deserted again as we drive up, but then the dogs come scrambling out from under the porch, hollering. I'm surprised when Lyndall speaks sharply to them and they promptly turn tail and go back under there. They crouch there, eyeing us, but they stay put.

No one answers the front door, but this time we have cause to search the place thoroughly, which means we can follow the path worn through the weeds in the vacant field behind the house into the thicket beyond. Before, I suspected that Borland might have a meth lab back there, but we didn't have a legal reason to follow my instinct. This time, we're within rights.

We've gone about twenty steps into the high, yellowed weeds when I hold out my hand to stop Lyndall and point to a wisp of smoke coming from the stand of trees. The air is dead-still, and the column of black smoke is shooting straight up, with particles of something flying up into the air surrounding it.

"Uh-oh," Lyndall says. "That doesn't look right."

A few seconds later we hear yelling from the vicinity of the smoke, and a door slams. Scott and Jett Borland come charging toward us through the trees. Behind us, I hear the dogs yelping. The Borlands barely make it out of the tree line and into the clearing when it feels like all the air is sucked out of the surroundings and all sound and sights pause for a few seconds. Then in a rush I see the Borlands sprawl forward just before I feel the force of the explosion hit me. We're far enough away that it doesn't bring us down, but I stagger back and the vegetation momentarily sways toward us. Bits of debris swirl in the air through a cloud of shimmering dust.

"Let's get back," Lyndall yells. "This air could be toxic." We turn and hightail it back the way we came and around the front of the house. The dogs are hollering and run around like the explosion has disoriented them. Lyndall sends them back under the porch.

From a distance, I hear one of the Borlands crying out in pain. I start to go back to help, but Lyndall grabs my arm. "You can't go back there. No telling what kind of chemicals are spewing out of that cloud."

He's right. I don't know what kind of residue there might be from such an explosion, but the air is filled with acrid smoke.

I hear sirens off in the distance. Whichever Borland is hurt is still yelling, but Lyndall and I stay put. When the firefighters arrive, they'll have the right equipment to deal with the blaze and the injuries. I walk to the end of the house and peer around into the vacant lot. The trees beyond the lot have caught fire, and burning branches are falling into the weeds. One of the Borlands is trying to drag the other one to safety.

Lyndall sees them, too.

"We've got to help," I say.

"Well, hell," Lyndall says, "You're right." We take off our shirts and wrap them around our heads, covering our noses, and run toward the two men. Scott is dragging his unconscious son, whose hair and clothing are badly singed. Scott is hurt too, burned patches blistering on his arms and back.

"Get on up to the house," I yell to him. "We'll take care of Jett." The fire is hot, and the trees crackle and pop as they burn. Lyndall and I grab Jett's arms and drag him.

When we get to the front of the house, we lay Jett down and I hurry out to the street to flag down the fire trucks. They come barreling into the yard, men leaping out before the trucks are fully stopped. The dogs seem to be thoroughly cowed and stay under the porch, whimpering.

"What happened?" a firefighter says.

"Meth lab," Lyndall says.

"Ah, shit!" He runs to the back of the truck and starts hauling out gas masks. Another one runs out to the street, looking in both directions. He comes running back. "I don't see any fireplugs," he says. "We'll have to get up close and use what's in the tanks." He jumps back into the truck, and the others step up onto the side of it and hold on as he steers behind the house and starts across the vacant lot. The other truck follows. They get as close as they dare before they stop and get to work.

One of the men has stayed behind to tend to Jett Borland. He's conscious now and is moaning. A few seconds later an EMS truck arrives, and two men take over working on Jett. The firefighter runs to join his crew.

"Any way I can help?" I call out as he sprints away.

"Yeah! Stay out of the way," he calls back.

And that's when I realize that Scott Borland is not with us. "What the hell? Where's Borland?" I start up the two wooden steps to the front door of the house, but I know Borland has used all the commotion to make his getaway. Sure enough, the place is empty and Borland is nowhere to be found. Lyndall and I look at each other. "Fatherly concern," I say.

Jett Borland gets loaded into the EMS vehicle and is hauled off to the hospital. Fire trucks from a neighboring county arrive ten minutes later. Because the day is so still, the four units manage to get the fire under control quickly. Lyndall calls headquarters to tell the sheriff what happened, including that we lost Scott Borland in the shuffle. He snickers at something the sheriff says. When he gets off he says, "He's pretty sure that Borland is not smart enough to figure out a way to escape for good. We'll find him."

"Besides, he's hurt," I say. "He's going to need some attention. In fact, I have a feeling I know exactly where he'll head."

We go straight to Donna Mae Borland's place and stop down the street from it. I walk to her trailer and knock on the door. She answers it wearing the same dressing gown she was in the other day. "Now what do you want?" she says.

I tell her what happened and that we're looking for Scott.

"He's not here, and I haven't heard from him."

"If you see him, ask him why he ran out on Jett. He got hurt during the explosion. He's over at the hospital."

She snaps to attention and grabs the front of her dressing gown and holds it together. "Why didn't you tell me?" She slams the door in my face, and I go back and get into the car with Lyndall. Five minutes later Donna Mae comes tearing out the door, jumps into her old Pontiac, and roars away. We settle back to wait for Borland. In the distance I hear the roar of bulldozers going about the business of tearing down Bobtail Ridge subdivision.

After forty-five minutes we decide Borland probably isn't going to show. The smoky smell of our clothes and the sour smell that adrenaline left on us drive us out of there, and I head on home to clean up.

CHAPTER 31

"You really think I'm going to be afraid of Scott Borland?" Jenny and I are standing in her kitchen. The bottle of Jack Daniels, or another like it, is sitting open on the counter. Jenny has been drinking, although she isn't as drunk as she has been the last couple of times I've seen her. But tonight the drinking has made her belligerent.

"Jenny, I'm worried that after what happened this afternoon, he'll come after you because he's pissed off." I'd worry that he'll come after her horses, too, but Truly Bennett is back on the job with Alvin Carter, and they're on guard.

"Let him come," she says. "I'm sick of people thinking they can bully me." She has her hands on her hips and is glaring at me.

"At least lock your doors," I say.

"All right, all right. Is that it?" She hasn't invited me into the living room to sit down. I always come to her back door, but we rarely stop in the kitchen. It's not a place she spends much time in, not liking to cook.

I probably ought to let her alone, but I'm too frustrated to back down now. "There's something else I need to talk to you about," I say. "Do you know who Estelle Cruz is?"

She frowns. "Name is familiar."

"Your mamma may have mentioned her a long time ago."

She has a moment of realization and storms over to pour herself another drink. "How can I convince you to leave me the hell alone about my brother?"

"You knew he was married to this woman?"

Her expression is so angry that I can hardly look at her. "When are you going to get that I try not to think about him, ever. I knew he was married because Mamma told me. She also told me the woman ran out on him. Big surprise."

Disappeared, like her daddy. It could be coincidence that both these people disappeared from Eddie's life. But I'm beginning to doubt it. And only by pushing Jenny to find out more am I likely to get to the bottom of it.

"When your mamma told me she thought you were in danger, do you think she meant from your brother?"

Jenny opens her mouth and then closes it again, staring at me. Finally she says, "It's possible."

"Why?"

She's breathing heavily, and for a bare second I think she might haul off and hit me. Her eyes are wild, and she's gripping the glass of whiskey so hard her fingers are white. "You're bringing it all back. Eddie and his goddam friends. Pack of animals. I wish to hell you'd leave it alone."

There's only one thing I can think of that would put Jenny in such a state after so long a time. "Did your brother assault you?" There, I've said it.

"You're not going to give up, are you?" She pours another shot of whiskey and downs it. "No, he didn't assault me exactly. Not personally, at least."

She looks at me for a long time. I feel sized up in every way. I can tell that she wants to confide in me, but she has lived with the past for a long time. The thought of bringing it into the open after all this time is eating her up.

"You don't have to tell me the details," I say. "It's clear that whatever happened set you back badly."

She walks over to the cabinet, sets her glass down, and leans onto the cabinet with her back to me. Her head hangs down. She stays that way for several seconds. Then she gets a second glass out of the cabinet and pours a lot of whiskey into both glasses. She hands one to me. "Here. You're going to need it."

I follow her into the living room. She turns on one dim light and sinks into the sofa.

I sit down in the easy chair I always sit in, but I don't sink back in comfort. I lean forward, cupping the glass of whiskey.

"You told me you found out that Eddie was a big deal in high school. He had everything—looks, athletic talent, charm, and he was smart enough. But what no one paid much attention to was that he always wanted more—he wanted to be not just the best, but the only. Do you know what I'm talking about?"

"Like somebody with a billion dollars, and two billion still wouldn't satisfy him?"

"That's it. I, on the other hand, was . . ." she stops, shaking her head. "A lunk. I didn't know what to do with myself. I was smart, but not in the way a young girl is supposed to be smart about boys and clothes." She sighs. "There was this guy on the football team. A year older than me. Mike Tolleson. He was a shy boy, sweet-natured. Studious. Football wasn't really in him—he played to please his daddy. I had a big crush on him, and I think he liked me, too. I thought so at the time, anyway."

Her eyes are squeezed closed. When she opens them, she looks panicky. "I've never told anybody but Mamma about this, and I don't know whether I'll get through it."

"You don't have to, you know."

It's like she hasn't heard me. "Mike was popular in a funny way. People trusted him. They looked up to him. People would say, 'Ask Mike—he'll know what to do.'" Her eyes get a faraway look, full of pain and regret.

Then she snaps out of it. "Anyway, the football team voted him captain when he was a junior. Eddie was a senior and thought he was going to be captain. When he found out Mike had won the vote, he came home and tore his room to pieces. Like I said, he had everything—but he was furious over somebody else getting one little thing."

She looks at me finally. "That's not normal. I know that now, but at the time I thought that's the way men behaved."

"Your daddy?"

She shakes her head. "He never lost his temper. But he always stuck up for Eddie. He said Eddie was going through a phase and he'd get his temper under control when he got older. He told me Eddie had a bit of an inferiority complex and was jealous of Mike, and that Eddie would get over being upset before too long."

"And did he?"

"I thought he'd gotten over it, but it turned out he was just biding his time."

"What did he do?" I take a sip of the whiskey. It hits my throat and stomach like bile.

"I don't want to tell you what happened. Makes me sick to remember it." She slouches back on the sofa. Her mouth is a grim line.

"I may not be the right person to tell."

"I know that. But now that I've started, you're in for it." She looks up at the ceiling. "I wish I smoked. Seems like the right time for a cigarette." She actually manages a smile, but it fades quickly. "Somehow Eddie got wind of the fact that Mike and I liked each other. Eddie started buddying up to Mike. Way down deep I knew that was a bad thing, but I tried to tell myself Eddie was trying to be nice because he knew Mike liked me. Not that Mike and I went out or anything. It was mostly studying together and being moon-eyed." She laughs—it's a wistful sound. "I wish I could go back to being that naive. Anyway Eddie kept it up for the rest of the school year. One big happy family. I wish I'd had more sense.

"We've all been in that situation, especially when we were kids."

"Maybe. But not everybody has been in my situation. One night our folks were gone. Who knows where? They hardly ever went out. Next thing I know, Eddie's telling me he has a couple of his friends coming over. I told him he wasn't supposed to have kids over when

Mamma and Daddy were gone, but I couldn't tell him anything. He was a senior and it was all him, all the time. He'd just found out he was getting a scholarship to SMU, which fed his ego to the busting point. Anyway, I heard the boys cutting up in the living room. And after a while Eddie came to my room and said I ought to come talk to them. I said what about? He said they wanted to ask me how to treat their dates on graduation night. I was flattered." She takes a long pull of the whiskey. Her voice is strangled. "How could I have been so goddam stupid?"

I don't like the way the story is going, but Jenny seems calmer now, although she's talking fast, in a monotone.

"Anyway, I went into the living room and they had all this beer and some whiskey. They asked me if I wanted something to drink and I told them I didn't drink. One of them said he knew how to make a whiskey sour and he knew I'd like it. And he was right." She picks up her glass and brandishes it like it's proof of something. "I drank one and then another one. And after that I may have had another. I don't remember. When they got me drunk enough, his two buddies raped me."

"Oh, shit."

She doesn't seem to notice my exclamation. "Rape. Is that the right word? Is that what you call it when a girl is so flattered that she'll go along with anything? I was too tall, too gangly, and afraid to look anybody in the eye. They sweet-talked me, told me I was really getting to be cute, or sexy, or who the hell knows what. It was a like a dream come true. Is it rape when you are thrilled . . . until the last minute, when you see the look on their faces and know they didn't mean a word of it? Is it rape when you call out to your brother and you think he's left the room?" I wish Jenny were crying, but she's completely dry-eyed and her voice is dead.

"Sons of bitches," I mutter. I want to comfort her somehow, but I think she'd break to pieces if I did.

She heaves a few breaths. Her face has gone white. "You think that was the worst of it? Think again. Eddie had videotaped the whole thing. He filmed it! And he gave the video to Mike."

I can't even begin to imagine something like that. But I remember what the assistant coach said, that Eddie had a cruel streak. "What did your brother stand to gain by that? It's not like he could go back in time and get the position as captain of the football team."

"I wish I knew. You remember when you met him the other day he said I held a grudge against him? He was talking about himself. He could hold a grudge like you've never seen. When we were little, if I did anything that Eddie didn't like, he'd wait until there was something I really wanted, and then he'd strike. I got a doll for Christmas one year. I loved that stupid doll. One day it went missing. It broke my heart. Eddie told me I had been careless with it and that's what I got for not taking better care of it. Couple of years later—years, mind you—he asked me to bring something from his closet. I found the doll there broken to pieces." She leans forward, her eyes narrowed. "Here's the thing. He could have simply thrown it out. But I went into that closet because he asked me to get something for him. He put those pieces there for me to find."

The person she's describing is twisted. Is that what I responded to in Eddie that made me uncomfortable with him? "Were you ever afraid of him?"

"Not physically. I mean, he'd pinch me or shove me sometimes, but nothing serious." She shakes her head. "I don't know how to describe it. Sort of a psychological fear. Like I had a feeling he was capable of terrible things, even if he never really did anything. Does that make sense?"

It makes total sense because both of Eddie's wives said something similar. And then I remember the nurse saying that Vera seemed trapped when she was with her son. "Sure it does," I say.

I'm a small-town police chief, and I don't deal with deeply disturbed criminals. The criminals I deal with are people who've gone off the rails because they made a mistake, or because they were scared or greedy. What Jenny has described is a different kind of person. If what she says is true, he's got something wrong with him. And the damage he inflicted on Jenny has lasted for a long time.

"You told your mamma . . . did your daddy know?"

Jenny's lips are trembling. She puts a hand to her mouth to stop it. "I had to tell Mamma. She was a teacher and I was terrified that everyone in school would hear about it. At first I didn't want her to know Eddie was involved, but she pushed and prodded until I admitted his part in it. I begged her not to tell Daddy. I was afraid he'd hate me."

"What did your mamma do?"

Jenny gets up and leaves the room and comes back with a box of tissues. She blows her nose and sits looking off into the distance for several seconds.

"That woman was so smart. She didn't waste time fussing over me. I think she knew that would have sent me over the edge. She just went into action. It was finals week and she arranged for me to take all my finals in a couple of days. And the minute the last one was over, she had me on the bus out to my aunt and uncle in Lubbock. She told everybody her sister was sick and needed some help. My aunt worked at Texas Tech and she found me a part-time job in the law school for the summer. Best thing that could have happened. I buried myself in work."

"Did kids at the high school find out what happened?"

"Besides Mike?" She shakes her head. "I don't think they did, but I don't know why. I guess it was too close to the end of school and the boys who did it were graduating, and maybe they didn't think there'd be any percentage in telling what they'd done if I wasn't around for them to torment. Honestly, I think if anybody had ever acted like they knew, I would have killed myself."

"So your mamma didn't do anything to see to it that they were punished?"

Jenny thinks for a minute. "You mean go to the law? She wouldn't have done that to my brother. And my guess is she thought if she didn't do anything about him, she couldn't very well accuse his friends. I was gone the whole summer and as far as I can tell all she wanted was to avoid any fuss. Plus, just before I got home my daddy walked out. That was hard on her and distracted all of us for a time."

I think back to the photo I saw of Jenny's daddy and the cheerful look on his face when he was with his family. "You never had any idea why he left?"

"I know just why he left." Another shot of whiskey. She's starting to have trouble focusing on me. "It was exactly what I was afraid of. He couldn't face me."

"What do you mean?"

"Couldn't face me after she told him what happened. I was damaged goods. He wouldn't have been able to stand being in the same room with me, so he left. At first Mamma told me that they had a fight and that's why he walked out. A couple of years later, after I kept asking her if she'd heard from him, she finally told me the truth. She said she told him what happened to me, and he didn't want to talk about it. A couple of days later he up and left. She didn't think it was about me—she thought he was so disappointed in Eddie that he couldn't stand it. But I knew it was me. He was proud of Eddie, but I was the one he adored. Sometimes that was the only thing that kept me going, knowing how much he loved me. When he left, I decided I wasn't going to ever trust a man again."

"That's harsh."

"You think so? Why should I trust a man?"

"No. You misunderstand me. I don't mean your decision was harsh, I mean you're not giving your daddy the benefit of the doubt. You felt so bad about yourself with what happened with those boys that you thought your daddy would have the same reaction."

"Maybe so. But I guess I'll never know, because we never saw him again. Now you've heard my story. You know why I don't have much interest in men, and why I was so close to my mamma."

"You ever think about seeing a therapist? It was a terrible thing your brother did to you."

"Where am I going to find a therapist around here? Mamma wanted me to talk to the preacher. I can just hear what he'd have to say. Forgiveness and all that."

We talk a bit more until Jenny seems calm. I stand up and tell her I'm going. "You going to be okay?"

She shoots an anxious look at me. "Lot of stuff got stirred up."

"Listen," I say. "Sometimes when somebody tells somebody a deep secret, they regret it and a tension comes between them. Don't let that happen. You know I won't ever let this information get past my lips, don't you?"

"Never had the slightest question about that."

When I get home, it takes me a while to settle down enough to go to bed. I'm not only mad at Eddie, but at Vera, too. Why did she let those boys off the hook? Maybe she had her reasons. Maybe she didn't know whether Jenny could face the public airing of her ordeal.

Some mothers might have wanted the boys punished enough to drag it into the open and have them arrested, regardless of the price their daughter would pay. Which would have been better for Jenny's psychological state? Hard to say. Jenny has carried the weight of the incident for a long time. Would she have been able to let go of it easier if she'd known the boys were punished? I just don't know. Maybe Vera knew that her daughter didn't have the confidence to bear up under such an ordeal. Either way, what's done is done, and I'm hoping that getting it out in the open will help Jenny put it behind her.

I keep coming back to Jenny's daddy. Is Jenny right? Did he leave because he couldn't face Jenny's shame? Upstanding man, honest, hard-working, loved his family. I don't see it. From all I've heard of Howard Sandstone, he was a man who would have maybe been angry on Jenny's behalf, may have confronted the boys who violated her, would surely have had a talk with his son to get to the truth of what happened. But leave? No.

CHAPTER 32

I'm at headquarters early the next morning after a poor night's sleep. The phone is ringing as I walk in the door. "Samuel, it's Jim Krueger."

"Jim, what can I do for you? The kids getting a case of short-timer's attitude?" With the prom over, it's finals week at the high school, and you usually get a few incidents of hijinks the last week before school is out.

"I wish that's what I was calling about. You know Rodell had a heart attack?"

"Yes, I went over to the hospital to see him." I hear a car outside and see that Zeke has driven up.

"I got a call from Patty and she asked me if I'd let people know that Rodell went into a coma last night. She especially wanted me to call you. Said she thought you'd want to know."

"What's the prognosis?"

"She said the doctor thought he might have had a stroke. His system is worn out." The door opens, and Zeke comes in whistling. When he sees my face, he stops abruptly and stands there with the door half open.

"How is Patty doing?"

"She sounded okay. She said her kids got there when Rodell was still conscious."

I thank him for calling and ask if he'll let me know if he hears anything else. When I hang up, I feel like everything around me is suddenly unrecognizable. I've known Rodell a long time, most of that time fraught with problems. But I've come to respect his determination to go out sober—not easy for a man so wedded to alcohol. I've seen a side of him I never knew, and I regret that it was for such a short time.

I tell Zeke Dibble what happened. "That's a shame," he says. "But not a surprise. You going to be here for a while?"

"No, I've got something I have to do," I say.

"About that," Zeke says. He sits down in the chair next to my desk. "You've been gone a lot and. . . ."

"I'm sorry about that," I say.

"No, no. It's no problem. Odum and I don't mind the work. It's not like we've got a rash of serious crimes to deal with. No, I was just going to ask if there was anything I could help you with." He gestures to the rest of the room. "Sometimes it gets boring just hanging out waiting for something exciting to happen. I thought maybe you could make use of my time."

I think about it for a minute. "Yesterday turned out to be pretty messy." I tell him about the meth lab fire. "The problem is, we lost Scott Borland. That's his picture that's posted up there." I point to the bulletin board. "I'm worried he might come after Jenny. It would be good if you'd keep an eye out at Jenny's place to be sure there's nobody hanging around that ought not be there."

It takes a while, but eventually I find the information I'm looking for at the courthouse in Bobtail. Eddie Sandstone married Estelle Cruz at the courthouse with two witnesses—a girl named Graciella Cruz and a man named Charles Cole.

Back at Bobtail High School, the archive queen, Mollie Cleaver, doesn't seem particularly surprised to see me. "I had a feeling you'd be back once you got the lay of the land."

I tell her I'd like to see some yearbooks spanning two years before and after Eddie Sandstone's senior year. I find pictures of Estelle Cruz in the yearbook two years after Eddie's senior year and of both Graciella Cruz and Charlie Cole the same year as Eddie. Neither of the Cruz girls show up in any clubs or athletic activities. Charlie Cole, on the other hand, is in many of the same activities as Eddie. In candid shots, they are often together. I wonder if he's one of the boys Jenny says raped her. I show Mollie the photos of the girls. "Can you tell me anything about these two?"

"I didn't know Estelle, but Graciella had a part-time job in the front office. Good, hard worker."

"Neither of them seemed to have been involved in school activities."

"No. Back then a lot of the Hispanic children didn't participate much. We finally got a Hispanic principal, Hector Salizar. He pushed to get the students of color more involved in the life of the school. We have a Dia de los Muertos celebration every year now and I think it's good for everybody."

"You wouldn't happen to know what became of Graciella, would you?"

"I don't have any idea. Let me look up her records." She goes to the computer, and her fingers fly over the keys. "Here it is." She hits print, and after a minute a page oozes out of the printer on the table next to her. "This is where she lived and her phone number. Maybe she has family that still lives there."

"And how about Charles Cole?"

"That was a shame. Charlie was a popular boy. Went to the University of Houston, stayed there in Houston, married, and had a family. He had his pilot's license and was killed in a small plane crash somewhere out west with his whole family. A real tragedy. Everybody was talking about it for days."

I start to leave and she stops me. "I'll be interested to know what this is all about once you get it sorted," she says.

I tell her I'll let her know, although it's unlikely that I actually will. I drive over to where the Cruz family lived at the time that Graciella and Estelle were in school. The street is in a marginal part of Bobtail, with the majority of houses being rundown and in need of a good paint job. One of the exceptions is the Cruz house. Like the others, it's small, probably no more than three bedrooms, but the cream color with brown trim has been applied in the last few years, and the yard is neat and trim. There aren't a lot of flowers, but the beds are free of weeds. The one lone tree in the yard looks healthy.

A woman in her forties answers the door. She tells me the Cruz family moved out a few years ago. "Mr. Cruz passed away and I believe the mother moved in with her daughter. I don't know where they live, but the daughter is a pharmacist downtown. Either with the Walgreens or the CVS, I can't remember which."

It's the Walgreens. Graciella Cruz's name is on the placard announcing the name of the pharmacist. I ask the young woman behind the counter if I can speak to Graciella.

"You need a consultation?" she says in an officious voice. "I can help you. What do you need to know?"

"It's personal. I'm chief of police in Jarrett Creek and I'm following up on some questions about an incident a while back."

"I'll see if she has time to talk to you."

Graciella Cruz eventually steps up to the counter, pushing her glasses up on the top of her head. She has put on a good thirty pounds since her school days, but she's still a pretty woman, with dark, thick hair streaked with gray, and big eyes so dark they're almost black. Her face is round and cheerful, but at the moment she's frowning. "I'm sorry I don't have much time. What can I do for you?"

"Could I speak with you in private? It won't take long."

"May I see some identification?"

I bring out my badge, and she opens a side door to let me in so we can talk in her office. It's a cramped space, with barely enough room for her desk and a small armchair. She gestures toward the armchair and sits behind her desk with a sigh. "Oof. Nice to get off my feet."

"Thank you for seeing me."

"What can I do for you?"

"It's about your sister."

"Lupe?"

"No. Estelle."

She leans forward and frowns. "What about her?"

"I understand she walked out on her husband a long time ago."

She sighs. "Got to be nearly thirty years."

"Have you heard from her?"

She looks startled. "No. Did somebody tell you I had?"

"No, I'm looking into another matter and her situation came up. Can you tell me the circumstances of her leaving her husband as you remember them?"

"I haven't thought about this in a while." She knits her brow. "I was in graduate school at the time. Mamma telephoned me all upset. She said Estelle's husband called and told her that Estelle had run out on him and gone to west Texas, to Lubbock. He asked Mamma if we had any friends in Lubbock. He wanted to see if he could go out there and get her to come back. Mamma told him she didn't know anybody there."

"Did you talk to Estelle's friends to see if she had confided in anybody?"

"Oh yes. Absolutely. Mamma was so upset that I came home from school for a few days to be with her. We called all Estelle's friends, but nobody knew where she went."

"Did anybody consider foul play?"

"Of course. We considered everything. I went to the police, but they said there wasn't anything they could do since it looked like she left of her own accord."

"Did they ever question Eddie?"

She's fiddling with a paperclip on her desk and seems to be avoiding looking at me. She lays the paperclip aside and shoots a challenging look at me. "You think the police would question Eddie Sandstone about the disappearance of his little Mexican wife? That's not likely."

"I don't know if you're aware, but Eddie was arrested for assault the summer after he got out of high school."

She shakes her head. "Doesn't matter. There's no way anybody would have questioned Eddie without evidence that something had happened to Estelle."

"Did your sister seem happy with Eddie?"

She smiles sadly. "My sister thought she had died and gone to heaven when she married him. He was popular, handsome, charming."

"So it didn't strike you as odd that she would run away if she was happy?"

Graciella shrugs. "People have arguments. Like I said, we worried, but there was always that chance that she really did take off and leave."

"What would make you think so?"

"Estelle was a daredevil. That's probably what attracted Eddie to her. She had a sassy way about her." She smiles at her memories. "I didn't really think she had gone off to Lubbock, but I couldn't entirely put it past her, either. It was just . . ." She sighs.

"What?"

"Even if she did run away from Eddie, I figured when she cooled down she would get in touch with our family. We weren't especially close to each other, but we were all close to our mamma. I figured if nothing else she'd eventually call Mamma."

"But she never did get in touch?"

She shakes her head. "A few years after she disappeared, I tried to find her. I looked in the Lubbock phone book and called the police there. But I couldn't locate her. And by then so much time had gone by, I didn't know where to look. Why are you looking for her now?"

"Some things have come up. It got me interested."

Her eyes search my face. "You think he might have killed her."

"I don't know. What do you think?"

"That thought crossed my mind, of course, but I didn't know how to pursue it. Like the police said, there was no evidence."

"Did Estelle and Eddie get along?"

"I don't really know. They weren't married that long, and I wasn't around. I was off at school. I asked Mamma and she said she thought Estelle was happy . . . but she thought Estelle was a little afraid of him." She holds a hand up to stop my response. "You have to understand this was my mother talking. She thought all women were afraid of their husbands."

"You said you had another sister?"

"Lupe. She and Estelle were actually closer than Estelle and I were."

"I'd like to talk to her. Do you have a number for her?"

She gets a funny look on her face. "I do, but I don't know if you want to go to the trouble. She's been in a federal prison for several years. She got caught up in a mortgage fraud scheme." She shakes her head. "All those bankers making millions off of their shady business and getting their hands slapped for it, and my poor little sister goes to jail for eight years for some two-bit scam that her boyfriend got her into."

"Did you ever ask Eddie if he heard from Estelle?"

"I didn't really talk to him after I found out he had the marriage annulled. I mean, I guess he did what he had to do so he could remarry, but I didn't want any more to do with him." She gets up. "I'm sorry I can't be more help, but I've got to get back to work or I'll have to stay late. I don't like to leave my kids at home by themselves too long. They're good kids, but you know how it is these days."

"One last question. Do you recall where Estelle and Eddie lived when she disappeared?"

"Yes, it's easy to remember because it was a block away from my parents' house. They rented part of a house from a widow. A while after Eddie moved out the place burned down. It's never been rebuilt."

I find the address Graciela gave me easily enough. Although the lot is overgrown with weeds, the slab of the original house is still there. The house next door looks relatively new, and I wonder if the fire that destroyed this house took that one with it. I expect whoever lives in the newish house doesn't know anything about Eddie and his young wife. On the other side, though, the house is old. Its weathered porch has a rocking chair and about thirty potted plants on it. A tiny old woman sits in the rocking chair watching my every move. If it weren't for her stroking the cat on her lap, you'd think she was a mummy.

I walk over and stand at the bottom of the porch, hat in hand. "I wonder if I could talk to you for a minute?"

"What's that? You're going to have to come up here close. I can't hear worth a damn."

I walk onto the porch, and the cat flies off the woman's lap like it has seen a monster. "Sorry," I say, nodding in the direction the cat disappeared to.

"Doesn't like strangers," she says. She has a deep country accent.

"How long have you lived here?" I say, raising my voice and speaking clearly.

"You don't have to shout," she says. "I've been here forty years."

"Do you remember the woman who lived next door?"

"Mrs. Kolajecko?"

"She rented out part of the house to a young couple?"

"Mm-hmm. She sure did."

"Did you know Eddie Sandstone who lived there?"

Her eyes narrow. "Married a wetback."

"He married a young woman by the name of Estelle Cruz. Did you meet them?"

"I knew them to look at, that's all. Anna Kolajecko told me that girl up and left him. I said serves him right for marrying out of his race. It's not right them that go outside their own people. Causes everybody trouble. I would have put my foot down if one of my sons had brought home something like that."

This is a heavy trail for me to ride. "Did Mrs. Kolajecko ever mention the couple fighting?"

She sucks her lower lip into her mouth. "Can't say that she did."

"Do you remember if there was a big fuss over the wife leaving?"

"Why would he make a fuss? You ask me, she came to her senses before he did. I wouldn't have known she was gone if Anna hadn't told me."

"Anybody ever figure out the reason for the house burning down?"

"Faulty wiring is what I heard. That's no surprise—these houses is old. After it burned, my son came in and checked on my wiring and he said it was fine."

"Anybody die in the fire?"

"No, Anna was gone at the time. I think she lost her cat in the fire, though."

I thank her for her time and head back to the lot where the house stood. It's a deep lot. At the back it borders on a fence that's sagging badly. I walk to the fence and look around, considering the possibilities.

I used to work as a landman for an oil company and got to be familiar with the ways of terrain. I know what I'm looking for. I stand at the back and let my eyes scan the weeds that have grown up knee-high. Besides the concrete slab that the house sat on, there are weathered boards lying in a pile and a lot of random trash—torn newspapers, paper cups, and soda and beer cans. I don't see what I'm looking for, so I walk up to the slab and scan the area from there to the back fence.

From that vantage point, it's easy to spot exactly what I suspected I might find. If anybody had taken more interest in Estelle Cruz being gone, they would have looked to see if she was buried in the backyard, and they would have found her. Or at least I suspect it's her body buried back near the fence. The size of the plot is about right. What people don't know is that if someone is buried in bare ground without a coffin, the grass will never grow properly where the body was buried. It's like the land insists on displaying the evidence that a physical being has been abandoned there.

With the house burning down shortly after Estelle supposedly left, and Eddie moving out, it makes sense that attention never came in this direction. I could be jumping to conclusions. It could be that someone buried a big dog or some other animal back here, but one thing's for certain—there's a body of some kind here.

It's late afternoon, and I'll leave until tomorrow the task of persuading the sheriff that a forensics team needs to start digging.

CHAPTER 33

I t will soon be summer, and we've seen the last of the early morning cool air. My cows are listless this morning, as if they know they're in for a long, hot spell and they are gathering their strength for it. In the pasture next door, I hear one of the horses whinny, and I go to the gate to see what's up. Mahogany is galloping around the pasture with Blackie watching. When they spot me, they both trot over to me, sticking their noses over the fence for me to pat. I don't know that I'll ever love horses, but since the incident with the snake, I've come to have more respect for them.

Back at the house, Loretta is waiting for me, sitting on the front porch in one of the two rocking chairs. I can tell by her face that the news isn't good.

"Rodell?"

She nods. "Passed away early this morning without regaining consciousness."

I sit down in the other rocker and lean over with my arms on my knees. "Well . . ." There's a lot to say and nothing to say, and I'm caught between them.

"I'll get us some coffee," she says and goes into my house, easing the screen door closed behind her. When she comes back, she's got mugs of coffee with her. "I left sweet rolls on the counter. I didn't figure you'd want anything to eat right now."

"We all knew this was coming," I say.

"Still, you're never really prepared," she says.

We sit and rock for a few minutes without talking. Soon Loretta gets up and puts her hand on my shoulder. "I better get on. I've got a lot to do today."

After she leaves, I get up, feeling a little older than I did before I heard the news. Rodell was several years younger than me, but I've known him most of my life. Didn't like him much until recently. But still.

At work I spend a while returning phone calls. Mostly I talk to people about Rodell. Like me, everybody seems more shaken up than they ought to be. That's the trouble with a town fixture: it seems permanent, for good or bad.

But there's also a call from Wallace Lyndall telling me that on the advice of Jett they found out where to look for Scott Borland. "We picked him up about an hour ago. Figured you might want to have a word with him at some point. No hurry. He's not going anywhere."

"You sound amused. What's going on?"

He chuckles. "I know it's crazy, but I kind of like Borland. He's creative. Most criminals are too stupid to think up interesting stories, but Borland always comes up with some doozies. Wait until you hear what he has to say about the meth lab that blew up."

"Did anybody press him on whether he had anything to do with Jenny Sandstone's automobile accident?"

"I forgot about that. We've got evidence that will get his parole revoked and tack on plenty of time besides, so I didn't think it was urgent. You can ask him when you talk to him."

"I was going to call you this morning anyway. I've got another matter I need to bring up with you."

We agree to meet at the jail to talk to Scott Borland in an hour. After we get done with that, I'll present Lyndall with my evidence that Estelle Cruz Sandstone may be buried in the backyard of the house she lived in when she disappeared.

Scott Borland comes into the little interrogation room where Wallace Lyndall and I are waiting. He's looking pleased with himself. He's got bandages on both hands and some burn marks on his face and neck from the fire at the meth lab. Because of the bandages on his hands, he's got leg chains on instead of handcuffs. He's also got a restraint on his upper arms chained loosely behind so that his reach is limited.

"I can't seem to get any rest around here," Borland says as he flops into his chair. "Everybody is so damn chatty."

"There's an easy way to fix that," I say.

"What's that?"

"Tell us what we want to know without fooling around. Then you can get all the rest you need."

"If I'm going to have to talk to you, can I get a coke?"

Lyndall grumbles, but he gets up and goes to the door and asks the deputy in the hallway if he'll get his majesty a coke.

"Maybe you can answer a few questions while we're waiting," I say.

"I don't know if there's anything I can tell that would be of interest to you," Borland says.

"Why don't you tell the story of what you were doing in that meth lab?" Lyndall says. "That's kind of an entertaining story."

"You might be entertained," Borland says, looking pained, "but I'm the one who got hurt snooping around." He holds up his bandaged hands.

Borland's tale is that he and Jett were innocently walking around in the back of the vacant lot behind Borland's place, and they happened to notice smoke coming from a little shed way back there and thought they'd better investigate. Who was to guess that some unknown person had sneaked in there and set up some kind of laboratory?

"I know now," Borland says, "that I should have run out of there and called the police right away. But how was I to know somebody was out there doing something illegal?"

Lyndall laughs and slaps his leg. "That story gets better every time I hear it."

Borland gets a puppy-eyed look. "I don't know why you think I'm not telling the truth. I ain't done nothing wrong."

"We'll see."

The deputy sticks his head in and has brought not only a Dr. Pepper, but some chips as well.

Borland says, "I didn't want Dr. Pepper. That's a girl's drink. I wanted a Coca-Cola."

"Cool it," Lyndall says, an edge to his voice. "Take it or leave, but that's all you're getting."

"If you don't mind," I say, "I'd like to get you back in your cell for your beauty rest as fast as we can. So how about if you answer my questions."

"If I can, I certainly will."

"How did you know where Jenny Sandstone lives?"

The question startles him. He was most likely expecting to dance around the subject of the meth lab some more. "What makes you think I know where she lives?"

"Because I saw you sitting outside her house in your car."

"Oh, yeah, you said that before. What car are you thinking of?"

"A white Chevy. Looks like the same car that was parked in your front yard the first time I went there."

"Somebody must have borrowed it without me knowing it," he says.

"I see. Well I'd like to revisit some questions I asked you before to see if I can get a different set of answers. Did you cut the lock on Jenny Sandstone's gate and let her horses out?"

"I most certainly did not."

I've promised not to bring the two boys Jett paid to dope the horses into it unless I have to. But if it's necessary, their testimony will be bad for Jett Borland and will likely lead to Scott Borland. The vet who had the pills tested said they were pyrimethamine, and that a big dose could give a horse convulsions and even kill it. But for now, I'll keep the boys out of it.

"Did you or your son pay anybody to let the horses out onto the street?"

"Why would we pay good money for something like that?"

"I can't answer that. Did you?"

"Anybody says we did is lying."

I'll take that as a verification of the boys' story. "How about putting a timber rattler into the horse's stall? You ready to own up to that?"

"I didn't do that," he says, grinning, "But I sure wish I'd thought of it. Sounds like a fine idea. And even if I did do it, you'd never find out where I got that snake."

"Well, one thing is for damn sure. We know you had something to do with attacking Truly Bennett with a pipe."

Borland licks his lips. "I don't know any Truly Bennett."

"Black man. Keeping an eye on Jenny's horses. There's no way out of this one. Your fingerprints are there."

"Somebody set me up. They got a pipe from my property that I'd been handling and took and put it there."

Lyndall says, "Borland, everybody knows you hate anybody who isn't lily white. You're just the person to have done this."

"How was I to know there was a nigger there?"

"So you admit you were there?"

"I don't admit nothing. What I was saying is like a hypothetical." He smirks. "Either of you got a smoke? I could use a cigarette."

I gesture toward his hands. "Looks to me like you've had enough to do with fire lately."

"Is that all? 'Cause I'm ready to be done talking to you."

"No, there's one more thing I need go over with you again. You said you didn't have anything to do with Jenny Sandstone's car being rammed and run off the road. You sticking by that story?"

"You're damn right I am. I'm not taking a rap for something I flat did not do. I'm not saying I don't rejoice in it, and I think whoever did it is a hero, but it wasn't me. I might mess around with a person's belongings, but I'm not about to do anything that might get me an assault charge."

"Except for Billy Hinton," Lyndall says, referring to some case I know nothing about.

"That was different." Borland frowns and glares at me again. "You've got to believe me on this. I didn't have nothing to do with Jenny Sandstone's car. And neither did my son."

I think I believe him, so Lyndall and I decide that's all we need for now. I tell Lyndall I have something else I need to talk to him about. We go out for a sandwich and while we eat I lay out for him the history of Eddie Sandstone's two disappearances—first his daddy and then his first wife. And what led me to suspect that we'll find her body buried in the backyard of the house they lived in.

"I have to go along with you," he says. "You have one person disappear on you, it's a shame. But a second person, you start to think maybe somebody's getting a little careless."

"Problem is, all this happened a long time ago. I'm worried that the sheriff won't take this seriously. What do you think? We need to get a forensic team out to dig up the body. If the sheriff isn't on board, that could be a problem."

"Let me talk to Sheriff Hedges. He knows I'm usually not one to be impulsive."

I started out not caring for Lyndall much, but it turns out that it's his way to be cautious in the beginning. When we get to his office, he goes down the hall to talk to the sheriff and comes back with him.

The sheriff, Mike Hedges, is thin guy with a military haircut, mostly gray. He wears horn-rimmed glasses that make him look studious. I've met him a few times but don't know him well.

"Wally tells me you think you've got an idea where a body is buried. Things must be pretty quiet around Jarrett Creek for you to be looking for bodies in Bobtail."

"I didn't go looking for trouble. One thing led to another."

He laughs. "That's what we get in our business. Tell me how this came about." He pulls a chair up, sits down, and crosses his legs with one ankle propped on the other knee.

I tell him what led me to think I've found where Eddie Sandstone's first wife, Estelle, might be buried, including my interest in Howard Sandstone's disappearance.

When I wind up, he nods a few times. "One thing at a time. We're not going to jump to any conclusions here, but it sure would be interesting to see what's buried on that vacant lot."

"Might be somebody's German shepherd," I say.

"You don't think that any more than I do," he says, getting to his feet. "I'll call over to San Marcos and see if we can't get a forensic team here pronto." He disappears back to his office. I go get coffee for Lyndall and me while we wait. Hedges is back in fifteen minutes.

"They're going to have somebody over here later this afternoon. You know how they are."

We laugh. Any other law operation may have taken a while to send someone out, but the people who do anthropology forensics always seem excited by poking around in places where they might find old bodies. They drop everything for a good dig.

The first forensic man to arrive does a few bore tests in the soil and confirms there is biological matter somewhere down below. He says he'll have a team out tomorrow morning to start digging. He's like a hound dog on a scent, poised to go in for the retrieval. Sheriff Hedges and the forensic man discuss whether to set up crime scene tape overnight. Finally they decide they don't even know yet if there is a body or a crime here, and either way after all these years one more night without marking the spot won't matter.

I'm dog-tired when I get home and don't want to have anything to do with anybody. I don't have the heart to go to Jenny's tonight. If I did, I'd have to tell her that we might have found her sister-in-law's body, and I don't know how she'll react. I have to wait until I'm not so low about things before I break it to her. And by then there might be more to tell.

CHAPTER 34

I wake up the next morning with a question on my mind. Even if the body on the vacant lot is Estelle's, how is anybody going to prove who killed her? I remind myself that first things have to come first.

I spend a short time in the pasture and then I dress quickly, in my short-sleeved uniform and khaki pants. It's going to be hot today.

When I get to the dig site where the forensics team has set up, I have to park down the street and wade through gawkers. A team of three men is already at work. Yesterday the forensic man told me their procedure. It's tedious when they're considering historical remains. They have to document everything found in the vicinity of the body. He said you never know what might show up that will be used for criminal prosecution if it gets that far. And the longer the body has been there, the more tedious the work.

There's a tent set up over the suspicious area, but digging has not yet begun. First they photograph the area and gather all the artifacts. I know it will take hours before anything concrete emerges, but I've come to feel that I have some responsibility for Estelle Cruz, so I settle in to wait.

At noon they've just gotten around to digging when Lyndall comes by and takes me to get a sandwich. We kick around the situation with Scott Borland. It has been confirmed that the shed behind the property was being used to manufacture methamphetamine. Jett Borland was released from the hospital and immediately taken into custody, although the charges against him aren't as clear.

I'm relieved to get back to the dig site. I don't feel like I should be anywhere else right now. In the midafternoon they find the first bones.

Human bones. Now the work proceeds more slowly, as they have to sift all the surrounding soil for anything that might give some answers as to what happened here. Within a couple of hours, though, they know that we are dealing with a young woman who was wearing a light dress when she was put in the ground. The fabric is almost rotted away, but there's enough of it to get the general idea. The flesh is gone, and all that remains are bones, still arranged more or less like a skeleton, and snatches of brown hair.

One of the diggers brings me over to show me the most important part of the find. "You see the skull?" He points to the back of it. "Somebody hit her hard enough to crack it."

The easy part has been done. Now the remains and surroundings have to be taken to a forensic lab for identification. At least I'm able to supply a possible ID, which makes their job easier.

At the end of the day, Lyndall and I go back to his office, where Sheriff Hedges is waiting.

"We have to talk to Estelle Cruz's family and find out if we can get dental records or a DNA sample to make a positive ID," Hedges says. "You know where I can find them?"

I tell him that Estelle's sister works at the pharmacy downtown. As soon as I leave his office I go to talk to her. I feel better telling Graciella myself that we may have found what happened to her sister all those years ago, rather than leaving it to someone she doesn't know.

Her reaction is muted, as you would expect after so many years of not knowing. "I think about poor Mamma wanting to know why Estelle didn't come and see her when she was sick. I don't know how we could have known, though."

"Remember, they still have to identify her. It may not be Estelle."

She shakes her head. "You don't believe that."

"No, not really. The sheriff will be asking you for some DNA or dental records . . ."

"I have a box at home with her old things in it from when we sold the house after my daddy died. If there's anything like dental records, it will be in there. We'll have to see about DNA."

The Bobtail police will investigate the crime, but that doesn't mean I can let go of it. I have questions plaguing me. This whole thing started when Vera Sandstone told me she wanted me to find two missing people. She also said she was worried for Jenny's safety. If she had never brought up either of these things, no one would ever have found Estelle's body. Did she have an idea that Eddie had done away with Estelle? And that brings me to Howard. Did she think Eddie had something to do with his disappearance as well?

The Bobtail police will wait until they have an ID in hand before they start their investigation. But I don't have to wait for that. And the first thing I want to know is if Eddie really was gone when his wife disappeared, like he says he was. Where was he, and is there anybody to corroborate his story?

CHAPTER 35

Eddie Sandstone agrees to meet me at Vera's house. I had forgotten that Nate Holloway was going to move everything out, and it's already done. Eddie is stunned.

"What the hell?" he says. "Jenny didn't even leave me a lawn chair to sit in. I thought she was still recovering from the accident."

We're standing on the back deck looking out a Vera's garden, which is drooping without anyone to care for it.

"She hired someone to move things out. She didn't want to waste time. We could go to a coffee shop and talk, if you'd like."

"No, let's sit on the back steps here."

When I was driving over, it occurred to me that it was stupid to meet Eddie and confront him with what we found yesterday if no one knew where I was. Suppose he gets violent on me? I called Wallace Lyndall and told him my plans. He said he didn't think the sheriff would approve, but that he wasn't going to tattle on me.

"Now what did you get me over here for?" Eddie asks.

"I have a question to ask you. It's about your first wife."

"Marlene?"

"No, I'm talking about Estelle."

If I hadn't been looking for it, I wouldn't have noticed his flinch. "Estelle! I haven't thought about her in years. What about her?"

"At the time she left, you told people that you were out of town and when you got back she was gone. Can you tell me where you were?"

Color flares along his neck. "I was in Austin taking care of some business. What difference does it make?"

"Can anybody vouch for that?"

He looks outraged. "That was a helluva long time ago. How am I supposed to know whether anybody remembers seeing me back then? Why do you want to know?"

"There's been a body found in the backyard of the property you and Estelle lived in after you got married."

Eddie's mouth falls slack and he pales. "What? Who found it? What were they doing digging around there? Have they identified the body?"

"Not yet, but it would be a big coincidence for some other woman to be killed and buried in the backyard the same time your wife disappeared."

The red flush has reached his face. "I'll be damned. How was she killed?" Then he lets out a bark of laughter. "Wait a minute. I know what this is about." He gets up and walks down the steps into the backyard and turns to face me.

I don't know what he's talking about, so I need to tread carefully. "What do you think it's about?"

He shakes his head, his mouth twisting. "After Estelle left, Jenny got this idea that I had done away with her."

"You mean killed her? What would make her think something like that?"

"Jenny was always making up stories about me. She put it into Mamma's head, too. Is that what happened? You told Jenny there'd been a body found and she said she thought I killed Estelle?"

What happened is that Jenny told me she was away at college during this time, so I ignore the question. "If it is your wife, how do you think she died?"

He walks around a few paces, thinking, and then comes back to stand in front me. "I don't really want to say what I think."

An odd statement. "You understand why I'm asking if anybody can vouch for your story that you were in Austin when she *supposedly* left?"

"You think I killed Estelle. That's crazy. I didn't have any reason to kill her. I loved her." He has moved to stand over me, and I have to crane my neck to look up at him.

"Did you make any attempt to find her?"

"Of course I did. I called her sister and asked if she'd heard from her."

"Graciella says that you told her Estelle had gone to Lubbock. What made you think that?"

"She left me a note!" He slams his hand down into his fist, agitated. "She said something like it was a mistake for us to get married and she was leaving. Said she was going to Lubbock and not to try to find her."

"You know why she said she thought it was mistake to marry you?"

"We had a big argument. I was going hunting and she didn't want me to go. That's why I was in Austin, to firm up plans for the hunting trip. When I found the note, I thought she'd just gotten mad and gone off for a while. Never occurred to me that she wouldn't come back."

Just like his daddy went off and didn't come back. "Who did she know in Lubbock?"

He throws his hands up. "How am I supposed to know?"

"Do you still have the note?"

"Of course not! I was royally pissed off. I threw it in the trash."

"Shame you didn't keep it. You sure it was her handwriting?"

He blinks. "I never thought about it. Why would..." His eyes dart back and forth as if he's calculating. "You think whoever killed her wrote the note?"

I shrug. If there really was a note, it's long gone. "You have any idea who might have killed her?"

He looks down at his hands and when he speaks, his tone is bleak. "Like I said, I don't want to say what I think happened."

"Go ahead. I'm interested to hear your ideas."

He comes and sits back down. "Let me ask you something. Didn't it ever occur to you to wonder why my sister was so close to my mamma?" His tone is wheedling.

"Not really. Vera was a nice person. I think mothers and daughters can be close."

"You might consider that Mamma felt like she needed to keep an eye on Jenny."

"Why is that?"

He stares at me as if he's running some things through his mind. "I told you Jenny was always making up stories about me, and she was jealous of me. She was jealous when I married Estelle. I think she knew good and well she'd never find a man herself, so she didn't want me to be happy with my wife."

"You think Jenny killed Estelle?"

"All I'm saying is that Jenny had it in for me."

"That's not exactly the way she tells it."

He studies my face. "Oh, wait a minute. Did Jenny tell you some story about something that happened to her in high school?"

"She might have mentioned something about it."

He points at me. "That's exactly what I figured. Look, I don't know what she told you, but I want you to consider that it didn't happen the way she said it did."

"Why don't you tell me your version."

"It makes me sick to think about it." He screws his face up.

"Get it off your chest."

He gets up and starts pacing on the lawn again, hands shoved into his back pockets. "It was toward the end of school, and myself and two of my friends were celebrating in the living room."

"Celebrating what?"

"Graduation was coming up. Anyway, I guess Mamma and Daddy were out somewhere. And after a while Jenny came sashaying in and plunked herself down and asked if she could have a beer. I told her I didn't think she ought to, that she was too young, but she persuaded one of the boys to give her one. After a while she had another one, and before I know it, she was cozying up to one of them. And one thing led to another and they went in the bedroom."

"By themselves?"

"Yes."

"Jenny told me you videotaped her having sex."

"Oh, Jesus! She told you that? I didn't have any idea she would come up with a story like that. I knew she told Mamma something, but Mamma wouldn't talk about it."

"Who did she have sex with?"

"His name was Charlie Cole. My best friend. She flat-out seduced him."

Convenient that Charlie Cole is dead now so he can't corroborate the story. "And you didn't try to stop him?"

"Of course I did!"

"You tell him what he was doing was statutory rape?"

"We were kids. What did we know about that?"

"You said there were two boys there. Who was the other one?"

He puts his hands up to stop me. "These questions are coming thick and fast and I can't help wondering if maybe I ought a call a halt to it. I didn't do anything, and I'm beginning to think you're trying to railroad me."

"So you're not going to tell me the name of the second boy who was involved?"

"I don't think it's fair. He didn't do anything. He left before Jenny and Cole went off to the bedroom. Besides, he doesn't live here anymore and I've lost track of him."

"Let me worry about tracking him down."

He's shaking his head. "I'm sorry, I'm not going to drag him into this. I don't think it's right."

I leave it for now. I have another source I can use to check on the facts. "You're right, your story is different from Jenny's. And now you're telling me you think Jenny might have killed Estelle?"

"I didn't say that. I don't know who killed Estelle—if it really is Estelle that you dug up. All I know is that Jenny was always jealous of me, and she didn't like me being with Estelle. I thought it was because

Estelle was Mexican, but pretty soon I figured out that Jenny wouldn't like me marrying anybody."

I don't believe Eddie's version of what happened, but I he's got a persuasive way about him. How much do we really know about people? Jenny and I have forged a good friendship, but it's based on the present—the funny outlook she has on life, her interesting line of chatter, and partly it's because she's a convenient friend, living next door. But what do I really know of her? She has never revealed much of her innermost self. Now that I'm questioning so much about her and her family, I have to face facts. Anyone could have bashed in Estelle's skull—including Jenny.

CHAPTER 36

It turns out that Mike Tolleson, the guy Jenny had a crush on in high school and who supposedly was the recipient of the rape film, is easy to track down. The trouble is he lives in Houston and is an engineer working on a project at NASA. He tells me he works about ten hours a day and doesn't really have time to talk to me. "What is it you want from me anyway?" I can't tell if he's pompous or overworked.

"I need some help on a case I'm working on in Bobtail that involves someone you knew back in high school."

"High school? I don't really keep up with anybody from high school."

"Do you your folks still live in Bobtail?"

"No, they moved to Houston after my sister and I both settled here. Who is it you're asking about?"

"Do you remember a family by the name of Sandstone?"

The line is so silent I'm thinking for a minute it's gone dead. Finally he says, "What do you want with me?"

"It'd be a lot easier if I could talk to you in person."

I could ask him on the phone if he ever saw a videotape like the one Jenny described, but I want to be able to see him in person. I may be kidding myself, but I think if he's lying I'll be able to spot it.

He finally agrees that if I come to his work tomorrow he'll slip out for a half hour and talk to me.

He meets me at a sandwich place near where he works. We grab a table in the back of the café.

He's a goofy-looking guy who stoops as if he's used to being in a position hunching over a computer screen or a microscope. I'll never know which, because I don't waste valuable time chatting. I want to get down to business.

"I'll tell you straight out, I'm here because I've got two different versions of a story and I need you to tell me which one is right."

"Suppose I don't know anything?"

"That'll be a different kind of answer."

He takes a bite of his sandwich and chews patiently.

"Jenny Sandstone told me that you saw a video of an incident that involved her. If that's true, I'd like you to tell me what's on the video."

He swallows, but it looks like he's trying to swallow a lot more than he was chewing. He puts his sandwich down and takes a drink of his iced tea. "I'm not sure what you're talking about," he says. This is why I wanted to see him in person. There's no question he's trying to dodge the truth. His cheeks are lit up, and he won't look at me.

"She told me, so it's no surprise. I just need to hear your version."

"I don't really want to talk about it. I'm not one of those men who likes to watch things like that. My wife and I don't go in for X-rated movies and such."

"What you're saying is that the video had sex in it?"

"If you already know what's on it, why are you asking?"

"I told you, I'm trying to corroborate a story. Who showed you the video?"

"Eddie Sandstone."

"Why did he show it to you?"

"I don't know what his purpose was, but I wish he hadn't."

"I need you to tell me what you saw on the video."

He starts to get up. "I have to get back. That's all I can tell you."

I grab his arm. "Sit down. It'll be a lot easier on you if you tell me privately than if I have to get a subpoena. And it'll be easier on Jenny, too."

So he tells me. It's a relief to me to know that Jenny's story holds up and that Eddie Sandstone is a liar. If he lied about this, I'm pretty sure he's lied about other things as well. And I'm pretty sure that his wife's disappearance and his daddy's disappearance are no coincidence.

I've decided to make one more stop while I'm in Houston. Even though Rodell will never know what I'm up to, I feel like I have to honor him by following through with something he said the last time I saw him.

I call to make sure Ellen's husband, Seth, is in his office today. I stop for coffee at a Starbucks to fortify myself and then locate the office where Forester works. It's a warehouse-type building large enough to house huge road graders and bulldozers. The offices take up a small portion of the vast structure.

A scrawny clerk directs me to Forester's office without asking what my business is. Forester's office is open to anyone to walk in. The man himself is ensconced behind a massive industrial-grade metal desk covered with piles of papers. At the sound of my footsteps he looks up and freezes. He glances over to another desk that takes up the other side of the room. There's no one sitting there, and I suspect Forester is as glad as I am that there's no one to witness our conversation.

"What do you want?" he says. He plunks his beefy arms on the desk and glares at me.

"I'm here to see if we can come to some agreement so I don't have to keep chasing you out of Jarrett Creek."

"Maybe if you'd mind your own business that would do the trick."

"The well-being of people in my town is my business, and I can't have someone coming in and creating problems."

Forester's smile is nasty. "Oh, I get it. You're making Ellen your business. Well, I can tell you that you aren't the first man to come sniffing around my wife. And my guess is she took somebody up on it a time or two."

237

If I were inclined to escalate the situation, I'd ask him why he'd make such a crude suggestion about a woman he supposedly still loves. Instead, I say, "She isn't your wife anymore. But that's beside the point. What I want you to understand is that I keep a peaceful town and you have been disturbing the peace and I want it to stop."

He gets up, and I'm reminded of how much bigger a man he is than I am—not to mention the ten years I have on him. "You have a lot of nerve coming in here ordering me to stay away from my wife," he says.

At that moment another large man of forty or so steps into the room. "Excuse me, gents," he says, "Sorry to interrupt, but I've got to get some blueprints out of my desk." He is so intent on not looking at us, that it's pretty clear he has sensed a heavy atmosphere in the room and wants nothing to do with it.

I clap my hat on my head. "That's okay, I was just leaving. I had a message to deliver and I've delivered it."

I expect I haven't seen the last of Seth Forester, but at least I've put him on notice. The only part of the exchange I didn't like was his insinuation that the reason I warned him away was because I have designs on Ellen. For the first time, I wonder if I'm fooling myself by thinking I would have done the same for anyone. Would I? I've known women who loved to get men into trouble with each other, playing the poor helpless female. I don't want to think that's what Ellen Forester is up to, but I don't know enough about her background to judge that.

Back in Jarrett Creek I stop by Ellen Forester's gallery. There's no class going on, and I find her in her little office. She's startled to see me, but I'm beginning to think she's always startled when a man shows up.

"I need to warn you that I've done something that might blow back on you."

"I already know," she says. "Seth called me as soon as you left his office."

"I imagine he wasn't too happy."

She stands up. "Neither am I. I know you're trying to protect me, but with Seth it's better if you leave things alone. He's a man who craves attention. If you ignore him, he's likely to get bored and stop making trouble."

"I can't have somebody coming in to my town and causing that kind of trouble."

"Your town?" Her voice is cold. "I feel like I'm in an old western. The town doesn't belong to you. You're interfering where you shouldn't be."

I feel like I've been slapped. She's right, I suppose. The town is different from the way it was the first time I was chief of police. More people live here that weren't born here. My sentimental tip of the hat to Rodell Skinner seems to have had me overstep myself. "I didn't intend to cause you trouble," I say.

She crosses her arms and glares at me. "Let me handle Seth in the future, if you don't mind."

"That's not the way it's going to work. Like I told Seth, I can't have him coming around here causing a ruckus and harassing you. In case you haven't noticed, I'm chief of police here. It's not interfering when I'm keeping the peace."

Her cheeks flare. "It is when you're acting like a couple of teenagers. I don't belong to anybody and I won't have two men fighting over me." All of sudden she stops, looking panicky. "I shouldn't have said that."

But she did say it, and now it's in front of both us and I don't know why I didn't notice before that I was showing more interest than I even knew I had in her. "Sorry if I overstepped," I say. I turn on my heels and I'm out of there like a scalded dog.

It has been a couple of days since I checked in on Jenny, and it's time I brought her up to date on everything that's gone on. After I've changed into my jeans, drunk a cup of coffee, and gone down to the pasture to check on my cows, I give her a call. She doesn't sound wildly happy to hear from me, but she says she's doing better and that I should come over.

She's morose, but at least she's not drunk. We sit in her living room, and she doesn't offer me a glass of wine, which is fine with me.

First I fill her in on the Borlands. "Scott's back in jail and I think he's going to be there for a long time to come. We've got an assault charge on him, which revokes his parole and adds a few years. As for Jett, they're putting together evidence that he was involved in a meth operation."

She nods but doesn't seem particularly impressed. "Have you gotten anywhere on finding out who hit my car?"

"Highway patrol says they don't think they're going to be able to track down whoever did it, but I'm not ready to give up on it. I have an idea, and if I'm right, it won't be long before we'll know."

She shrugs. Suddenly I'd like to shake some sense into her. She's behaving like a child, pouting and refusing to be communicative. "Look," I say, "I know you've had a rough time, but . . ."

"Eddie called me." Her voice is like poison. "He said you talked to him and that you don't believe me about what happened with those boys."

"He told you that?"

"You're damn right he did. I thought I talked to you in confidence. It never occurred to me that you'd go blabbing to him about what I said."

"That's not exactly how it happened." How can I tell her that Eddie's part in her rape is the least of the things I believe he's guilty of? And that as of now I have no way to prove what I believe he's done. I don't want to tell her that I went to Mike Tolleson and that he confirmed her story. I can't help thinking that if she knows I spoke with

Tolleson, she'll feel even more violated. "Do this for me," I say, rising. "Reserve judgment for now."

"Judgment on what? On whether you can be trusted? Whether with my mamma dead there's no one I can trust? Did you tell anybody else what happened to me in high school? Are you blabbing it all over town? Did you tell Will?" She's almost crying.

"Of course I didn't tell Will or anybody else. It hurts me that you think I would do that."

She doesn't say anything, but she looks desolate.

"Are you going back to work soon?"

"I have to. If I don't, I'll lose my mind."

"I hope you do. It will be good for you. And meanwhile, stay away from Eddie. And be careful."

"Careful?"

"There are things I'm not talking to you about. But until they're resolved I want you to be alert."

Her features soften a little. "Maybe you should tell me everything."

"I'm not going to do that. Not right away. But I want you to know I have your best interests at heart, whether you think so right now or not."

She searches my face, and for a moment I see the old Jenny. "I'll take your word for it."

CHAPTER 37

With a little pressure, Eddie gave me the names of the two people who can corroborate his story that he was in Austin when his wife disappeared. I'll need to make a trip to Austin to interview them. I'm reluctant to make the drive, not even sure if it's worth it. After all, even if they say he was with them, it doesn't mean he didn't kill Estelle before he left. But I know I have to follow through. If we're ever able to charge Eddie with killing his wife, we're going to need every scrap of evidence we can find to make the charge stick.

Eddie said he used to go hunting with the two men, and the reason he went to Austin was to discuss their next hunting trip. The first one I reach laughs and says he doesn't remember anything about it. But the other one, a serious-sounding man named Hank Parker, says he does remember. He says he'll meet with me in a couple of hours and gives me the name of a café where we can have lunch while we talk.

He's a paunchy man with a couple of extra chins. He attacks his sandwich with gusto.

"Have you talked to Eddie recently?" I say. I'm suspicious that maybe Eddie called him and urged him to "remember" their meeting around the time Estelle disappeared.

"No, I haven't. Well, I mean until he called me and told me he'd given you my name."

"Did he remind you that he'd been here to discuss a hunting trip that weekend?"

"He did, but I would have remembered anyway." He looks uneasy.

"Why do you say that?" I say.

"I don't want to talk out of turn and get Eddie in trouble. But I have to be honest with you. There were things about that visit that always bothered me."

"Like what?"

"First of all, it was unusual for Eddie to come all this way to talk about a hunting trip. We always arranged the trips over the phone. Not that that's a big deal, but I thought it was odd."

"Did he say why he came instead of calling?"

"No sir, but I got the sense that he was feeling a little trapped. He'd just gotten married, and he said his wife wasn't happy with him leaving her to go hunting. . . ." His voice trails away.

"Seems strange that if she didn't want him to go on the trip, he'd rub it in by leaving her to arrange it."

"That's what I thought, too," he says eagerly, seizing on my suggestion as a way of explaining himself. "Eddie seemed to want to be sure she knew who was boss. It wasn't the first time I'd seen Sandstone act that way. We used to call him The Big Bull. We all went to high school together."

Big Bull, as in bully, I think to myself.

"You said there were other reasons why you remembered the incident?"

"That's when his wife left. Funny thing was, he didn't tell me himself. He called to say he wasn't going to go through with the trip and never mentioned that his wife was gone. I found out later from John, the other guy we go hunting with. I thought it was odd, that's all. Excuse me a minute." He's done with his sandwich and goes back to the counter and comes back with a piece of lemon pie and coffee.

It looks good, so I go get myself the same thing. When we're started on the pie, I say, "When was the last time you saw Eddie?"

"That was the last time I saw him—when he was here to plan the trip. For some reason, after that we let things drift. John and I still go every year, but Eddie kind of dropped out."

"I know this is a stretch to remember," I say, "but when Eddie was with you for that planning session, did you get the sense that anything was troubling him?"

He's quiet for a while, working on the pie. Finally he lays his fork down. "I wish I had something concrete to tell you, but all I can say is, when I think about that weekend, my mind shies away from it. I've always had an itchy feeling that things weren't right—but I can't tell you why."

Alice Blackman is one of those women who turn ethereal looking as they age. She wears her straight white hair long and has on a loose gray dress that makes her hazel eyes look smoky. Her smile is soft and her voice a husky contralto. "I'm happy to talk to you about Howard. He was such a good friend."

Her living room is old-fashioned, but I find it comfortable and easy to be in, with its pale, stuffed chairs and highly polished mahogany furniture. She tells me that her husband died a few years ago, and that although her house feels too big, she hasn't had the will to move.

"You and Howard were in the choir together, I understand."

"Howard had a lovely tenor voice. He stood right behind me and I loved hearing him sing."

"I don't mean to make you uncomfortable, but there are people who thought you and Howard had a bit of a flirtation going on."

She chuckles. "I knew those rumors were going around, and I won't deny I had moments—hearing his lovely voice behind me—that I wished that we could be spirited away somewhere back in time and meet before we were both joined with our beloved spouses." Her smile lights up her gray eyes. "I don't know if Howard ever felt that way because we never talked about it. Howard was a gentleman through and through. He would never have cheated on his Vera. Just as I never once cheated on my husband."

"How do you suppose the rumors got started?"

She arranges the folds of her dress, as if she is arranging her ideas about how to proceed. "Howard and I had a kind of sympathy between us. Do you know what I mean by that? A deep understanding. We sometimes talked with one another about things that troubled us. And I suppose people thought we were flirting when we'd sit off by ourselves. But it wasn't that way. We simply understood each other."

"What troubled Howard?"

She looks startled. "Oh. The usual things. He worried about his daughter. She struggled with feeling awkward, as many young girls do at that age. It didn't help that her brother was so handsome and had such confidence."

"Did he worry about his son as well?"

"Not usually." She clasps her hands in front of her. "But something happened not long before Howard went away. He told me he was very angry with his son. He didn't say why and I didn't want to pry. Teenaged boys are always at odds with their fathers. My husband and I raised two boys, and as regular as a clock, they discovered around age fifteen or sixteen that their father was dull and stupid and that they were brilliant and knew everything there was to know about the world." She laughs gently. "But of course they got over it. I told Howard that Eddie would get over it, too."

"He disappeared soon after he told you how angry he was with his son?"

She sighs. "I always wondered if maybe he went for a drive to think about things and maybe he had an accident and was never found. It may be that one day his car will be found in a lake, submerged with his body in it. It could be something as simple as that."

It could be that simple, but I don't think so.

"The sad part," Alice says, "is that after Howard left, I heard that Eddie acted out a great deal. He needed his father, and Howard wasn't around. A shame, really. Eddie had a good future. Howard was so proud that he was going to SMU. Howard was a smart man, but he was ashamed of being a carpenter. He hoped that Eddie would make more of himself than he was able to."

Eddie Sandstone told several people that he wanted to help tear down the Bobtail Ridge subdivision for sentimental reasons, but if there's anybody feeling sentimental about the subdivision coming down, it's Rich O'Connor, the original contractor. As soon as I drive through the gates, I see him standing by his SUV looking out over the worksite, hat tilted back on his head. He's standing on a slight rise of ground, watching the far end of the subdivision where dust is rising from bulldozers attacking houses.

I pull in behind him and get out to say hello. "They're going right ahead," I say.

"Once backers get the financing together for something as big as this shopping center, they don't waste any time," he says. There's a wistful sound to his voice, even though he told me he knew the materials were shoddy and he wasn't proud of this subdivision.

"Seems like they barely got the contractor nailed down," I say. "LoPresto told me a week or so ago."

"That's right, but that was part of the deal. LoPresto said he could get started right away. Not like some of these old boys who drag their feet. I've seen LoPresto work before and he's not one to fool around."

"Did you put in a bid for the job?"

"Me? Hell, no. I retired a few years ago and I spend every second I can fishing. Only reason I'm not down at the gulf right now is because the realtors who put the deal together are paying me a fat consulting fee. What are you doing here? You a demolition groupie?"

I laugh. "No, I need to talk to one of the guys I know working on the demolition crew."

Back in my truck, I drive toward the area of houses that are being torn down. Most of them I pass are empty and the streets deserted, a contrast to the last time I was here when people were packing up cars and moving vans and heading out. There's an eerie feel to the place, as if ghosts are drifting through the streets. I chuckle to myself. Fanciful thoughts.

Halfway through the subdivision, movement catches my eye. I glance over to see Eddie Sandstone walking down the street dressed in coveralls and a baseball hat. Just the man I wanted to see, but he seems oddly out of place, and I wonder what he's up to. I slow my truck and hang back, watching. He stops in front of one of the houses and peers at it, then walks along the side of it and disappears into the back. When he comes back to the street, he goes to the next house and walks back into the backyard, then repeats the process with a third house. This time when he comes back, he glances down the street and sees my truck. He freezes, reminding me of a deer startled by headlights at dusk.

I drive up and stop at the curb next to him. His face and clothing are covered with red dust. "Hey, Eddie, I thought you were working demolition."

He takes off his baseball hat and sunglasses and wipes his brow with his handkerchief. "Yeah, I'm taking a break. Thought I'd walk around and take a look at some of the houses. What are you doing here?"

"I'm looking for you. A question came up with regard to your daddy's disappearance. Thought maybe you could answer it for me."

His sunglasses are back on, so I can't see his eyes, but his jaw tightens. "I don't think I have much to add."

"It's about your daddy's car."

"What about it?"

"The day he walked out on your family, that morning he hitched a ride from his boss, Curly. He said his car wouldn't start. What I want to know is, how did it get repaired?"

He gives a sharp bark of laughter. "How the hell should I know?"

"Did he have a regular service station he went to for car repairs?"

"Shame you didn't think up that question before Mamma died. She might have known the answer."

"When your daddy left, he drove off in his car?"

Eddie clears his throat and spits off to the side. "That's exactly what he did. How he got the car running again is anybody's guess." He glances at his watch. "Sorry I can't help you more. I better get on back. Break time is over."

"Let me drive you back down there."

"I won't turn down a ride."

I pull up a half block from the site, and we watch as a bulldozer works. There's something violent about the way it edges back and then rams the house. The driver seems to have it down to an art, hitting it at just the right spot. As soon as the dozer backs up, the house starts to crumple in on one corner. Down the block, other equipment is pushing debris into a huge heap, leaving behind clean concrete foundations.

"How do they get rid of the foundations?" I say.

"A pile driver comes in and breaks it up. They clear a block at a time and then come in with the pile driver." He swings the door open and climbs out. A guy in a hardhat waves him over.

I drive away and stop in front of the houses Eddie was so curious about and retrace his steps, going into the backyard of each of the houses. Eddie was looking for something. For a wild moment I wonder if it's possible that another body is buried in one of these backyards. But the signs that led me to Estelle's body aren't apparent here. What was Eddie here for? Is he thinking of stealing something? Copper or fixtures? I walk inside one of the houses. If that's what he was planning, he's too late. The house is stripped bare. And besides, he didn't come inside.

I go back out and stand on the sidewalk and look from one house to the next. Three houses that will soon be down to the concrete, and a day or so later, even that will be gone. It occurs to me that maybe Eddie was interested in these house because that's where he and his daddy were working when Howard walked out on the family. And then I remember why Curly said he was annoyed when Howard walked out the day he did. They were pouring concrete that day. A shiver catches me. Ghosts in the street may not be so far off.

I get back to O'Connor just as he's walking to his SUV. Apparently he was here to meet someone, because he waves at a pickup that's just pulling away. I honk at O'Connor, and he stops to wait for me.

"Let me ask you something," I say. "Do you keep any records of when your foundations were poured on the original subdivision?"

He stares at me. "Why would you want to know a thing like that?"

"I have a good reason. Did you keep those records?"

He pulls his hat off his head and scratches his thinning hair. "Funny you should ask. I've had my wife going through my files to make sure there was nothing that the new people need to know in terms of problems we found—Indian remains, stuff like that. After that, we're fixing to throw out all the paperwork. Once these places are all torn down, there's no reason to keep any of it."

I follow him to his house, where he said the records are in his home office. My heart sinks when we walk in. There are boxes of files and stacks of folders lying on every surface, including a couple of card tables that have been set up. "Look at this mess," he says. "If I had to find something in here, I'd be in big trouble. But my wife can find any piece of paper you want. I don't know how she does it. I'll go get her."

His wife is a stout woman who carries her belly out in front of her like she's got pillows stuffed into her clothes. Her handshake is as firm as a man's. "Rich says you need some concrete pour records. Is that right?"

I give her the approximate date I'm looking for.

"Hold on. It might take me a minute." Instead of diving in like some people might do, she stands with her hands on her hips and surveys the room. Then she points at a couple of stacks of paper on one of the card tables. She bustles over and starts pawing through them, and within three minutes she says, "Here we go."

"If everybody kept records this good, I suspect there'd be a lot less trouble in the world," I say.

She grunts. "All it takes is one time being sued by somebody. After that you keep every piece of paper that ever comes through. I don't mind telling you, I'll be glad when that subdivision is flat and we can haul all this junk out of here."

I jot down the addresses of the places where the concrete was poured at the same time Howard Sandstone disappeared.

"Is that it?" O'Connor says, frowning.

"Who's in charge of bringing those houses down? I'd like to know when these particular ones get razed."

"I'll talk to the dozer people. They'll have a schedule. I'll call you with the info."

I drive back to the subdivision long enough to assure myself that the addresses I jotted down are the very ones Eddie was looking at.

CHAPTER 38

As soon as I leave Rich O'Connor, I go straight to talk to Wallace Lyndall. I've come to see him with a plan that sounds cockeyed, but when I lay it out for him, he's game. "It gets a little boring dealing with people like that dingbat Borland. You're talking about a little excitement."

We agree it won't do to leave the sheriff out of it. I explain to Hedges what I suspect and that I've enlisted Lyndall to help me do a stakeout. He's not entirely onboard but he says, "You're due a pass for finding that girl's body, so I'll go along with you. If you two geezers want to do a stakeout, go ahead. Just don't get yourselves killed."

O'Connor calls with the information I need. He says the bulldozer schedule is loose, so I check back every day in case I'm off by a house or two. Yesterday bulldozers cleared the surface of the lots I'm interested in, and today the pile drivers broke up the concrete foundations, leaving rubble behind to be scooped up by earthmovers. It's time for Lyndall and me to make our move.

There's not much moon tonight, but with the houses gone in the area Lyndall and I are watching, there's plenty of ambient light. We hole up in a house still standing down the street and take turns keeping a lookout. Lyndall says he'll watch for a couple of hours while I get some sleep and then we'll switch. Next thing I know, he's poking me. "Got some action," he says. "Let's see if it's just somebody stealing wood."

I rub my face to wake myself up and stand next to Lyndall, looking out at the street. A big, dark car drives past slowly and continues down the street. "This guy drove by a minute ago," Lyndall says. "He turned around down at the corner and came back. That's when I figured I ought to wake you up."

The car pulls to the side of the road near the area we're watching, and we hear the engine turn off. You'd think the night would be silent after that, but it's alive with the sound of mosquitoes and tree frogs and cars on the freeway.

A man gets out of the car dressed in dark clothing. He's turned so that I can't see his face, but he's the size and shape of Eddie Sandstone. He opens the trunk and takes some things out. I watch through binoculars and see that he's carrying a shovel and a black bag that looks heavy. Finally he turns just enough so I get a clear look. "Bingo," I whisper to Lyndall.

At first Eddie stands still, moving his head only enough to look from one ruined foundation to the next of the three in front of him. Even as far away as I am, I can almost sense the agitation he must be feeling, wondering exactly where he should dig. He walks over and picks up a couple of chunks of rubble and tosses them aside. He paces back and forth, stopping once and putting his hands on top of his head, looking at each of the three lots.

He comes to some decision and paces off several steps toward the back of one of the foundations. There he starts picking up concrete and hurling it away. He moves faster and faster until his motions are frenzied. For thirty minutes he doesn't pause, clearing the area. Then he stops for a minute and takes something out of the black bag. Turns out to be water. He drinks and wipes his forehead. It's a hot night, and I imagine sweat dripping off of him.

When he starts back to work, this time he uses the shovel. And before long he stops and crouches down, shining a flashlight. Then he stands up abruptly and walks away to the sidewalk where he pauses for a few seconds, looking at the sky. Then he goes back to his dig site. At one point he stops, comes to an alert position, and peers around like he senses that he's being watched. When he resumes work, his movements become faster again. He must have a substantial hole by now. He stops, turns on the flashlight again and shines it around where he's working. He shuts off the light, crouches down, reaches out with his hand, and pulls something out from the earth which he then drops like it was on fire.

"Jesus," Lyndall breathes.

Sandstone sinks back on his haunches and is still for moment and then reaches into the earth again.

"I guess it's time," I say.

As Sandstone goes back to his grisly job, Lyndall and I ease out of the vacant hull of the house where we've been watching and walk toward him. His back is to us, but suddenly he either hears or senses us because he stops cold.

I've brought a powerful flashlight and I shine it on him. "Eddie, you might as well put the shovel down," I say. "Your work is done here."

He throws his arm up to cover his face. "What the hell are you doing?" he says. His bravado has always served him well.

"We could ask you that," I say.

I shine the flashlight into the pit. It's a shallow grave, with the body of a man partly exposed. The body is better preserved than Estelle's because of the concrete that has protected it all this time. There's still a lot of dirt covering part of the body, but you can see that Howard Sandstone was wearing blue jeans and a short-sleeved shirt when he was buried. His hands have been crossed over his chest. I'm surprised Eddie took the time to do that. There must have been some regret about what he did.

Eddie has a grip on the shovel, and I see him calculating whether he can get in a good blow and manage to break away.

I ease my Colt out of my holster and hold it where he can see it in the light. "Put the shovel down."

"I've got every right to be here," he says, "There's no need to point a gun at me."

"Eddie. The shovel." I motion with my gun for him to get rid of the shovel. Sandstone tosses it aside, and Lyndall steps away to call for a squad car as backup. Sheriff Hedges told us he'd have officers on the alert waiting for the call.

"They'll be along in a minute," Lyndall says to me when he comes back.

"Turn around now, Eddie. I need to put these cuffs on you," I say.

"You can't arrest me. I didn't do anything."

"Just being here at the scene, digging up a body looks suspicious enough to take you in. We'll sort it out at the station."

Eddie's head drops forward onto his chest. "I don't believe this," he mutters, but he turns around anyway, and I have the pleasure of clipping the cuffs on him. "You think you know what's going on, but you don't," he says. "I can explain everything."

"We've got a few minutes. Go ahead and spin your tale." I train the flashlight back on the scene so he doesn't have a chance to forget that we are talking about his daddy lying there.

"I got to thinking about my daddy disappearing when we were working on these houses, and it occurred to me that somebody could have done him in and buried the body here, knowing that they were going to pour concrete the next day."

"Uh-huh. And who do you think might have done such a thing?"

"Somebody like that Greevy guy. The one who made fun of my daddy leaving us."

"Eddie, I'm pretty sure you're the one who buried your daddy here."

"Not me. Oh no, not me. I didn't touch him. Whoever did this had a grudge against him. You know, maybe it wasn't Greevy. Daddy was flirting with some woman. Probably her husband got wind of it and . . ."

"Must have been hard on you all those years knowing your daddy was lying here," I say. "And then to find out they were going to tear this place down. Scared you. You figured they'd find the body. So you got yourself hired on the demolition crew to keep an eye out for when they got close to the area where you'd buried him. My guess is there'll be evidence of what you did. You were probably in a hurry."

Sirens are coming in the distance. Eddie's head jerks toward the sound. "Whatever happened, I didn't have anything to do with it. You can't prove a thing."

The sirens wind down as two squad cars turn off the road into the subdivision. The revolving lights on the cars makes this scene of destruction look like something out of a war movie.

CHAPTER 39

Rodell's funeral is a fine affair. He would have been pleased. All his old drinking buddies show up in suits and ties and act like they are saying good-bye to Saint Rodell Skinner. There is a wake afterward at Bill White's place, but I don't have the heart to attend. There will be a lot of carousing and rehashing old drinking stories.

Instead, I take Loretta out to eat at a barbecue place between here and College Station. I tell her I'll take her someplace fancy another night, but I need to unwind after all that has gone on in the last few weeks. She's a good sport, and she goes along and acts like all she wants out of life is a good plate of barbecue. I ask how she's doing with her painting.

"I don't want to talk about it, Samuel. It embarrasses me. I know how important art is to you, and I don't really feel like what I'm doing is art. I just like the way watercolor goes onto the paper. I like how the brush feels in my hand and the way . . ." She laughs. "I said I wasn't going to talk about it, and here I go sounding like I know what I'm doing."

"Is Ellen a good teacher?" I'm still feeling the sting of Ellen's anger over my confrontation with her ex-husband, and I wonder if and when she'll forgive me.

"I like her, but I don't have a teacher to compare her to. She's been a little skittish lately, what with the window being broken." She puts her fork down and looks me in the eye. "Speaking of skittish, I want to ask you how Jenny is. I haven't seen her since all that stuff came out about her brother. I left some coffee cake and sweet rolls on her porch a couple of times, but I haven't heard from her."

The day after we caught Eddie digging up his daddy's body, I sat down with Jenny and told her the circumstances of Estelle's and Howard's bodies being found. I kept it short, knowing that hearing it all would be a shock and details could be filled in later. "I'm sorry to have to tell you all this," I said. "I know you didn't trust Eddie, but even so finding out he is suspected of killing his wife and your daddy is a lot to take in."

She showed hardly any emotion. "I feel numb," she said. "I only wish Mamma was still alive so she could know that Daddy didn't just walk out on us."

After that, Jenny more or less disappeared for a while. She hasn't been answering her phone, so I've left messages telling her I'll be here when she's ready to talk. The only time I see her is when she's leaving for work.

"She's had a hard time," I say to Loretta. "First her mamma dying and then finding out her brother might have killed his wife and maybe her daddy, too. Not to mention needing the time to heal from that accident."

"She doesn't take kindly to people fussing over her, does she?"

"Give her time. I know she appreciates what people do for her; she's wrung out, that's all." I don't tell her that Jenny has kept me at arm's length, too.

When I get home that evening, I find a note stuck on my door that reads, "Samuel, I'm unhappy with the way our last conversation went. If you're free, I'd like you to come to dinner one night so we can talk about it. Ellen." I almost call her then and there but decide it'll keep a day or so.

Eddie Sandstone is cocky and seems to be confident that no evidence will be found to merit charging him with murder. The fact that he was caught digging up his daddy's body is enough to keep him in jail for the time being, but nothing incriminating him has been found at either of the gravesites so far. We need more evidence to pin one of the murders on him.

I go back to Temple and talk to his ex-wife and his estranged wife. I sensed that Marlene was afraid of him, but no matter how I push, I can't get her to admit to it, much less to tell me why.

I've come to the point where I feel like it's a personal crusade to get Eddie off the street, and Lyndall and Hedges aren't far behind me in that feeling. But we're at a dead end.

I suggest to Sheriff Hedges that we make a more thorough sweep to find the shop that repaired Eddie's car after Jenny's accident. "If we can at least get him on attempted murder, he'll spend time in prison." Hedges says he'll put more men on it.

What I keep coming back to is a question: if Eddie did try to kill Jenny, why? Why right after Vera died? He could have attacked her anytime, so why wait? Is there something Eddie was afraid that Jenny would find when she was going through Vera's things that might implicate him in Howard's death? Maybe Jenny knows something and doesn't even realize what it is.

I call Jenny at work and tell her I don't want to intrude, but that I really need to talk to her.

"I'm sorry I've been standoffish," she says. "I needed some time to process everything. Mourning Mamma. Trying to figure out how to go on with my life."

"I understand. You don't have to apologize."

"I was going to call you," she says. "Eddie plans to sell Mamma's house. I'd like you to go with me to see it one last time."

When I arrive at Vera's, Jenny is standing by her car waiting for me. She looks good, although she's lost a little too much weight. I was afraid we'd have an awkward moment, but she reaches out and takes my hand and squeezes it. "I really appreciate your coming over. You've done so much. I promise you, I'm going to get over all this. It'll just take some time."

She's quiet as we walk through the empty rooms of the house. Then we go out on the back deck and sit on the steps.

"I had a reason for calling," I say. "You know we haven't been able to make a case against Eddie for either of those deaths. I know he's guilty, but we just don't have enough."

She nods. "He was always able to weasel out of things."

"I also believe it was Eddie who ran you off the road that night. But I don't know why."

She looks at me and shrugs. "General principles, most likely. He always hated me."

"But why then? Why right after Vera died?"

She smiles and the Jenny I knew before peeks out at me. "You've got a theory, I can tell."

"Not so much. But a question. You need to think hard about this. What could he have been afraid that you might find in Vera's things? Something to implicate him in Howard's death—or even Estelle's death."

She shakes her head. "I never found anything that would fit that."

"You didn't go through all of her belongings, though. Some of them were in boxes in the garage."

"I don't know if I'm up for going through all those boxes just yet."

"It wouldn't have to be all of them. Did Vera keep a journal? You said you found stories she wrote. Maybe she . . ."

I stop because Jenny grabs my arm, her eyes wide. "Those stories. They were in folders and there was a folder marked "Eddie." I quit before I got to it. I almost threw it away. I wasn't sure I wanted to read it."

"We're going to have to go retrieve that box from storage," I say. "I'll do it, if you can tell me anything that might identify it."

"No." She gets up abruptly. "I'm going, too. And we're going now."

"Wait, slow down," I say. "Don't get your hopes up. It's a real long shot."

"I know it is, but I have to find out."

We have to drive all the way back to Jarrett Creek to retrieve the key to the storage area. It's late afternoon when we get back, but the manager of the storage area says they're open until 10 p.m. and we don't have to rush.

Once we get the door of the unit open, Jenny stands for several seconds. "Gathering my courage," she says, but her voice is resolute.

Nate Holloway has stacked everything in neat rows, and Vera marked most of the boxes, so we can eliminate a good number of them. I open the ones that look promising, and Jenny paws through them. Two hours pass, and we've gone through all the ones that looked like they would hold what we're looking for. Jenny is sitting on the floor, her face flushed. "Dammit, where is that box?" Suddenly a look of horror comes across her face. "Could Eddie have taken it?"

I think about it. Eddie tried hard to get the key to Vera's place, but he wasn't successful. I wouldn't give him Jenny's key, and Nate Holloway didn't have one. "He would have had to break in," I say, "and there's no evidence that he did that. He only got the keys after the house was cleaned out." We stare at each other, and then I say, "Wait, you had some boxes at your house. I saw them."

Jenny smacks her forehead. "I'm an idiot! I brought several to my place and put them in the spare bedroom closet. That's got to be where it is."

I try to persuade her to stop and meet me somewhere on the way to her house for a bite to eat, but she's adamant. "I have to get home and look through those boxes. I have to know."

While she goes inside her house to start checking through the boxes, I go to my house and grab a plastic container full of chicken and dumplings out of my refrigerator. I take it to her place and put it on the stove to heat up and go back to the spare bedroom.

Jenny is sitting on the bed, tears leaking out of her eyes. She hands me a couple of pages that have been folded. "It's all there," she says. "She left it in an envelope for me."

My dearest Jenny,

I hope you find this letter after I'm gone. Please forgive me for not telling you what I have to say before I died. I know you won't think it's fair, but there are some things a mother simply can't do. I couldn't send your brother to prison. If I had thought he was a threat to society, I would have forced myself to go to the police, but I honestly thought what happened was a terrible tragedy and that having him spend time in jail would do no one any good.

Eddie had not been married long when his wife Estelle came to me for advice. She said Eddie was drinking one night and he told her he killed his daddy. He swore it was an accident—they fought and Howard fell and hit his head. She said Eddie felt guilty, but he was afraid that if anyone found out, he would go to jail. She asked me if I thought she should go to the police. I will always regret that I told her I needed time to think about it. Before we spoke again, your brother told me that Estelle had run away. Did she really run away? I don't know. I have a horrible fear that your brother became afraid that she would go to the police and he killed her. But I have no way to prove that, and I was too cowardly to pursue it.

What I didn't tell Estelle or anyone else is that I had always harbored suspicions that Eddie had something to do with Howard's disappearance. I knew Howard would be furious about Eddie's role in what happened to you, so I didn't tell him at first. But he knew something was wrong because I had sent you to my sister's house. Just before you came home, I finally told him. He was angrier than I've ever seen him. He said he had coddled Eddie too much and made excuses for his bad behavior and that it was time to call Eddie to account for his behavior. That night he told Eddie that he wanted the two of them to take a ride so they could talk. His car wasn't running, so they took Eddie's car.

Neither of them came home that night. I finally went to bed early in the morning, and when I got up the next day Howard's car was gone. I questioned Eddie about what happened between them and why Howard's car was missing. Eddie told me that Howard said he needed to get away for a few days and they used Eddie's car to jumpstart Howard's. I wanted to believe him, but the longer Howard stayed gone, the more I was certain that something terrible had happened, and that Eddie was to blame. I have been a little afraid of him ever since, not on my behalf but on yours.

I plead with you not to use this information. I am afraid of what he will do if he finds out you have an interest in what happened all those years ago. I'm writing this because I know you've always believed that Howard left because he was ashamed of you. That was never true. He loved you more than anything.

Love, Mamma

"It might surprise you to know that I've seen Eddie," Jenny says.

We're sitting in her living room a few weeks after she found the letter, having a glass of wine. Jenny's life as a drunk was short-lived, but she still likes her wine.

"How did that come about?" I say.

"He called and asked me to see him. So I went to the jail and spent about twenty minutes with him."

"How was that?"

"Better than I thought it might be. Somehow knowing everybody sees him for the scumbag he is takes the burden off me. I swear, he really believes the lies he tells. He tried every which way to convince me that both of the killings were accidents. He said Daddy was yelling at him and then started shoving him and he shoved back. And he said Estelle attacked him. He doesn't realize that me being a prosecutor, I've heard every excuse in the world."

Jenny thought long and hard about whether to go the police with her mother's letter, but she decided in the end she couldn't live with what she knew. And neither could I. I went back to Eddie's ex-wife Marlene and showed her the letter. She confessed that Eddie had hinted that he had a dark past. She also admitted that Eddie told her he needed the bumper on his car repaired because he had accidentally bumped another car. Confronted with the letter, Eddie confessed— not to murder, but to killing two people accidentally. He'll get man-slaughter at the very least. Maybe even second-degree murder.

"Who's going to prosecute the case?"

"My boss wants to do it, but with me being so closely involved, I'm sure Eddie will get a change of venue. His lawyer has already applied for it." She laughs suddenly. "Do you know Eddie tried to get Will to be his defense lawyer? I told Will he should have agreed to it and made sure he did a bad job of defending him."

I laugh with her. It feels almost easy between us again.

"Eddie is using the money from the sale of Mamma's house for a defense fund." Jenny shakes her head. "I wish the money from it was going to something more useful than to defend a murdering scoundrel, but I don't have the heart to contest the will."

"I'm glad," I say. "You need to put this behind you and get on with your life."

"I suppose I will, eventually," she says. "But for now, all I can do is put one foot in front of the other. I wish Mamma was here to talk to."

ACKNOWLEDGMENTS

I am delighted to acknowledge my wonderful readers, the people who share my affection for Samuel and the people who surround him. There is nothing in the world like getting a note that is some variation of "I loved this book. When do I get to read the next one?" It's gratifying and terrifying in equal measure. I hope always to live up to your praise and expectations.

ABOUT THE AUTHOR

TERRY SHAMES is the best-selling author of *A Killing at Cotton Hill*, winner of the Macavity Award for Best First Mystery; *The Last Death of Jack Harbin*; and *Dead Broke in Jarrett Creek*. She lives in Berkeley, CA, but her imagination is always stirred by the vast landscape and human drama of Texas, where she grew up. Visit her website at www.Terryshames.com.